CATCHING BODEL

Nikole Carol Jalbert

Booktrope Editions
Seattle, WA 2015

Cover Design by Laura Hidalgo
Edited by Cecile Jagodzinski

*This is a work of fiction. Names, characters, places, brands, media, and
incidents are either the product of the author's imagination or are used
fictitiously. Any resemblance to similarly named places or to persons
living or deceased is unintentional.*

PRINT ISBN 978-1-62015-770-1

EPUB ISBN 978-1-62015-791-6

Library of Congress Control Number: 2015934566

To my husband, Kyle

For Gabe and Brian,
the best brothers
anyone could ask for

CHAPTER 1

I LUGGED MY LAUNDRY up the basement steps and through the kitchen. My two hundred pound mutant sheepdog, Mop, stood in my way while I juggled the basket and tried to open the back door. I noticed a pair of Bugs Bunny boxers had found their way into my laundry. Two days of living with James and I felt like I had known him for weeks. He reminded me of my brothers.

I managed to get the back door open and stepped out onto the tufts of crabgrass that made up the back yard. A stockade fence bordered the space and allowed me to sunbathe topless when the mood struck me. The clothesline was strung between two trees in the yard. I tried to hang my laundry until it was too cold. There was nothing like the smell of line-dried clothes, despite the fact that it made jeans stiff enough to walk on their own. Seeing as it was only mid-September, I would be using the line for a while longer.

I set my basket on the ground, wincing as my bare feet found a rock. The pair of cut-off sweatpants that ended just below my knees had slipped down to expose the top of my butt. I was out of clean underwear, hence the laundry. I was wearing my ratty uncomfortable bra with a tank top over it. There was a built in bra in the shirt but the flimsy elastic didn't have the strength to hold up my C luggage. Between the shirt and the old bra my breasts were behaving somewhat.

Mop lazily loped after a squirrel while I hung my clothes on the line. I made sure to hang jeans and shirts on the front string so I could hide my underwear on the next one. I had a fashion sense only slightly better than that of an adolescent boy, but I had a penchant for sexy underwear. I wanted to keep said underwear out of James's view. He had enough ideas in his head without me giving him pretty pictures.

I hung everything but the underwear when Mop started barking. I told him to shut up. He shifted his head in my direction and his eyes caught on my laundry. He loped over and stuck his head into my basket. He pulled his head out and grinned at me, a lacy pink thong hanging out of his mouth.

"Dammit, Mop. Drop it!" I ordered.

Sensing a great game in the making, the lunatic dog bounced away from me. I gave chase. He was old, how fast could he really go? He ran in tight circles around me, panting happily and staying just out of reach.

"I'm going to skin you and make you into a rug," I yelled at his fluffy butt as he evaded my grasp. I lunged for him, lost my balance when I missed and slipped onto my ass. I produced a creative string of profanity that died suddenly when I noticed the pair of work boots that were planted about two inches from my bare feet. I looked up at the gigantic man who was standing over me. He was a wall of broad chest and thick arms wrapped in a T-shirt and worn jeans. I felt like an unlucky quarterback about to be clobbered by a runaway tackle.

Mop had noticed the man standing there and bounced over. He barked his greeting, dropping my lacy pink thong onto the man's boots. I glared at the dog.

"You are so dead," I muttered.

I looked up at the man again. Maybe it was the fact that I was sitting on the ground that made him look so big. His body was impressive, but I realized who he was when I looked at his face. He was a bigger, bolder version of James. His brown hair wasn't styled and he let it grow long enough to brush the collar of his shirt. His eyes were green instead of blue but the shape of them was the same. He wore a full beard that was neatly trimmed and only made him look more primal. I swallowed hard.

"Problem with your dog, ma'am?" he said. His voice sent a stab of pure lust through me. It was deep and thick; two words that came to mind along with associated nasty thoughts. James adjusted his drawl to the situation. He toned it down to blend in, and blasted it when he was flirting. His brother, who had to be the man standing over me, was obviously not the kind of man to play those kinds of games. His voice was pure Georgia and was far too close to a caress than a voice should have been.

I snatched the lacy pink panties off his boot and held them behind my back as I scrambled to my feet. I knew I was blushing like an idiot and my long brown hair had fallen out of its clip while I chased Mop. I went to push my hair back forgetting about the thong in my hand. I quickly returned my hand behind my back but his eyes followed the movement of the pink panties.

"Hi," I said as brightly as I could. "You must be Zach."

"Zachary Cutter, ma'am." He offered his hand. "It's a pleasure to meet you, Bodel." He mispronounced my name. I'd heard a variety of attempts at it, but he was the first to pronounce it *Bod-el*.

"It's Bodel, actually. And I prefer Bo."

"Sorry, ma'am."

I sighed, hating being called ma'am. It'd taken me several reminders to get James to stop doing so, but I had a bad feeling Zach wouldn't abandon his manners as easily.

"Try it," I suggested.

He raised a dark eyebrow in question.

"Say Bo."

He looked down at me, crossing his arms. Now that I was standing I couldn't pretend that he only seemed big. I was five six but he was about a foot taller. I was used to big guys but he was the first one who had ever made me feel small. He was the only one who had ever made me feel feminine.

"James said you were a handful," Zach said.

I couldn't stop myself. I looked down at my breasts that were on display in the low cut tank top. "I'm two."

He didn't smile. This was definitely not going as smoothly as I hoped.

I put on my waitress smile and blasted the charm. "I didn't realize you were going to be here today. James said you weren't gonna get here till tomorrow."

"I got an earlier flight."

He wasn't giving me much to go on. He looked at me with a mix of befuddlement and distaste. James had warned me that Zach could come off as abrasive and cold. I hadn't thought he was serious. How could two brothers be so completely different? I needed him to like me. If I couldn't find a way to appease him, he'd tell me to pack my stuff and sell the house out from under me. Recently inherited or not, it was still his house to do with as he pleased.

I blasted the charm again, though I'd always been more comfortable with sarcasm than courtesy. "Well, welcome to Cape Cod. I have to finish hanging the laundry, but I was going to make James some lunch before I headed to work. Are you hungry?"

He looked at me a minute the way most people would look at a jigsaw puzzle. I liked the color of his eyes. They were a shade of dark green I had never seen before. For a man with no sense of humor he was still extremely attractive. It was a shame.

"You don't need to trouble yourself," he said.

"It's no trouble. I'm making food anyway."

"All right. I'd appreciate a meal, thank you, ma'am."

"My name is Bo."

The corner of his mouth turned up the slightest bit. I was sure I could pry a smile from him if I put my mind to it.

"Say it," I suggested.

He raised an eyebrow at me.

"Will it kill you to say my name?"

"No, ma'am."

I glared at him and reached out to poke him in his barrel chest. It wasn't until after I had done so that I realized I was still holding the pink thong. I whirled around to hide my blush, but not before I saw him smile. I muttered some profanity and finished hanging the laundry. I hung the pink thong on the front line prominently displayed against a white T-shirt. If I was going to make an ass of myself, I was going to do it big.

CHAPTER 2

I TOOK A MOMENT to calm myself before going inside. I looked at the house and sighed. I'd lived there for the past two years, taking care of Walter, a good-hearted if grumpy old man whose failing eyesight provided me with a job. His need of a driver, cook, and general companion gave me a way to escape living with my parents. A month ago, Walter collapsed at the Elks Lodge while playing poker. He died with a smile on his face and a royal flush in his hands.

Walter left the house to his estranged step-grandsons, James and Zach Cutter. Due to the bad blood between Walter and his ex-wife, Walter had never been allowed to see his grandsons in person. Regardless, he spoke of them often, and I'd helped him wrap their Christmas gifts the past two years.

The brothers decided to come see the house to determine what they wanted to do with it. I didn't know if they planned to sell it, live in it, renovate it, or burn it down. I didn't know if they would allow me to keep living there, since I had only been paying two hundred dollars a month for rent.

I found James sitting at the kitchen table when I walked back inside. He seemed smaller and less attractive now that I'd met Zach. My first impression of James had been negative, due to his taste for designer jeans and watches that cost more than my truck. He styled his hair with more skill and enthusiasm than I did. He had grace and charm and classic blue-eyed good looks. I assumed I'd never be able to get along with him, but his easy-going nature and sense of humor won me over quickly.

Zach was nowhere in sight and I was relieved. I was out of charm.

"So you met Zach," James mentioned.

"I think I offended him," I said, heading to the fridge to start making sandwiches.

James laughed. "What did you do?"

I considered my answer carefully. "Breathe?"

"I'm sorry, Bo. He's just got a stick shoved up his butt."

I rolled my eyes, amused that he wouldn't swear in front of me. "Will he eat a Reuben?"

"He'll roll over and let you rub his belly if you feed him that. And if he is ever really angry, corn bread will fix it."

I had a very naughty image of Zach that I pushed aside. "Good to know," I said. I made three sandwiches and placed two in the toaster. Mop whined at me and I tossed him some small scraps of corned beef.

"You feed the dog table scraps?" Zach's disapproving voice startled me. He moved silently, especially for a guy his size.

"Mop's old. I don't deny him simple pleasures," I said, checking the sandwiches.

"It teaches dogs to beg."

I had the distinct impression I was being criticized. Knowing it was a bad idea rarely stopped me from doing something. I tossed a piece of corned beef in Zach's direction. Mop was so eager to catch it that he barreled right into the tall man and knocked him back into the wall. James laughed, turning it into a cough when Zach glared at him.

"He's old, doesn't see that well anymore," I said innocently, pulling the sandwiches from the toaster and onto plates. I decided that I needed to stop harassing my new landlord. If I didn't stop he would likely toss me out on my ass within an hour. I turned to see him looking at me with narrowed eyes. He didn't look angry, just confused.

I smiled as I placed the sandwiches in front of the brothers. "My specialty. Hope you both enjoy it."

"She's an amazing cook," James chimed in, with his mouth already full.

"Are you not eating?" Zach asked me.

I indicated the third sandwich as I slipped it into the toaster. "Working on it."

Zach pushed his plate toward me. "I'll take the last one. You eat."

"Its fine," I began.

"You cooked, and you have to go to work. Sit down and eat. I can get that." Zach stood up and moved to the counter. He didn't give me much choice. I had to move or be stepped on. I sat down at the table, biting back a sarcastic comment. He was being gentlemanly. The idea was creeping me out. The only time the men in my life acted that way was when they needed money or broke something that was going to be hard to replace. I had to shower and get ready for work though, so I picked up my sandwich and wolfed it down. I felt Zach watching me but didn't look at him. James had started talking about football.

"The game's at one on Sunday," I supplied. I glanced at Zach. "My brothers usually come over to watch. Is that, ah, is that OK?"

"This is your home, ma'am," Zach said, taking his sandwich carefully out of the toaster. "We may own the house, but that's different. I honestly don't know how to deal with this situation. I feel like my brother and I have invaded."

"I don't know what is considered the normal thing in this situation either," I said, licking dressing off my finger. I pretended not to notice the way Zach's eyes followed the motion of my tongue. "But I only rented a room here from Walter. I barely paid rent. I mostly just cooked and cleaned for him. It's your house and it makes sense you stay here while you decide what to do with it."

"Still, I appreciate you accommodating us, ma'am," Zach said, pausing to finally take a bite of his sandwich. He chewed for a moment and produced a deep rumbling sound of approval. It was far too sensual a sound for a man who didn't smile.

"See what I mean?" James collected the crumbs from his plate with his fingers. "I'm going to marry her. I don't care if she never touches me as long as she cooks for me."

I laughed and kicked his shin under the table. "I'd sooner marry Mop."

"Adopt me then."

"I'm only a year older than you," I pointed out.

"Fine. Just please..." He dropped to one knee in front of me. "Please cook for me."

"You're ruining my appetite," Zach muttered.

I knocked James over with a careful sweep of my bare foot and stood up. "I love to cook, so you have nothing to worry about unless you decide to kick me out on the street."

"What has my little brother been telling you? That I'm an ogre?" Zach glared at James.

"I'm not little," James said from the floor. Zach looked down at him and the corners of his mouth did the small twitch that I decided was as close as Zach got to smiling.

"You should smile more," I said.

He looked at me like I had suggested he dye his hair green.

I laughed. "Well, if you want to mope around like an ogre, that's your deal. I have to get ready for work." I didn't quite run out of the room, but I moved quickly enough to ensure I got the last word in.

CHAPTER 3

I WOKE UP with Mop draped over my chest, as usual. I squirmed out from under him, adjusting my cotton pajama pants. They were red with pink hearts on them. They were a gift from my brothers, given with the intention of ridiculing me for wearing them. I checked myself in the full length mirror that hung crooked on my door.

My shoulder length brown hair fell without style or grace in a tangled mess. My naturally tan skin was still a few shades darker from the summer sun. I was big-boned and had inherited broad shoulders from my mother that resulted in my love of sleeveless shirts. My odd-colored gray eyes were slightly slanted, courtesy of my Thai grandmother. I may not have been a supermodel, but I was definitely an original.

I stepped out into the hall and jumped when I heard voices downstairs. I'd hated being alone in the house, but hadn't gotten used to sharing it with the brothers. There were three small bedrooms on the second floor and a functional but uninspired bathroom. The stairs creaked as I went down them. Mop thundered down behind me, gaining momentum and losing his footing on the second to last stair. He skidded into the front door with a thud.

"Is he OK?" Zach asked through the archway leading into the kitchen.

"That's how he always goes down the stairs," I said. I walked through the living room into the kitchen. James was eating a bowl of cereal with enough sugar dumped on it to make it unhealthy. Impressive metabolism allowed him to stay as thin as he was. I could relate. By all rights I should have weighed two hundred pounds the way I ate. I couldn't be called skinny; my body type didn't recognize that term. I was curvy and soft, a bit too soft around my belly, but there was only so much I could ask from metabolism alone and I was allergic to organized exercise.

"Good morning," I said, pretending to be a morning person. Seeing the full coffeepot was a welcome shock. I assumed it was Zach who made it, because James hadn't gone near the machine since he arrived. I poured myself a mug and opened the fridge. I stood in the cold for a moment.

"Are you looking for something?" Zach asked.

"She does it every morning," James said. "It's how she wakes up, I think."

I grunted and shut the fridge. The truth was that every morning I opened the fridge and considered making a big breakfast, and almost every morning, opted for cereal instead. I loved to cook, but not when it was only for myself.

I poured some cereal and took the chair across from James at the table. Zach sat beside James, where the local paper was spread. I stared at it a moment. I didn't get the paper. I had never actually read one in my life. It was only eight in the morning. Zach had already been out of the house to buy a paper and he looked wide awake. I wouldn't be able to pretend to be that awake for another two hours.

"I guess we should talk about the house," James said while I chewed.

I didn't want to have that particular talk while my brain was still curled up in bed, but it didn't look like I had a choice.

"Well, what do you think of it?" I asked.

We glanced around the kitchen with its peeling counter-tops and ancient stove. The fridge was that ugly color of puke green that someone in the seventies had declared appealing. The pattern was worn off certain sections of the linoleum floor. The kitchen was a good representation of the whole house.

"It's in decent shape," Zach said. "It needs work, but structurally it's sound."

"The septic was brought up to code last year," I said. "And the roof was replaced three years ago."

"The electric and plumbing are up-to-date too," James said.

"The bedrooms are too small," Zach mused, scratching his beard. "The bathroom needs a complete overhaul. And the back yard could use some landscaping."

I assumed he was referring to the two small overgrown gardens in the back yard. I did my best to grow my own vegetables and flowers, but every summer I ended up working too much to maintain the gardens. I bit back my instinctive bitchiness and didn't try to explain my lack of landscaping skills. I forced myself to ask the hard question. "So what are you going to do with the house?"

James wouldn't look at me, finding a sudden intense interest in his cereal. Zach, on the other hand, looked right into my eyes. "Would you be interested in buying it?" he asked.

I choked on a startled laugh. "I'm a waitress." His lack of response led me to elaborate. "I can't afford to buy new shoes, never mind a house. Especially this time of year."

He frowned. "Why this time of year?"

I rolled my eyes at him. The fact that he was independently wealthy made me uncomfortable, and I wasn't sure I could explain without sounding defensive and bitchy. But I tried anyway.

"This is a tourist community," I said. "For three months a year, there are jobs, people, and money. Then September hits and everything closes, the people go away, and the locals hunker down on unemployment for the winter."

"Everyone?" James asked.

"A lot of us," I said. "Everyone loves to visit the Cape, but living here is something else entirely. Housing is ridiculously expensive; work opportunities are limited to manual labor and service jobs. There isn't any real industry here. And it's a ghost town in the winter. A lot of people work two or three jobs during the summer and budget it to survive the winter. That's what I do. I'm lucky enough to work at a year-round restaurant, but my shifts get cut way back in the winter."

Zach nodded. "I never really thought about it. Sounds like a tough way to live."

"We manage. Well, we try. Honestly, most people my age are forced off the Cape in search of year-round work and affordable housing."

Zach took a long sip of his coffee. "If we sold the house, do you have somewhere to go?"

I stared down at my cereal. "Sort of."

"Sort of?" Zach prompted.

"I could move back in with my parents," I admitted miserably. I was twenty-five years old. Moving back home would be humiliating and I'd have to share the bathroom with my father again. I kept talking because my brain was still in bed. "Or I could move in with my brothers, Gage and Mason. They rent a place in Eastham. But it's a bachelor pad and I'd end up as the maid. I could try living with my brother Axel. He just bought a house down the street. But his house is under construction and his perky new wife is four months pregnant and I'd rather sleep in my truck than live there."

I glanced up at Zach and James, startled to realize I'd spoken my thoughts aloud. Embarrassed, I continued, "I have a big family, and I love them. But they all seem to think my life needs fixing. And I don't want to live with any of them. I, well, I want to live here." I forced myself to meet Zach's cool stare. "I've lived here for two years. I love this house. It's home."

Zach looked at me for a while, calmly sipping his coffee. I couldn't read his expression, and couldn't keep from fidgeting. I played with my cereal, no longer hungry. Mop was curled up under the table, and he licked my toes. I patted his head with my foot.

"I'll be honest with you," Zach said at length. "My original plan was to sell the house as soon as possible. But now that I've seen it, selling it as is would be a waste. The value could be significantly increased with renovations."

"But you still plan on selling it?" I asked.

Zach sat back in his chair. "I'm not sure."

James' head snapped in Zach's direction. I had a feeling Zach was normally sure about everything. He oozed confidence without seeming egotistical, which was an interesting and attractive combination. I had a sudden need to know more about Zach.

"Come again?" James said.

Zach's lips twitched in a smile. "I know. Shocking, right?" He took another sip of coffee. "I could use a break from Georgia. Charley's business is thriving now and he doesn't need me there. I need a new project. Most of the renovations I can do myself." He scratched his beard and looked around the kitchen again.

"You want to stay here and renovate the place?" James asked, his mouth hanging open.

Zach nodded. "Well, you said you liked it here. You said there were some work opportunities for you."

"I applied at a nursing home yesterday," James said. At my inquisitive look he continued, "I have a degree in nutrition and exercise science, and I'm a CNA."

"Oh, there's plenty of that kind of work since the Cape started turning into Florida," I said.

"I figure we give this place a try," Zach said. "We'll do the renovations and see how we feel about the place when the work is finished."

"What about me?" I asked.

"You are free to continue renting your room," Zach said.

"For the same price?"

Zach opened his mouth but James interrupted him with, "As long as you cook for us."

Zach narrowed his eyes at his brother, but when he looked back at me he smiled. "I like your cooking."

"I'll clean too," I said, not entirely believing I was going to get to stay.

"James and I will do our part. You are not hired help. This is your home."

"So I can stay?"

Zach leaned back in his chair, a surprising gleam in his eyes. "Like I said, I like your cooking." There was something in his tone that gave me the distinct impression that wasn't the only thing he liked. Suddenly, I wasn't sure being allowed to stay was a good thing or not.

CHAPTER 4

AFTER THE FIRST WEEK I figured Zach's impeccable manners and respectful distance would crumble, but they didn't. He never said my name, only referring to me as ma'am or Miss Tavish. He kept his distance physically as well. I had taken to lying on the couch with James, with my head or my legs in his lap, depending on my mood. Zach always sat in one of the two big armchairs and made sure not to brush against me when we passed in the hall. Despite that, I felt him watching me constantly. I pretended not to notice. I couldn't figure out what he wanted from me. It was a relief when he flew back to Georgia on business. But on the other hand, he had been gone for two days and I was startled to realize I missed him.

James was out on a job interview and I had the house to myself. I tuned the little radio in the kitchen to the local country station and turned it up. I did a little standing dance in front of the open fridge while I considered what to make for a snack. I selected ham and cheese and swung my butt against the door of the fridge to close it. The move turned me to face the room and I almost screamed when I saw Zach standing in the archway. I blushed as I realized I was clutching the deli meat against my chest. I threw the meat on the counter and turned the radio down to a reasonable level.

"Zach, you scared me," I said. "I didn't think you were coming back so soon."

"Sorry, ma'am. Didn't mean to frighten you," he said.

"I have a name," I muttered. That won me the slight curl of his lips.

"I finished my business back home early. I wanted to check over what James has done so far. I'm a bit more knowledgeable than he is about remodeling."

He had a large bag slung over one shoulder. He set it down and stretched. His gray T-shirt rode up. He had a slight gut, nothing too noticeable, but James harassed him about it regularly. It made him less perfect and more attractive somehow. Apparently, he didn't agree with my opinion because he quickly tugged the shirt back down.

"James spent most of his time drinking beer and watching bad movies," I said.

Zach grunted. "I figured. I hate to agree with my grandmother about anything, but James is lazy."

I ignored the criticism of James, latching onto the other part of the comment. "Why do you hate to agree with your grandmother?" She was married to Walter for five years. He described her as bitter and unhappy. Walter loved her son, Zach's father, much more than Roberta.

Zach sighed and sat down in a chair. He ran a hand through his thick brown hair.

"My grandmother is a harpy," he admitted. It was rare to hear him say anything negative about someone. He continued, "She hated Walter so much. All we ever heard about was what a failure he was. She used to scream at my father when he gave us the presents Walter sent. She's mean as a snake."

"Sorry to hear that," I said, thinking of my two sets of grandparents. They were both loving and accepting. I didn't know my mother's parents very well, seeing as they lived in Ohio. My dad's parents had been a regular fixture in my life since I was a baby.

He shrugged. It wasn't in Zach's nature to share what he was feeling. He was the most self-contained person I had ever met. It drove my inquisitive nosy nature to hysterics.

"Have you eaten anything?" I asked.

His lips did the twitch that passed for a smile, but there was a light in his green eyes that made me wonder.

"I had coffee this morning."

I checked the clock. It was three.

"I'll make you something," I said, heading back toward the fridge.

"Don't trouble yourself," he said.

"How many times do I have to tell you, Zach, I love cooking."

"You're making me fat," he muttered.

One of my favorite songs came on the radio. It was sassy and fast and gave me bad ideas. I walked over to Zach, who was slouched in the chair looking sexy and ruffled. I poked the slight belly above his jeans with my fingers.

"You are not fat," I said. I couldn't help myself. Rather than simply back away, I let the back of my hand run up his chest. I skillfully turned the move into a flamboyant dance step and danced my way back across the kitchen. I could feel Zach staring at me, and I tried not to concentrate on the way his muscular chest had felt under my fingers.

I wasn't trying to put on a show, but I loved to dance. I couldn't keep myself from getting into the music. I threw together a ham and cheese sandwich for Zach while I danced in place at the counter. I jumped when I turned around because James was standing in the doorway.

"Dammit, I'm going to put a bell on each of you," I muttered.

"I'll wear a damn collar, just don't stop moving your hips like that." James grinned. Zach elbowed him sharply in the gut. It was harder than I thought the comment deserved. James rubbed at his ribs, looking confused for a moment. But the look passed and he resumed grinning.

"Seriously, Bo, where did you learn to move like that?" he asked, sitting across from the table from his brother, out of elbow range.

"I took belly dancing classes with my mother," I said, putting together a second sandwich for James.

"Really?"

"Yeah. The guys on my Dad's crew, he runs a construction company," I reminded them. "They were giving my Dad shit for marrying my mother."

"Why?"

"Because she's a mechanic," I said, rinsing my hands. "They said he was married to one man with breasts and was raising another. So we took belly dancing classes, dressed just shy of harem girls, and proved them wrong."

I was shocked to hear Zach chuckle. It was a quick sound and drowned out by James, but I had heard it. I turned to see a full smile on his face. The smile reached his eyes and took him from handsome to breathtaking. It wasn't fair.

I placed the food in front of them.

"Enjoy, boys."

"Don't you eat?" James reached out and pinched at my belly. I jumped away.

"I ate lunch earlier."

"Salad?" He rolled his eyes.

"What?" I asked. "I'm trying to save some money by working my way into a couple pairs of old jeans."

"While fattening us up?" James rolled his eyes. "She's evil."

Zach's mouth was full but he nodded agreement.

I shook my head, checking the clock. "I have to go to work at four. You want me to bring home some dinner?"

"No thanks," James said with his mouth full. "I don't like eating that late."

"I'm gonna tell Rosey how bad your manners have been lately," Zach said. James actually looked frightened.

"Don't you dare." He pointed a finger at Zach.

"Who's Rosey?" I asked.

"Our housekeeper," James said. "Well, she's more than that. She's like a mom to us. She was our nanny when we were kids. Our parents are both doctors so they weren't around much."

The subtle reminders of their wealth always made me feel uncomfortable. While Zach said I wasn't the hired help, I still felt like a charity case. I forced myself not to think about it.

CHAPTER 5

I WOKE UP SLOWLY, realizing it was late because my room was fully illuminated. The clock said it was ten. I normally woke up around eight and stumbled downstairs. Mop was still sprawled across me. He was enjoying his retirement from the rigors of young dog-dom. I loved that about him.

After freeing myself from under his bulk I headed for the bathroom. The door was open and Zach was crouched down under the sink, his head stuck into the cabinet underneath. I assumed he was checking the plumbing. I took the opportunity to give his ass my full attention. Mop loped down the stairs but suddenly erupted in harsh barking. I recognized it as his 'the mail is here' bark. Zach misunderstood the sound, interpreting it as, 'Fire!' He jumped up, or tried to. The back of his head slammed into the porcelain edge of the sink so hard I was surprised it didn't crack. He dropped to his knees and swore. It was the first profanity I had heard from him. It was only one word, but it was said with such passion it made up for his normal good manners.

I was by his side instantly, reaching for his head.

"Zach, are you OK?" I pushed his hand out of the way, knowing it was serious because he let me.

"Ouch," he muttered. I ran my fingers through his hair, searching for a cut or blood. I didn't find a cut, though he was going to have a huge bump. I noticed something on the back of his neck and couldn't stop myself from brushing his hair aside to get a better look. It was a date written in flowing script: *2-18*. I wondered what it meant to him.

"Let's get you downstairs so I can put some ice on your head," I said, forcing myself not to ask about the tattoo. "Can you stand up?"

"I'm seeing double," he admitted.

"OK. Well, no stairs for you then. Sit down. I'll be right back."

I didn't want to chance moving Zach while James was out of the house at a job interview. If Zach fell down, there was no way I was going to move him. He would stay where he fell until he woke up. I ran downstairs and retrieved a bag of frozen peas from the freezer. Zach was leaned against the wall, his hand on his head when I returned.

"Still seeing double?" I asked as I crouched beside him.

"No."

I pushed his hand aside and pressed the bag of peas against his head. He flinched. I pushed his hand away when he tried to take it from me.

"I got it," I said. "You hit your head so hard I thought you broke the sink."

"I didn't?" He tried to smile but grimaced instead. "I don't like that dog much right now."

"Don't blame Mop. He was just saying hello to the mailman."

Zach let out a shaky breath.

"Come on, we can't sit on the bathroom floor all day." I stood up, offering my hand. He looked up at me.

"You're kidding, right?" he asked.

I knew it was physically impossible for me to help him up. He outweighed me by at least a hundred pounds. But the gesture was automatic. I told him as much and he smiled at me. He took my hand and picked himself up, swaying only a bit.

I walked with him into his bedroom and settled him down on the bed. His room was messy, with clothes discarded on the floor. His bed was unmade, and there was a collection of empty soda cans on the bedside table. He looked around the room, obviously embarrassed. It was a good thing he'd never seen the mess that I called a room. Still, I'd had years to accumulate clutter.

"You've only been back for two days," I said, looking around. A pair of Superman boxers was on prominent display, hung over the chair in the room. Zach caught me looking and actually blushed.

"Rosey," he said, adjusting the peas on his head. "She buys James and me boxers every Christmas. She has eclectic tastes."

I laughed. My attention was drawn to the gold necklace around his neck. He normally tucked it under his clothes but it had slipped free of his white T-shirt. The cross and the simple gold band stood out against the white. I realized I was looking at a wedding ring. Zach followed my gaze.

"Raised Southern Baptist," he said, fingering the cross. "I don't go to church anymore, though Rosey screams about me burning in hell for all eternity." He sighed, moving the peas on his head again. They were starting to melt. A bead of moisture trickled down his forearm.

To distract myself from wanting to lick the droplet away, I said, "My parents worship football and beer. I think I would burst into flames if I walked into a church. Guess I'll be keeping you company in hell someday."

He smiled, but his fingers had left the cross and were holding the ring. I wanted to ask but I could see he didn't want to talk about it. It took everything I had to let it go. I pushed the bag of peas aside to inspect his head again.

"I think you'll live," I said. I enjoyed the feeling of his hair. It was soft and thick. I wanted to rub my cheek against his beard to see how it would feel. I didn't. I just took the bag from his hands and told him to relax. I talked to him about the renovations for a while. After a few minutes, he sighed.

"I know you want to ask," he said.

"Ask what?"

"Don't play dumb, it doesn't suit you."

I stood up. "If you want to tell me something you will. It's not my place to pry. I'm going to go do some laundry. If you're OK?"

"I'm feeling a lot better, thank you."

He wasn't going to explain the wedding ring or the tattoo. I had a feeling the two were connected. I left him sitting on his bed looking very lost and sad.

* * *

James came running into the back yard, picked me up off my feet and let out a whoop. I laughed as he set me back down.

"I guess you got the job," I said.

"Was there ever any doubt?" James grinned. "Who could resist this face?"

I rolled my eyes but congratulated him.

"You need to make me something amazing for dinner to celebrate," he said.

"Sure."

He sobered. "What's wrong?"

"Nothing."

"Liar. What did my brother do?"

"What makes you think Zach has anything to do with my mood?"

"Call it a hunch."

I turned away from him and resumed hanging laundry.

"He hit his head this morning, really hard. Mop scared him while he was checking out the plumbing under the sink."

"Is he OK?"

"He's fine."

"So why are you, well, not fine?"

I shouldn't ask. I should respect Zach's privacy. But I just couldn't.

"Why does he have a date tattooed on the back of his neck? And why does he have a wedding ring on his necklace?"

James tried to hide the emotional pain my question caused, but he didn't entirely succeed. I was glad I hadn't asked Zach directly.

"He didn't tell you anything?" James asked.

"No. I'm trying to be good, but I'm curious by nature. It's driving me crazy. Was he married? Is he married?"

James hesitated a moment, stuffing his hands in the pockets of his khakis. "His wife's name was Alice. She kil—she died in February a year after they got married."

I stood motionless, afraid of what he had started to say but stopped.

"She was a childhood friend of ours," he continued. "Her father is the chief of staff at the hospital my parents both work at. He was twenty-one when they got married. I never understood why."

I wanted to ask how she died, but I didn't. I was afraid of the answer. I was afraid that the answer was the reason that there was often so much sadness in Zach's beautiful eyes.

"It's been nine years since she died. Zach's never been the same. He used to laugh all the time, joke around with me. But after Alice, well, he shut down for a while. He's much better now than he used to be. In fact, he's smiled more in the past two weeks than I think he's smiled in years."

I forced myself to smile despite the grief I felt in my chest. He'd been a widower at twenty-two, three years younger than I was now. I couldn't bring myself to ask what had happened to Alice now. The fact that the date of her death was tattooed on his neck said all there was to say.

"I wish I hadn't asked," I said.

"It's better you know. It'll help you understand Zach more. This way he doesn't have to talk about it. Why don't you make us some corn bread tonight? It's his favorite."

I shook off the depression. It was hard to stay down with James grinning at me.

"Sure. And I'll even bake a cake."

"Cake?" James shifted from foot to foot like a small boy who had just been told he was going to the fair.

"What's your favorite?"

"Chocolate of course. And just so you know, Zach loves carrot cake."

"I'll keep that in mind."

CHAPTER 6

I WAS NERVOUS about my brothers meeting James and Zach. I kept them away last weekend, trying to give James and Zach a chance to settle in. But Mason, Axel, and Gage were frothing at the bit and I couldn't hold them off any longer. The three were due in any minute for football and chili.

I was gathering my clothes from the line. James and Zach were outside on the lawn, taking measurements for the porch. Mop was loping after a squirrel that must have been as old as he was. The two seemed to be enjoying their slow-motion game.

I heard my brothers coming, but it was too late. I turned in time to be tackled by Mason, the biggest of the three. I twisted at the last moment, managing to squirm out from under him before being pinned to the ground. Mason was almost as big as Zach. Axel was shorter and leaner, but I didn't feel the difference when he collided with me. Gage, the baby at six feet and an athletic flexible one hundred sixty pounds, caught me when I elbowed Axel and squirmed free. The four of us fell in the grass, yelling profanities, punching, kicking, and shoving. I ended up crushed at the bottom of the pile, gasping for breath and crying uncle. Mop had been circling us, barking like a lunatic the entire time.

James and Zach stood staring at us like the circus sideshow we were. Mason was the first to get up, seeing as he had been on the top of the pile of Tavish siblings. Axel groaned and complained that if he ended up with a black eye his wife was going to give him another lecture. That left Gage draped across my lap. He was wearing faded jeans and a tight white tank top. He had the sculpted body of a dancer. Instead of casually standing up, he pushed himself up into a handstand

and did a graceful flip to regain his feet. Gage was always showing off. He held a hand down to me.

"Did you miss me?"

I allowed him to help me up. As soon as I was on my feet I jumped onto his back, wrapping my arm around his throat in a solid hold. He gasped out a plea to our brothers. We ended up back on the ground, laughing.

James and Zach were still watching us. The four of us noticed at the same time and brushed ourselves off. We made an attempt to look dignified as I introduced them. Hands were shaken and nods exchanged. My brothers all looked startlingly alike. Each had straight brown hair cut short in only slightly different styles. They had similar builds and varied only marginally in height. Mason was the biggest and heaviest, and he was the only one with my mother's blue eyes. Axel and Gage had brown eyes, like my father.

The five men looked at me. I imagined most women would feel intimidated or small. I had never felt that way. I grew up being tossed around by big men. I could be surrounded by giants and be as calm as a Hindu cow. That being said, placing me in a room full of women scared the hell out of me.

"How did you end up with the name Bodel anyway?" James asked.

"What do you mean?" I asked.

"Well, Mason, Gage and Axel aren't that uncommon, but I've never met anyone else named Bodel."

"She was named after our great grandmother, who was Norwegian," Mason explained.

"Only Mom and Dad got it wrong," Gage added. "The name is actually Bodil, but they spelled it wrong on the birth certificate and didn't realize it for years. By then, it was too late."

"The game's gonna start soon," I said to change the subject. "And I made chili."

"You didn't make it too spicy, did you?" Gage asked.

"You are such a baby," Axel said, holding the door open as we all trooped inside.

"Am not," Gage whined.

"How are classes going?" I asked.

"Not bad. I almost ate shit yesterday. Scared the hell out of everyone."

James and Zach looked confused, so I decided to clarify. "Gage goes to the Boston Conservatory." That didn't seem to explain anything.

"I'm a dancer," Gage said, his hand stuffed into a bag of chips. "And before you ask, I'm not gay. Feel free to make fun of me if you want."

James stole the bag of chips. "Dance? As in ballet?"

Gage made a face. "I concentrate more on modern style, but I've been known to do a *fouetté* or a *grand jetée* from time to time."

"He looks so cute in his pink tutu," I teased.

Gage glared at me, grabbing me and tickling the back of my neck. I struggled to get away from him.

"Don't listen to her," Gage said, unconcerned with my struggling. "She thinks she's hot shit with her belly dancing. If I hadn't suggested that class you and Mom would still be known as men with tits."

"Yeah, thanks to you now every guy who meets Mom thinks she's hot." Mason shuddered as he heaped chili into a bowl.

I watched Zach while my brothers joked and dished out food. We were a loud touchy-feely bunch. Zach's normal reserve wouldn't mix well. But I was surprised to find him smiling and talking. He settled in one of the overstuffed armchairs and asked Gage about his classes. He and Mason engaged in a serious discussion about the merits of different power tools. With Axel the conversation veered more toward his plans to fix up the house he had recently bought.

I relaxed as the football game started. James and Zach joined in the cheering, heckling, and general yelling that football inspired in my family. Zach and Axel claimed the overstuffed chairs; Mason, James and Gage claimed the couch while I was in the kitchen dishing out more chili. I thought about dragging a chair in from the kitchen but discarded the idea. Gage was done eating so I settled myself on his lap.

I loved all of my brothers and honestly couldn't say I had a favorite. Mason and I were the closest in age and he was usually the one I confided in. Axel had drifted away from us since getting married, but he still came over regularly for football and food. Gage and I had grown extremely close over the years, as his love of dancing confounded our brothers. I was the one to go to dance classes with him. Because of the dancing I was completely at home curled up against him. Axel and I had never been as comfortable with that kind of physical closeness.

Mason was too macho for that kind of affection to be acceptable for long. But Gage would cuddle with me.

Gage's arms wrapped around my waist and he adjusted me on his knee so he could see the TV. "Dammit, throw the ball, you pansy," he yelled.

I basked in them. I loved being surrounded by my brothers. I was relieved James and Zach had blended so well. The five of them bonded easily over chili, beer, and football. They discussed the Atlanta Falcons as opposed to the New England Patriots. Beer flowed freely as the game continued. I noticed that Zach only had two beers. I wondered what he would be like drunk. My brothers had worked magic on him. He was quiet by nature, but his usual stoic seriousness was gone. He didn't yell like my brothers, tending to respond to good or bad plays with grunts and nods. But he talked freely and I enjoyed hearing his heavy Georgia drawl blend with my brothers' New England slang.

I picked up the empty bowls and cans and headed into the kitchen. Mason followed me with his arms full of more empties and dishes.

"Don't do any of these," he said. "We can clean them, or better yet, your new boy toys can."

I rolled my eyes. Mason had been arrogant and controlling since he was old enough to walk. He was aggressive by nature and I was relieved he hadn't already picked a fight with Zach. "They are not my boy toys," I said, dumping everything in the sink. "I'm glad you're all getting along."

"You do realize that Zach has spent more time watching you than the game, right?" Mason asked, his voice quiet. The TV in the other room coupled with James and Gage recapping a bad call from a referee ensured that Mason and I were not overheard.

"I'm not sleeping with Zach." I rolled my eyes.

"Maybe not, but it's on his mind."

I sighed. Mason was overprotective, and he wasn't afraid to physically harm anyone who showed interest in me. There was a wildness in Mason that he managed to hide day to day, but it would come out from time to time when he got into a bar fight or went surfing during a hurricane. He had appointed himself as my guard dog when I grew breasts, and my Dad encouraged him. It drove me crazy.

"I'm a big girl," I reminded my brother.

"You're my baby sister."

"I'm younger by ten months."

"Still, younger."

"Look, Zach is the perfect gentleman. His nanny drilled in the whole southern charm and respect thing so hard I've only ever heard the man swear once, and that was when he nearly cracked his skull open on the sink."

"I need background info on him," Mason said.

"Let it go, Mason."

"Dad's gonna ask. I can't go to him empty-handed."

Axel walked in, heading toward the fridge and, I imagined, a fresh beer.

I grabbed his arm. "No more beer for you. You have to drive home to Maxine tonight. If I send you home drunk she's gonna call me and whine. I hate that."

"Axel, you still friendly with John Wallace?" Mason asked.

I whirled to face my bigger brother. "Don't you dare."

"What?" Mason tried to look innocent.

"Don't you dare ask John to do a background check on James or Zach."

"Wouldn't think of it," Mason lied. I looked over my shoulder at Axel, who grinned and took another beer from the fridge.

"I'll sleep here tonight," Axel said. "I think our baby sister needs a chaperone."

I stomped on his foot and he yelped. Mason dodged the fist I sent at his shoulder. I muttered some profanity as I stalked back into the living room. Halftime was over and the third quarter was starting. I lay down on the couch between James and Gage. I settled my legs on James and rested my head on Gage.

Mason and Axel walked back into the room at the same time. They looked at the one remaining chair and engaged in a quick scuffle to get to it first. Mason won, landing in the chair with a triumphant grin. Axel muttered and looked at the couch. I was sprawled comfortably and I gave him the finger.

"You guys suck," Axel muttered. He dragged a chair in from the kitchen table and straddled it moodily.

I knew better than to think my brothers would let the matter of Zach and James drop. Especially if Zach kept looking at me like he did. I thought maybe I was just imagining it, but having Mason say something killed that theory. Zach was quickly becoming the most irritating man I had ever met. He was the king of mixed signals. I settled comfortably on the couch with James and Gage and did my best not to notice his dark green eyes.

CHAPTER 7

WE SETTLED into a comfortable routine. I cooked and cleaned and worked my sparse shifts at the restaurant. James got a part-time job working at a nursing home and spent the rest of his time working on the house. Zach carefully organized and detailed the renovations, starting with the back porch and the stone-walled gardens. He hired Axel to do the masonry.

Gradually I pieced together the life of Zachary Cutter. He had always done exceedingly well in school and started taking college courses while still in high school. He graduated with his first degree in accounting at the age of twenty-one. That was the year he married Alice. But he grew restless and bored with the work despite his skill at it and the money he made. He went back to school part-time, studying architecture. Somewhere along the way he also earned a degree in business.

He continued to manage a few large accounts he established at the accounting firm that hired him out of college. He bought and sold a few houses and knew more about the stock market than I wanted to ask. After getting his degree in architecture, he made a name for himself and became in demand. But even that didn't hold his attention.

James had graduated from high school by that point. Having no solid goal in mind, he started working for Charley Walsh, an old college friend of Zach's. Charley had started a construction company, borrowing heavily. By the time he hired James he was nearly bankrupt despite having work coming in. Zach saw the floundering company as his new project. Investing a sum of money he wouldn't disclose pulled Charley's company out of the red. With some careful marketing and

Zach's name as architect attached to the business, it won a few high-profile government bids and was now flourishing; which meant that Zach was bored with it and looking for something new.

Renovating the house was his new project. He had worked closely with Charley to learn construction and was determined to do the work himself. He agreed to hire my dad to do any of the work that needed tools or expertise he didn't have.

His plans for the house were impressive. The basement would be finished, adding a bedroom. The wall that separated the kitchen and living room would be removed, making it one large room. Zach was still discussing the changes to the second floor with James. He wanted to take down a wall and make two of the small bedrooms into one large master bedroom. He wanted to have the bathroom attached to the master bedroom and create a second smaller bath for the other bedroom.

Zach was in no hurry to complete the project. On a rare evening where he had consumed four beers instead of two, I found myself sitting at the kitchen table with him after everyone else went home or to bed.

"I want to take my time with this," he'd said, looking around the kitchen.

"The house?" I guessed.

"Yeah. I've spent the past ten years working myself into the ground. I'm tired, and old."

"You're thirty one."

He smiled at me, scratching at his beard. "I feel older. I'm tired of feeling tired. I'm tired of juggling ten things at once. I like it here. I can relax here. For the first time in my life I don't feel this nagging itch to be *doing* something. I like it."

"We put something in the water," I said.

He chuckled quietly. I wished he would laugh. The closest he came to a laugh was the quiet chesty rumble. I loved the sound but I longed to hear a full blown laugh from him.

"I'm glad you're happy here."

He blinked at me in surprise. "Happy?" He seemed to consider the idea like it was a foreign concept. He sat back in his chair. "Yeah, I guess I am."

"You weren't happy back in Georgia?"

"Not really. Not since . . ." He trailed off, his hand touching the ring that was under his shirt. He shook himself like Mop did after rolling in the dirt. "It doesn't matter. I'm tired. Goodnight, Miss Tavish."

"My name is Bo," I called after him.

CHAPTER 8

I LOVED THE FALL and winter, not only because of the weather but because of Halloween, Thanksgiving, and my all-time favorite, Christmas. James and Zach disclosed that their Southern Baptist grandmother referred to Halloween as the devil's day and never let them participate in the festivities. I promptly decided to throw a Halloween costume party.

Zach resisted the idea, as I knew he would, but James convinced him in the end. James was thrilled and happy to meet some local people our age. I didn't know too many, seeing as most had been forced off the Cape due to the price of housing and lack of jobs. It was mostly family and friends that my family worked with. Which meant it was a bunch of mechanics, masons, and construction workers with a smattering of fishermen, wait staff and house cleaners.

I dressed in my harem girl outfit, pale blue to contrast with my mother's pink. James put together an impressive pirate costume that resembled the guy on the Captain Morgan bottle. Zach put on a Coke shirt and called it a day. Despite Zach's lack of enthusiasm, the Captain and Coke brothers, as they became known, was a big hit. My father always cross-dressed for Halloween and I had long ago gotten past my mortification over this fact. I think the experience of seeing my six-foot-two, two hundred and fifty pound father stuffed into a red-sequined dress with a slit up to mid thigh scarred James and Zach for life.

I continued to get mixed messages from Zach. Despite literally staring at me in open-mouthed obvious lust in my harem girl outfit, he never made a move toward me. He stayed formal and distant and firmly friendly. The looks he gave me were anything but friendly.

James and Zach went back to Georgia for Thanksgiving, although neither was very enthusiastic about it. They described their Thanksgiving as a group of polite acquaintances searching for common ground. Their parents would criticize Zach for his inability to settle on one profession and stick with it. They would criticize James for choosing to work at a nursing home instead of something more lucrative. Despite what sounded to me like bad parents, Zach and James defended them. They said while they were formal and distant, they were loving in their own way. I couldn't understand what that way was, so I was glad they had Rosey too. They described her as open and affectionate, and they both talked to her on the phone regularly.

My own Thanksgiving was a hectic loud drunk fest hosted by my grandparents and attended by my parents, brothers, aunts, uncles, and cousins. There were over thirty people there and grace meant 'Go!' While guarding my food from the thieving hands of my brothers I thought about Zach and James dressed in suits and ties sitting around a table making polite conversation. I was surprised how much I missed them while they were gone.

The back deck was completed after Thanksgiving. Axel used cobblestones to border the gardens that had been expanded and now bordered the deck. I had no idea how I was going to maintain them the following summer but I didn't say anything. They looked too good to protest.

Seeing as there were three of us living in the house, Zach chose to start finishing the basement first. We could all go about our normal lives while he hammered away downstairs. He wanted to have the basement finished by the spring, at which time he would start with the kitchen and living room.

I was only working a few days a week, seeing as it was the off season. James only worked part-time as well. Zach did his accounting work and did some consulting, not that I knew what that meant. Some days he would sleep in until noon and spend the rest of the day walking the beach or the bike path. He didn't seem like there was anything to hurry about.

I was cleaning the kitchen, listening to the radio warn about a possible snowstorm when the phone rang. The land line was a new addition; I had never needed one before. None of my friends or family even had the number. Since Zach was in the basement and James was working, I figured I would answer their phone.

"Hello?"

"Oh. I'm looking for Zachary or James Cutter." The voice made me picture an old cranky lady with crazy hair and a cane she wanted to hit you with.

"James is at work. Zach's working in the basement; want me to get him for you?"

"Who is this?"

"My name's Bodel Tavish."

"And what are you doing at my grandson's house?"

I blinked at the phone. Her tone made it sound like she was accusing me of witchcraft and sodomy.

"I live here. I rent a room."

"Get Zachary for me. Be quick about it."

I was tempted to hang up the phone but refrained. I set it down loudly and opened the basement door. Country music and a skill saw were battling for dominance. Yelling wasn't going to do any good. I went down the narrow stairs. Zach was covered in sawdust and looked irritated.

It took some yelling and hand motions to get his attention. He pulled off the safety glasses.

"What?"

"The wicked witch of the west is on the phone for you," I muttered.

He grimaced. "My grandmother?" He ran a hand through his hair, dislodging some wood chips. "How did she get this number?"

"I don't know, but she's mean. And holding."

Zach looked like he might swear. I followed him back upstairs and stood in the kitchen, shamelessly eavesdropping.

He braced himself and picked up the phone. "Hello, Grandmother." He pulled the phone away from his ear as yelling erupted from it. He glanced at me and shrugged, setting the phone on the counter and getting a Coke out of the fridge. After opening it and taking a long sip he picked the phone back up.

"Glad you got that out of your system," he said. "Why should we have told you? What does it matter? You hated him, what would you want with his house? It's a nice place. James likes it here." There was more yelling. "She was living with Walter before he died. No . . . No. . . No. Did you miss the fact that I am thirty-one years old?"

The comment seemed to light a fire under the bitter old woman. Zach set the phone back down with a resigned sigh and leaned on the counter.

"She sounds lovely," I said.

He rolled his eyes. "I never answer the phone when she calls."

The yelling on the other end of the phone quieted and I distinctly heard, "Zachary Ethan Cutter, did you walk away?"

Zach snatched up the phone. "No, ma'am."

I couldn't help it. I started to laugh. Zach clamped a hand over my mouth, shaking his head. He was so distracted by his grandmother he didn't realize what he was doing. I wanted to run my tongue along his long calloused fingers. That would give his grandmother something to bitch about. I knew I shouldn't do it, but he was so close. He smelled of sweat and sawdust, which had always turned me on. I gave in to impulse and licked my tongue along his fingers.

He swore right into the phone. The dead silence on the other end was ominous. He pulled his hand away, covering the receiver.

"You are evil," he said through clenched teeth.

The screaming resumed on the other end of the line but with more enthusiasm. Zach shoved me roughly away from him.

"Sorry, Grandmother. I, ah, stubbed my toe," he said.

"That was lame," I said.

He covered the mouthpiece again. "Stop helping me, dammit."

Two swears in one day. I must be really pissing him off. Either that or his grandmother was. I relented and sat down in a kitchen chair.

She was still yelling at him. He glanced at me. "Do you have to sit there and listen?"

"Absolutely."

He literally twitched, but his attention returned to the phone. "I'm fine. The house is torn apart right now, so there's nowhere for you to stay if you came for a visit. I'm not lying to you. No, ma'am." I stifled my laughter by clamping a hand over my own mouth. Zach glared at me, which only made me laugh harder.

He let out a large sigh into the phone. "I have to go now, Grandmother. I was in the middle of something. Work. It is work. I'm not going to argue with you about it." He had to hold the phone away from his ear again. When she relented, he continued, "I'm going to hang up now, Grandmother. It was nice to talk to you. Yes, ma'am. Goodbye." He turned off the phone and placed it gently on the counter. It was the gentleness that warned me. In my experience, if a man was merely angry he might throw something or be rough; if he had gone beyond angry and into blindly furious, he became gentle and quiet.

Before I could get up and run, Zach's heavy muscular arms bracketed me as he gripped the arms of my chair hard enough I felt sympathy for the wood. He seemed to double in size as he loomed closer and I instinctively slumped lower in the chair. It wasn't until he settled over me so close I could feel his breath on my lips that I realized his legs were between my knees.

"You are going to drive me crazy," he said.

There was a look in his eyes that made me feel very small and female. I wasn't afraid of Zach. He would never hurt me. But the look in his eyes was domineering and very possessive. It was extremely intimidating. I had never been intimidated by a man in my life.

"What did I do?" I demanded.

The sound he made was the best expression of derision I had ever heard. I didn't like feeling trapped in the chair. I put my hands on his chest and shoved. It was like shoving against a wall. He didn't move an inch. His eyes were so impossibly green and intense. My mouth went dry and I licked my lips. His eyes traced the movement and I shivered.

I don't know what would have happened, but the front door opening broke the spell. Zach stepped away from me. He was back to being angry instead of, well, whatever emotion had nearly made him kiss me.

"I'm home!" James yelled cheerfully as he walked in the front door.

"We noticed," Zach said, his tone so harsh that James flinched.

"What did I do?" he asked.

Zach ran a hand through his hair. "Nothing. Grandmother pissed me off. And you." He glared at me with renewed anger. "You need to grow up."

I stuck my tongue out at him.

He stomped over to the basement door and slammed it after him.

James hadn't moved from the doorway. He stared after his brother with his mouth open in shock.

"What the hell did you do to him?" he gasped.

"Nothing," I snapped. "Why do you think I did anything?"

"Because I haven't seen Zach that mad in years. My grandmother irritates him, but never like that. Which means it was you."

"I didn't do anything," I muttered rebelliously. I could still taste his fingers on my tongue.

James shrugged. "Oh well. I think some corn bread is in order."

I sighed, looking at the closed basement door. "Corn bread might not be enough."

"Put bacon bits in it."

CHAPTER 9

ZACH EMERGED from the basement and acted as if nothing had happened. He accepted the bacon speckled corn bread with charm and grace but no affection for me. It was driving me crazy. He was so much the southern gentleman; until you noticed the look in his eyes when he looked my way.

But there wasn't much I could do. And it was almost Christmas so I didn't let him spoil my mood. We decorated the house, stringing up lights inside and out. James and Zach joined my brothers and me selecting the Christmas tree and setting it up. I'd pilfered some of my parents' old ornaments and started a collection of my own. Walter always insisted I hang five ornaments on the tree. One was a picture of Walter, his bitter ex-wife, and his stepson. The other four were pictures of Zach and James. Their father sent the pictures to Walter secretly, not wanting to upset Roberta.

James loved the holidays but Zach seemed immune to the merriment. I tried dancing around singing Christmas carols but he only graced me with a placating smile. So I danced with James and my brothers. Zach usually parked himself in one of the overstuffed chairs, drank his single beer, and went to bed early.

He and James flew back to Georgia on December twenty-third; neither left with any enthusiasm. They were less excited about Christmas than Thanksgiving because their grandmother had decided to fly up from Florida to join in the non-festivities. I wasn't surprised to get a text message from James on Christmas Eve. I detangled myself from Gage and escaped the frivolity of my drunken happy family for a bedroom.

Hey Bo. I need a favor. Give Zach a call. He and Rosey got in a huge fight and I'm worried. Thanks, J

I didn't allow myself to hesitate. I called Zach's cell phone. He picked up after two rings.

"Hello?"

"Hey, Zach. It's Bo."

"Oh. Hi."

There was something wrong with his voice, but I couldn't figure out what it was.

"James just texted me that you had a big fight with Rosey."

"Yeah. She was pissed."

"About?"

"I refused to go to church. I don't want to go there, dammit. I don't believe in that crap anymore. And everyone just gushes about how good it is to see me. And they don't talk about Alice."

I settled on the bed in the spare bedroom of my parents' house.

"I'm sorry, Zach. You've had this fight before, right?"

"Not like this. Rosey went off on me. And the bitch of it is she was right. It's hard to fight with someone who's nailed your sorry ass to the wall."

I stared at my cell.

"Zach, are you drunk?"

"Yep. At least I hope so. I drank a bottle of Jack Daniels. If I'm not drunk, I can go get some more."

"Where are you?"

"At my parents place. Lying on a bed. I think."

"You think?"

"The room is kinda spinning."

This conversation was making my head spin and I'd only had two beers.

"Are you OK, Zach?"

"Me? Hell no. Haven't you heard? I live in the past, blame myself for everything. I'm a failure. I just keep running."

"You're not a failure."

"I failed her."

I had a bad feeling he was talking about his dead wife. I wish I knew what happened so I could say something comforting and intelligent.

"You're a good man, Zach. You're smart. Hell, you're brilliant."

He grunted.

"Look, I know you feel like shit right now. But Rosey loves you. This much I'm sure of. She just wants you to be happy."

"How do you know Rosey loves me?"

"Because she raised you. And you are a man who's been loved. It shows."

"That sounded pretty."

I realized with some astonishment that it had been a little poetic. I should drink more often.

"The point is that Rosey and you may have fought, but it's only because she loves you and wants the best for you. You are a wonderful man, a good friend, and a fantastic brother. Not to mention an excellent landlord."

He chuckled.

"I miss you," he said.

"I wish I was there right now."

"Why? So Rosey can throw a shoe at you when she gets back from church?"

I laughed. "No. So I could be there for you. So I could distract her with my hedonistic Yankee ways. She'd be so shocked and horrified by my impropriety she'd forget your various sins."

He laughed. It was an impossibly beautiful sound, full and coming from deep in his chest. It washed me in warmth and accomplishment. I had made Zach Cutter laugh out loud. It was the best Christmas gift I could have received.

"Thank you," he gasped, after his laughter subsided.

"For what?"

"I thought I'd forgotten how to do that. But I didn't count on you. You always find a way to make me smile. And now you've made me laugh. Hell, I think I'll fly next."

I smiled at my phone. "Don't even think of it. Stay away from the windows."

He laughed again. The sound nearly made me cry.

"I don't think I'll be getting up. I am drunk."

"I'm not."

"Shame. We could have some fun." There was a teasing note to his voice I had never heard before.

"Why, Zachary Cutter, are you being naughty?"

"Only when no one's looking."

It was my turn to laugh. "Are you feeling better now?"

"Much better. I don't know how you do it, but you always do."

"It's a talent."

The door to the room I was in opened and Gage stuck his head in. He gave me an inquiring look and I nodded to him that everything was fine. He blew me a kiss and was gone.

"I have to get back to the party, if you're OK?"

"I'm more than OK, babe."

"How much did you have to drink again?"

"A lot."

"That explains it. Are you sure you're OK?"

"I'm lying on a bed. My shoes are off. What more do you want?"

I forced the image of him lying on a bed naked out of my mind.

"I'm glad you're OK. I'll call you tomorrow, Zach. Merry Christmas."

"Merry Christmas, Miss Tavish."

I glared at my phone. "Dammit, Zach. Say my name."

"Goodnight, ma'am." He let me hear his great booming laugh one more time before hanging up.

CHAPTER 10

"YOU ARE a miracle worker," James said when I answered my cell phone Christmas day.

"Merry Christmas to you too."

"I'm serious, Bo. I don't know what you did, but I owe you."

"For what?"

"My brother is acting like a human being. Rosey was in a snit all through church. She was dead-set on getting home and starting the fight right back up. But when we walked in the front door we heard Zach laughing. I haven't heard Zach laugh in years, Bo. Years. Rosey started crying."

I didn't know what to say.

"And this morning he walked downstairs with a big smile on his face and picked Rosey up off the ground in a hug. He hasn't even let my grandmother spoil his good mood. And I know it's because of you."

"You're giving me too much credit. I just cheered him up is all."

"I've been trying to cheer him up for years. But you did it. I feel like I got my brother back. And when I get back there I am giving you the biggest hug in the history of the world."

I laughed at his boyish enthusiasm.

"I'm looking forward to it."

"Oh, here, Rosey wants to talk to you."

"What? Wait," I began, but the phone had been passed. I sighed. "Hello."

"Hello, dear." The voice was motherly and made me think of cookies in the oven and hot chocolate. "So you're the Bo that made my boy laugh."

"He made me work for it."

She laughed. "I just needed to hear your voice. I have no idea how you did it, but Zach is actually acting happy. It is the best Christmas present I have ever received. Thank you."

I was blushing furiously and glad no one was around to see. "I don't know what I said or did. He was so sad, and I just wanted to cheer him up."

"Well, you did. I wanted to talk to you about one other thing. I want to come up for a visit. It's your home, and I didn't want to invade it without speaking to you first."

"I just rent a room," I protested.

"Ha. Both boys have told me about the place and how much work you put into making it more than just a place to sleep. It's your home. I would love to come and see it, to meet you."

"I'd love to meet you too."

"It's settled then. I won't be up till the spring though. My old bones don't like the cold you have up there. But come spring I'll come for a spell."

"I'll be looking forward to it."

"I knew I would like you. Oh!" She produced a startled sound and the phone was lowered from her mouth but I could still hear the conversation.

"You know better than to sneak up on an old woman, Zachary Cutter," she scolded.

"Sorry, ma'am," Zach said. I could hear the grin on his face.

"I was just talking to that lovely girl, Bo."

"How do you now she's lovely?"

"Is she?"

"Absolutely."

"Well, here, you can tell her yourself."

I heard the phone move.

"Hello?" Zach sounded tentative.

"Hi, Zach. Merry Christmas."

"Merry Christmas to you too."

For a moment, I was lost for words. "You don't sound as hung over as you should."

He laughed. The sound came easily this time.

"I'm fine. Thanks."

"Well, good."

I had no idea what else to say.

"You going to your parents' house soon?" he asked.

I checked my watch. "Shit, I'm late."

"The way you talk, I'm surprised Santa didn't bury the tree in coal."

"Ha ha." I drew out the sound dryly. "I have to go."

"OK. James and I will be back tomorrow afternoon."

"I'll have the lights on for you."

"And corn bread?"

I laughed. "And corn bread. Merry Christmas, Zach."

"Merry Christmas, Miss Tavish."

He hung up before I could correct him.

CHAPTER 11

JAMES THREW OPEN the front door and yelled, "Honey, we're home!"

I laughed as I heard him literally run through the living room and into the kitchen where I was finishing dinner. He rushed right to me and picked me up off the ground. He spun me around with a whooping cheer and gave me a noisy kiss on the lips. He set me back down and I nearly lost my balance.

"So." He leaned on the wall smugly. "Best hug in the world?"

I laughed. "I'd say so."

"Good. I'd hate to disappoint." He moved back to me and hugged me again, but more calmly. Then his eyes caught on the stove.

"What is that?" he asked.

"Cod piccata. You'll love it. Trust me."

"Anything you make I'll love. Do I have time to shower quick before dinner?"

"You've got about ten minutes."

James saluted and ran upstairs.

"Where's Zach?" I called after him.

"Finishing a work phone call outside. He'll be right in."

I checked the concoction on the stove and the corn bread in the oven. Everything was perfect. I heard the front door open and I wiped my hands on a towel and turned to see Zach standing in the archway of the kitchen. His large duffel bag was slung over one massive shoulder. He set it down.

"Hey, Zach," I said. I wasn't sure what kind of reception I would get. He looked at me and I caught my breath. I could see the change in him. It was in his eyes. That horrible sadness was gone. His smile wasn't strained.

We walked toward each other and I went with instinct and wrapped my arms around his waist. I had never hugged Zach before and I expected him to pull away. But his brawny arms settled around me, pulling me closer. He picked me up off the ground so that my body fit more comfortably against his bigger, taller one.

It felt impossibly right being in his arms, like I had been there a thousand times before. His chin was resting in my hair and he held me effortlessly. The moment dragged out and neither of us seemed interested in separating. But eventually he set me back on my feet, pulling back enough to smile at me. It was instinct and not conscious thought that had my lips brushing against his cheek.

"I missed you," he said.

"I missed you too. I'm glad you're back."

I realized that his arms were still around my waist. He let his hands drop casually and looked over my head at the stove.

"Dinner smells good."

I went back to the stove to check on it. I was confused as to exactly what was going on. I didn't know what Zach was thinking or feeling. I didn't know if anything had changed, and if it had changed then how?

"How was the flight?" I asked.

We made small talk while I cooked and James showered. We didn't discuss anything important. He described his quiet polite Christmas and I made him laugh with the antics of my crazy family.

Zach felt the same but different. He moved with a masculine grace that was constant, confident, and relaxed. I spent most of the meal trying to figure out exactly what had changed about him. It was extremely subtle but glaringly obvious at the same time.

Aside from hugging me, he acted the same as he always did. He was polite and friendly but not romantic in any way if you ignored his eyes. But when I handed him his plate he touched my fingers. He wasn't avoiding my touch anymore. I figured it was progress, but on the downside, it was making me want him to touch me a lot more.

CHAPTER 12

I RAISED MY GLASS and clicked it against Mason's beer.

"Happy New Year." He grinned at me.

"Not for another five minutes," I pointed out, looking at the TV. Gage was snuggled on the couch with his new girlfriend whose name I had forgotten. She was a fellow dancer, willowy beautiful and, unfortunately, brainless. Axel and the eight-months-pregnant Maxine stopped in, but fatigue and swollen feet had sent them home early. I made a point to talk to my sister-in-law, searching for common ground. Maxine was pretty, blond, and girly. But she loved my brother, and I did too, so we talked about Axel and the coming baby.

James earned my attention by stumbling into the room with a yell. He glanced at the TV.

"Oops. Pretend I did that in four minutes," he slurred. I had never seen James that drunk before. I helped him into a chair. Once I was sure he was going to stay in it and not fall on the floor, I went back to enjoying Mason's mostly sober company.

"You're a good babysitter," Mason pointed out.

"I'm like Mom that way," I admitted.

"You'll make a great mom someday."

The idea made me choke on my mudslide.

"Someday. In the very, very, very distant future."

Mason clicked his beer against my glass and finished it. "Amen. Mom's been giving me that *when are you getting married look* lately."

"Better you than me."

"At least you have prospects." I saw a sadness in his eyes that he would never admit aloud. He didn't like being a bachelor. He wanted a wife and kids and everything that went with it. I hated that he was so lonely. But he was wrong about me having prospects. Wasn't he?

I blinked at him. "What?"

"Don't *what* me. You know exactly who I'm talking about."

I did know. And thinking of Zach made me realize he was missing. He had been sitting in one of the big armchairs a little while ago. I was on a mission to get him drunk, which was why I pulled out the blender and made mudslides. After about an hour of pestering Zach I managed to get him to drink one. Then another. Then I handed him another for good measure. He grew quieter and quieter the more he drank, settling in the armchair and watching things move around him. It was a disappointing result to my get-Zach-drunk experiment.

My attention was drawn to the TV. The countdown was starting. I adjusted my silver party hat and joined my brothers and James in yelling out numbers. After yelling zero I threw my arms around Mason and kissed his cheek. I leaned over James, who was too drunk to get out of his chair.

"Happy New Year, you lightweight," I said. I gave him a friendly kiss on the mouth. He grinned at me as I removed my party hat and slipped it over his head.

"You're purty." He exaggerated the southern drawl and winked at me. I laughed and gave Gage a kiss on the cheek. I looked at my empty glass and started toward the kitchen.

"Oh, purty one, mind getting me another beer?" Mason grinned.

"You are so lazy."

"Is that a yes?"

"I'll get you a beer, you loser."

"That's a new record. You made it a whole minute into the year before insulting me."

I laughed at him as I placed my glass in the sink. I was done with mudslides. The room was looking a little too bright and spinny. The beer was in a cooler on the back deck. Mop was sound asleep under the kitchen table. I nearly tripped on an outstretched paw as I walked out the back door.

I bent down to open the cooler and paused, hearing a slight movement behind me. I turned and jumped with an indignant squeak. Zach was leaning against the house in the shadow under the light.

"Dammit, Zach." I was embarrassed for the squeak. "You scared me. What are you doing out here all alone?"

He shrugged. I couldn't see his face due to the shadows cast by the light.

"Well, Happy New Year."

I took the three steps separating us. I wanted to give him a friendly kiss to celebrate the holiday, try and pull him back into the party with the others. He was too tall and I placed my hands on his shoulders to pull him down so I could reach his lips.

It happened so fast my brain couldn't process it. The air left my lungs as my feet left the deck and I was pressed solidly against the house. Zach's hot hard body trapped me up off the ground. His hands on my hips slid around to my ass as he lowered his head and kissed me. I had been planning on a friendly kiss. Zach's kiss wasn't friendly.

He invaded my mouth, stealing any protest with his tongue. His kiss was filled with passion, desire, and need. My brain jumped ship and I drowned in emotion. He was so big, so strong, and so completely in control. I couldn't move with him pinning me so forcefully against the wall. I didn't want to move. I wanted him to keep going. My hands had found their way around his neck, tangling in his hair.

One of his hands slid more fully under my ass, pulling me firmly against him. His other hand traveled up my body. Without any preamble his hand slipped under my gray sweater and traced fire over my belly and ribs. He bit at my lower lip, changing the angle of the kiss. His hand caressed my breast through the lace of my bra.

My body shivered at the touch of his large claiming fingers. I should have protested. I should have done something. But I just tightened my fingers in his hair and pulled his mouth harder against mine. He tasted like chocolate mudslide and desire. His hand explored my breasts through my bra, his fingertips curling around the edge of the material. His thumb rubbed against my erect nipple and I bit his lip in surprise and pleasure. He pulled his mouth away from mine and ravaged my neck. I tilted my head, giving him better access. I wanted to feel him naked against me. I wanted to feel him naked inside me. A part of me was frightened of how much I wanted him, but most of me was too wrapped up in pleasure to care.

His mouth burned on my neck. His teeth grazed my skin and his tongue caressed my ear. It was too much. It wasn't nearly enough. He bit down gently on the spot where my neck met my shoulder. I moaned his name.

Zach's head shot up the second I spoke. The desire in his beautiful green eyes burned out into concern. His hand slid out from under my shirt and he set me on my feet. He didn't move his body away. He was breathing hard and trembling.

I touched his face, wondering what I had done wrong.

"Zach?"

He let out a shuddering sigh and leaned his forehead against mine. He had to bend down to do so, placing a little distance between our bodies. There was something even more intimate about his forehead resting against mine than his body being pressed against me. His eyes were closed, his hands resting on my hips.

"Zach? What did I do wrong?" I asked.

His eyes opened but he didn't move his forehead from mine. "Wrong? Nothing. You didn't do anything wrong. I'm sorry."

"What are you sorry for?"

He stood up straight, breaking the contact between us except for his hands on my hips. I rested my hands on his chest. He didn't pull away.

"I practically attacked you." He sighed, looking down.

"I wasn't complaining." I rolled my eyes. "Hell, I've been flirting with you for months hoping you'd do just what you did."

He still didn't look at me. I moved my hand to his face. His full beard was an interesting sensation against my palm; soft but wiry. I remembered the way it felt against my face. He was looking down stubbornly at his work boots. I tilted his face and ducked a little so he had to look at me.

There was desire in his eyes, but also regret and pain. I wanted to know everything that he was feeling. I stroked his cheek and he leaned his face into my touch.

"What is it? What's wrong?"

Without his body pressed against me I was starting to notice the cold. But this conversation was going to happen here and now. If we went inside our brothers would interfere.

"I don't know what to do," he admitted.

"About me? Cause at the moment taking me upstairs and ravaging my body sounds like a great idea." I was only half-teasing. He smiled but it didn't reach his eyes.

"You don't understand." He sighed, trying to lower his eyes. I didn't let him.

"Explain it to me."

He sighed again. "I've never felt like this before. I don't know what to do about it. About you. I'm a traditional man. From the moment that idiot dog dropped your panties on my foot I've wanted you. And you're so . . ." He paused.

I smiled. "I'm a Yankee harlot?"

He let out a small chuckle. "To say the least. You're so different from anyone I have ever been attracted to. And you live here. I wanted to take you out on a date, but . . ." He trailed off.

"We live together already. It'd be a bit weird," I admitted. I shook my head. "Untraditional. Which is me in a nutshell. Why didn't you tell me? Why didn't you just ask me to go to dinner?"

"I'm not good at this." He removed a hand from my hip to run it through his hair.

"Obviously."

"Thanks for your support."

"Come on, Zach. I've lived with you for four months. I've flirted with you constantly. I've hinted and flaunted and given you a thousand opportunities."

"I haven't been on a date in years," he admitted. He pushed me a few steps away from him. "This is hard to say, so bear with me."

I nodded, wrapping my arms around myself to keep from reaching for him. He looked so wounded.

He took a long moment before speaking. "I've been really messed up since Alice died. I don't know if I ever really got over it. I'm not sure it's the kind of thing that can be gotten over. I tried to date but I could never get myself to trust a woman again. I had given up on anything more than a one night stand." He blushed but continued. "And then I met you."

"And you want more than a one night stand?"

The look in his eyes answered my question.

"Don't be stupid," he muttered.

"I'm not a mind reader," I said defensively. "You've been sending me mixed signals for months. It's been driving me crazy."

"I know. I'm sorry. I just don't know what I should do."

I stepped up to him, pressing my body against his massive warm chest. "You should kiss me again."

He smiled, his fingers tucking a stray strand of hair behind my ear.

"I don't know if I have anything to give you," he said. "I'm not exaggerating about Alice. I'm still mixed up about it. I never had the guts to really deal with it before. It was just easier to keep it locked up in the past. But I can't leave it there. Not if I want to really be with you." He paused. "I'm talking you out of this. My own worst enemy."

I smiled and stroked his cheek, wrapping my other arm around his neck. I let my fingers rest on the tattoo.

"I'm not stupid, Zach. I can understand that you have baggage. That you've got unresolved emotions about your wife." I sighed. I wished he didn't have them, but I was an adult and could handle it.

"I should have moved past it years ago," he admitted. "I've just been running. For nearly ten years I've been running. Filling my days with so much work I didn't have time to feel. But then I came here. I met you, and that shaggy mutt in there. And this place." He cupped my face in his large hands. "You made me stop running. You stopped me dead in my tracks."

I didn't know what to say. I smiled at him.

"Go out to dinner with me tomorrow night," I said.

He grinned. "I'm supposed to ask."

"A girl could go gray waiting for you to find your balls."

He laughed, throwing his head back. I couldn't help it but laugh with him. He lowered his head and kissed me. This kiss was calmer, gentle, a promise of more.

"I'll take you out to dinner," he said against my lips.

And I'll take you to bed I thought, but I didn't say it. I did say, "For now, we have to go back inside. How do you want to handle our brothers?"

Zach groaned and rested his forehead against mine. I loved the feeling and hoped it was something he would do often. "My brother is going to make my life a living hell."

I smiled, stroking his beard. "We'll try and keep it a secret," I said.

He grinned at me. "It'll never work."

I laughed. "For now, just come back inside with me and get warm."
He kissed my forehead and opened the door for me.

I turned in the doorway. "Do one thing for me."

"What?"

"The next time I ask you to say my name, say it."

"Yes, ma'am."

I laughed as I walked into the living room. Mason glanced at me.

"Where the hell have you been? And where's my beer?" he demanded.
Then his eyes caught on Zach, who had walked in close behind me.
"Never mind," he added hastily.

"I decided my big strapping capable brother could get his own
beer," I said.

Zach looked uncomfortable. He sat down on the couch because
Gage and James were taking up the chairs. Gage's girlfriend was on
his lap in a drunken stupor. I couldn't honestly tell the difference from
her normal look.

I yawned and settled on the couch next to Zach. I didn't exactly lean
against him but it was close. Mason watched me warily a moment
before sitting down on the other end of the couch. An action movie was
on TV. I was still cold from being outside. I pulled the blanket from the
back of the couch and shifted around until I was lying down with my
head on Zach's thigh and my feet on Mason's lap. I draped the blanket
over me and pretended not to notice the men in the room staring at me.

Zach draped an arm around me casually, resting his hand on my
side. I snuggled against his warmth and fell asleep. Let them all think
what they wanted. I was damn comfortable.

CHAPTER 13

I WOKE UP ALONE in my bed. Well, I wasn't alone, but the male in bed with me was furrier than the one I wanted. Mop looked at me with his chocolate-brown eyes and woofed, slapping his tail against the blanket.

"Morning, handsome." I sighed, feeling bad that I was disappointed to see my dog instead of my man. I shook my head. Zach wasn't my man, not yet. I wasn't sure what he was. But I couldn't wait to make something out of the previous night.

"How did I end up in bed?" I asked Mop. I had fallen asleep on the couch. On Zach's warm muscular thigh. I took stock of myself. I was still dressed in my jeans and gray sweater but my shoes were off. Someone had carried me to bed. My brothers would have simply kicked me awake, and James had been so drunk he would have dropped me if he tried to carry me. I smiled and changed into sweatpants and a tank top. Southern boys that they were, James and Zach kept the heat cranked much higher than I would have so I could wear my summer PJs in the winter.

I headed downstairs behind Mop's lumbering exuberance. He slipped on the last step in his haste and eternal grace and barreled into the front door. I ruffled his indignant old head but I was worried about his climbing the stairs as his age caught up to him. It made me think of Walter as I walked into the kitchen.

"Whoa, what's wrong?" James asked. He was standing at the stove next to a counter of cracked eggshells.

"Oh." I ran a hand through my loose tangled hair. "I was just missing Walter. It's nothing."

James looked relieved, probably because I no longer looked like I would cry.

"I wish I could have met him," he admitted. "You want eggs?"

"Did you pour hot sauce in them?"

James had a strange habit of trying to hide his lack of cooking ability by making everything so unbearably hot your taste buds were burned out before you could realize the food was terrible.

"Zach yelled at me not to," he muttered rebelliously.

I looked around the empty kitchen. "Where is he?"

"Downstairs, working." James stomped loudly on the floor, signaling that food was ready. There was a thump of a broom handle in response. We worked out the system after I grew tired of yelling down the stairs over power tools.

I heard Zach's heavy footsteps and wondered what I should do or say to him. Would he come into the kitchen and kiss me good morning? Would he give me a nod and sit down like last night hadn't happened?

Zach smiled at me as he walked into the kitchen. James's back was to us but I still wasn't sure how to greet him. He leaned down and gave me a quick kiss on the top of my head.

"Morning," he said. He moved around the table and sat down casually. He didn't want to make a big thing of it. I was in agreement. James would tease both of us mercilessly when he realized we were going on a date. James turned around, plates of overcooked peppery eggs in his hands. I sighed but took the offered food, watching James dump hot sauce over his own eggs.

James sat down. "So, how's the new year treating you so far?" he asked.

It shouldn't have been a loaded question but it was. Before Zach or I could speak, Zach's cell phone rang. It was the ring tone reserved for his accounting business calls. He looked at the phone and grunted. He opened the cell phone.

"Ciao, Marco. Come il nuovo anno ti tratta."

James let out a bark of laughter at the look on my face. Zach glared at both of us and left the room.

"He speaks Italian too? What the hell doesn't he do?" I groused.

"You should have realized by now that Zach never does anything halfway," James said. "He learned when my maternal grandmother came to live with us."

That information surprised me. It must have shown on my face.

"I know. From what we've said about my parents I guess it seems weird that they would take her in. My grandfather died when I was seven. My Nonna, that's grandmother in Italian, she had dementia. My grandfather had taken care of her, and I think my parents would have preferred to put her in a home, but she had forgotten how to speak English. My grandfather met her while studying abroad in Italy, married her and brought her home with him. But we couldn't put her in a nursing home, not if she couldn't speak to anyone. So we took her in. None of us could speak Italian, but she trusted us and settled in OK. But she was always confused and anxious. And so lonely. My parents were busy at the hospital and I was just a little kid, so Zach learned Italian."

I glanced at the doorway where Zach had disappeared. "How old was he?"

"Fourteen. Nonna couldn't teach him, she didn't always make sense cause of her dementia. So he found a tutor and worked at it every day. I don't remember really well, I was only seven, but he seemed to learn it overnight. And she was so happy. She could tell him what she wanted. When she was confused and upset he could understand her and explain what was going on."

I sat back in my chair. At fourteen years old, Zach had learned a second language so he could take care of his aging grandmother. Was the man a damn saint? What the hell was I thinking going after a man like him? He was too perfect for someone as jaded and cynical as me.

"My Nonna was the nicest woman," James continued. "I couldn't understand her, but she loved Elvis. Was crazy about him." He looked around and leaned closer to me, lowering his voice to a conspirator's whisper. "If I tell you this, you have to swear never ever to let Zach know I told you."

I nodded, leaning closer.

"My Nonna always wanted to meet Elvis. She was out of it enough not to realize he was dead and Zach figured that it wouldn't hurt to indulge her. Her health had been growing worse and we knew it wouldn't be long till she was gone. So on Halloween he dressed up as Elvis."

Despite the image of a teenaged Zach dressed in white rhinestone glory that flashed into my head, I had to blink back tears. The tears surprised me. I wasn't a crier by nature. But the fact that Zach would go to that length to make an old woman happy made my heart flip over in my chest.

"I know." James smiled fondly at the memory. "He pulled it off so well too. She didn't even think it was odd that Elvis spoke Italian." He paused, the smile lingering on his face. "She died three days later."

"I'm sorry," I said automatically.

"Don't be. She died peacefully in her sleep. It was her time. The day after Halloween she told Zach all about fulfilling her lifelong dream of meeting The King. She said she'd done everything she had ever wanted and was ready to go see Lawrence again. My grandfather," James clarified.

Nonna explained why I sensed such a strong sense of family from Zach, despite his distant parents. I knew within the first few days of meeting Zach that he was the kind of man who liked to take care of people. He was a rescuer of damsels, savior of lost causes, and friend to everyone. What did he think he was doing with me?

Zach walked back into the room. He looked at my face and glared at his brother.

"I leave the room for five minutes and you make her cry?" he growled.

James held up his hands. "I was just telling her about Nonna."

Zach looked surprised.

"I was surprised you spoke Italian," I said, feeling the need to rescue James. "He was telling me why you learned. Your grandmother sounds like she was quite a lady."

The look in Zach's eyes was full of warmth, pride, and love. "That she was. She would have liked you."

I blinked at him. "Me? The Yankee harlot?"

Zach rolled his eyes, a boyish gesture that made him look younger. "Nonna was Italian," he said, sitting at his plate of cold eggs. "She was scandalous. She told me more about my grandfather than I ever wanted to know."

I laughed. I laughed harder when Zach shoved the eggs in his mouth and grimaced. "They taste even worse cold, little brother. Seriously, how do you mess up eggs?"

James had eaten all of his and most of mine. They were overcooked and doused with so much black pepper that my eyes would have watered even if I hadn't heard about Nonna.

"I like them," James said defensively.

Zach slid the plate at him. "I'd rather chew on sawdust downstairs."

CHAPTER 14

ZACH STAYED DOWNSTAIRS for most of the day. I busied myself cleaning the house from the party the previous night. Gage showed up searching for one of his shoes. I fed him lunch.

"So," he said around a bite of sandwich. "You and Zach?"

I tried to keep my face passive. "What about us?"

Gage chewed his food and rolled his eyes at me, waiting for me to answer.

"Fine. We're going out to dinner."

"A date?"

"Yeah. So? What's it to you?"

He grinned at me and licked mayo off his thumb. "You're my sister. He better treat you like a queen."

I didn't feel much like a queen in my stained ratty sweatpants and threadbare tank top. I sat down with Gage, knowing I could say to him what I couldn't to Mason or Axel.

"I need a reality check," I admitted.

"Ready and waiting."

"Zach's a great guy. Hell, he's more than great. He's educated, bilingual, rich, generous, polite, screw it, he's perfect."

"He's not," Gage shook his head. "That's your first reality check. No one's perfect."

"I know. But he's just so much better than me."

"What?"

"Look at me. I'm a twenty-five year old waitress. I did one year of community college before dropping out. I have no money in the bank, no savings, and no plans. I have never done anything worthwhile in my life."

"And I have?" Gage rolled his eyes at me.

"You're twenty."

My brother looked at me like I was an idiot child.

"Bo, you can't look at it like this. He's not better than you. He's done well professionally. He also started college when he was seventeen and had his first degree when he was twenty-one. Hell, you were fifteen. And all that is just surface stuff anyway. It doesn't matter how much money he has or what he does for a living. That kind of crap doesn't make a man."

"Philosophical," I muttered. "But I agree. Still, he's better than me on the human scale too. He learned Italian to take care of his sick grandmother. He took care of James, bailed his friend Charley's business out of debt."

"You moved in here to take care of Walter," Gage pointed out. "A complete stranger who was mad as hell, bordering on cantankerous."

I had to concede the point. I couldn't pretend I was selfish. I hadn't ever been interested in college and figured if I dropped out my parents might be able to help Gage with school. Walter put up a flyer that stated: *Grumpy old man needs someone to cook clean and drive him around.* I met him at the local donut shop and we took Mop for a walk. I lived with Walter for two years. He hadn't really needed someone to care for him. He was just lonely and unable to drive. And if I hadn't met Walter, I never would have met Zach.

"I'm worried," I admitted.

"About?"

"Zach likes to save people. To help them. I don't think I need saving, but maybe he sees it that way."

Gage nodded, his food gone. "Personally, I don't think he sees you that way. I've seen the way he looks at you. Makes me want to punch him sometimes."

I rolled my eyes. My brothers were such boys.

Gage reached across the table and took my hand. "You're great. You're amazing and wonderful and beautiful and spectacular. And you're female, so you're automatically better than any man, even if he has money, charm, and a high IQ."

I laughed.

"That was just what I needed to hear."

"I know. I'm gonna head out now before I say something stupid and ruin it."

* * *

Zach emerged from the basement sweaty and coated in sawdust. He looked entirely too sexy in his torn jeans and ratty white T-shirt. I was on the floor trying in vain to get a brush through Mop's unruly fur. I had a plastic bag full of shed hair beside me. I knew there were tufts of fur sticking to my clothes and likely in my hair. He was sexy, and I was trying to impersonate Chewbacca.

"Done working?" I asked, checking the wall clock.

He was looking at me with an amused smile on his lips. Mop was draped over my legs, panting happily while coating me in loose fur. Zach reached down and pulled a large tuft of gray fur out of my hair.

"I'm not sure I like this new look," he said.

I glared at him.

"You have something against gray hair?" I muttered.

"No. But yours is such a beautiful shade of brown."

I had never learned to take compliments well. When Mason or Axel complimented me it was because they were preparing me for bad news. I shoved at Mop, who didn't seem inclined to move. Zach bent down and gently tugged once on Mop's collar. The giant dog elbowed me hard in the gut as he scrambled to do what Zach wanted, forcing the air from my lungs.

The next thing I knew Zach had pulled me to my feet, sending fur flying. We stood in a dog-fur whirlwind, but all I noticed was the warmth of his hand on the spot where Mop had elbowed me.

"You OK?" he asked.

His body was so close. I loved the smell of fresh cut wood and sweat. My hand had found its way to his chest.

"I'm fine," I said. I moved to rub at the spot on my belly but Zach's hand was still there. It made me self conscious but I didn't really want him to stop touching me. I looked up into his dark green eyes. The heat in them made my knees threaten to forget what they were supposed to be doing. That fact irritated me. I was not the kind of woman who went weak in the knees from a hot look.

"Are we going to dinner?" I asked, pretending my voice didn't sound husky.

"Yes."

"Then go shower. I need a shower too, so don't use all the hot water."

I had a sudden intense image of showering with Zach. The look in his eyes made me think he was sharing the image and taking it another step. I used the hand I had been resting on his chest to shove him, not that it moved his big frame an inch.

"Get. I have to clean up this mess."

He chuckled, and to my immense displeasure didn't throw me over his shoulder and drag me into the shower with him. I listened to his heavy footsteps on the stairs. Damn his southern manners. How was I going to convince this traditional gentleman to let me have my way with him tonight?

Mop gave me a look. I could have sworn there was reproach in the large brown eyes.

"What? Not all the males in this house had their balls removed."

Mop let out a tired moan and flopped onto his belly on the floor, sending out whirlwinds of fur.

CHAPTER 15

WE ESCAPED THE HOUSE before James returned home from work, succeeding in avoiding the explanation and resulting harassment. Zach had bought a new Ford F-150 with a casualness that unsettled me, but I had to admit sitting in the new car smell was an experience. I directed him to Fairway, which was the best and one of the only year-round restaurants in Eastham. It was also connected to the Hole in One donut shop, home of the spectacular donuts that contributed to the tightness of my jeans.

Zach wore jeans and a clean white T-shirt, sexy male personified. I dug out my nice-ass-jeans and a low cut shirt that hugged me in the right places and cleverly disguised my cookie intake over the holidays. I noticed Zach trimmed his beard, not that he ever let it become unruly.

"Can I get you something to drink while you look at the menu?" the waiter, who I had gone to high school with, asked. He glanced at my face and smiled. "Oh, hey, Bo."

"Hey, Carl. This is Zach, Walter's grandson."

The two men shook hands.

"So," Carl continued. "What can I get you?"

I was feeling nervous so I decided a beer wasn't going to cut it. "I want that fruity martini, the one that Jill recommended at my birthday."

"No problem. And for you, sir?"

Zach glanced at the drink menu. "I don't normally drink like the Yankee harlot here, but I guess seeing as she'll be getting smashed I have to order more than a beer." I kicked him under the table as he and Carl shared a knowing look.

"You look like a rum guy," Carl guessed.

"Mount Gay and Coke," Zach said.

Carl left us alone. I sat back in the booth, glad that it was a quiet night and we had the section to ourselves. Cape Cod in the winter had its benefits.

"So," I said, picking up a dinner roll. "Tell me about Alice."

Zach looked at me like I had suggested we discuss murdering puppies. "Ah, it's not really dinner conversation."

I shook my head. "No, Zach. I want to know about her. She was important to you. She was a big part of your life. And I want to know what she was like, not how she died."

Zach's green eyes lit with an emotion I couldn't name, but I was absolutely sure I said the right thing.

"Do you have a picture of her?" I asked. She had hurt him, of this I was certain. She wounded him so badly he ran for ten years. But when I said her name I saw the look in his eyes. I had to know her if I wanted to really know him.

Zach shifted on the booth so he could pull his wallet from his back pocket. He slid a small battered photo across the table at me. It was a picture of the two of them. Alice was tiny, probably not more than five feet. She was thin and small boned, with pale skin blue eyes and blonde hair. She was looking up at Zach with a huge adoring smile on her face. I'd figured she was beautiful, but I hadn't been prepared for just how beautiful. And she died at the age of twenty-two.

"She was so beautiful. Adorable even. Southern belle to the tee," I said, sliding the picture back.

"That she was. My Alice didn't have a mean bone in her body." He took a moment to look at the photo. The emotions in his eyes were too complicated for words. Carl arrived with our drinks and broke the moment. We ordered our food and Carl shuffled off.

"So," I said, trying to sound light and happy. "How did you meet?"

"We grew up together. My parents are doctors," he reminded me. "And Alice's father worked at the hospital with them. He wasn't chief of staff at the time, but he was on his way. He and my father were good friends. Alice was born six hours after I was." Zach sipped at his drink. "My mother went back to work as soon as she could. Alice's mother was a stay-at-home mom. So when my mother went to work she would drop me off with her."

I settled in to listen, knowing I didn't need to talk while he wandered down his memories.

"My mother-in-law, Charlotte, had miscarried twice before Alice, and Alice was born two months early. It was touch and go for a while. Alice was never very healthy. She got sick easily and was always small for her age. Charlotte practically worshipped her. She's more of a mother to me in a lot of ways than my own mother."

Zach paused. "I don't want to paint my parents in such a harsh light. I love my mother, and my father. But we're not close. They always made sure we had what we needed and they were there when we really needed them. But my mother isn't maternal. She's not warm and nurturing; she's a surgeon. Charlotte is soft and warm. She bakes cookies and folds the napkins at the table into little animal shapes. Alice was a lot like her.

"Alice was my shadow. She went wherever I went. Because she was shy and small, she got picked on a lot. Or she would have, but I was there," Zach said. His protective streak went to the core, apparently. "I didn't think anything of it. She was just always there. I started to realize something might be a bit off in middle school. If I was sick and didn't go to school, she would stay home. It was like she was afraid of the world if I wasn't there holding her hand."

He sighed and took a healthy swallow from his drink.

"She *was* afraid. She was afraid of spiders, snakes, thunder, the dark, everything. She was always trying to save things. She brought home stray after stray, but she couldn't keep any because of her father's allergies. She always insisted on finding them good homes. It was nearly impossible to say no to her."

"She sounds sweet." I tried to sound diplomatic. I couldn't understand a woman that was so afraid of the world she needed to cling to a man, but that didn't mean she hadn't been wonderful and kind.

Zach rolled his eyes at me. "I know what you're thinking."

"No," I began.

"It's OK." He smiled at me. "You're an independent confident woman. She wasn't. She was mousy and afraid."

"I don't want you to think I think badly of her," I tried to explain.

"I know that. I get it. She irritated me, trust me. I wished she could stand on her own. I dreamed of being able to stop holding her, protecting her from nothing. But she was so warm, so generous. She spent all her free time volunteering at soup kitchens, in the children's ward at the hospital, anywhere there was need. She would go door to door for charities, and no one could turn those big blue eyes away." He looked down at the picture that was still sitting on the table. He put it back in his wallet.

"As soon as I got my license I started going by her house and picking her up for school. She took all of the same classes as I did, except for shop because the tools scared her. Sometimes I resented her being there all the time, but she had a great sense of humor. She made me laugh and I didn't mind having a beautiful blonde shadow. But I knew something was wrong."

He sighed and finished his drink. Carl swung by with salad and Zach asked for another drink.

"What was wrong?" I asked.

"She was sad all the time. She tried to laugh and joke like the average teenager, but there were days that it was all I could do to coax her to get out of bed in the morning. She cried all the time, over nothing. I convinced Charlotte that something was wrong when Alice was sixteen. She started seeing a therapist and they diagnosed her as manic-depressive."

I had a really bad feeling about where this was going. I didn't want to let him get to the horrible end but I knew I couldn't stop him from talking. If he wanted to say it I needed to listen. I doubted he had spoken to anyone about Alice in years.

"It took them a few months to find the right medication and dosage before she started getting better. But she was never really OK. Always sad. She said that as long as I was with her, she'd be OK."

I reached for his hand.

"I hope I'm not making her sound pathetic." Zach sighed. "She was truly wonderful. When her meds were working and she was having a good day, she was amazing. There was no bad in her, none at all. People were drawn to her. No one could resist. I couldn't. Even though I should have."

"What do you mean?"

He sighed. "This is completely not first-date conversation."

"It's *this* date conversation. Now tell me what you meant."

"I was never in love with Alice," he admitted. "It's been long enough that I can say it without feeling like a horrible jerk. I loved her as a best friend. But I never felt the way she did. Hell, she worshipped me. I avoided her advances through most of high school. But she wore me down. She was so afraid and she needed me so much. So I told myself I would grow to love her the way she loved me."

I nodded. "That rarely works."

"I was seventeen. I thought I could save her."

Dinner arrived and broke the mood. I thanked Carl and made small talk for a second about his girlfriend. When we were alone again, I watched Zach's eyes to decide if he was done talking about Alice. I didn't think so.

"Are you OK talking about this?" I asked.

"Yes. It's actually good to talk about it."

"How did you end up marrying her?"

"I did dual enrollment in high school," he said. "I took some classes at the community college and the rest at the high school. Alice hated it because she didn't qualify for the program, and couldn't be in my classes. Her grades dropped because she wouldn't go to school without me. It drove me crazy. When I picked a college she panicked. She begged me not to leave her behind."

I really didn't want to dislike Alice. And after seeing her picture, and the way she looked at Zach, I couldn't. She had been weak and sad and very needy, but not bad. It was Zach's failure that he cared for her rather than get her the help it sounded like she needed. But I couldn't really call it a failing.

He cleared his throat. "So she moved in with me when I went to college. She didn't work, but she cooked and cleaned and volunteered. Getting married was just the next logical step. She was so good to me. There were still the days when I got home and found her curled up in bed crying, right where I left her. But it wasn't all the time. Most of the time she was OK. She ran to the door when I got home, dinner ready, eager to tell me about her day."

But he hadn't loved her. I could see it in his eyes. He felt guilty for not loving her back.

"The natural thing to do was marry her," he said again. "We had been living together for two years. She started talking about having a baby. So I got a ring and we got married. I had just graduated college and gotten a great job; it seemed like the right thing to do. I was happy enough even if I wasn't in love with her. I figured it would be enough."

But it hadn't been. And I had a terrible feeling the idea of a baby had been a desperate attempt on Alice's part. If he couldn't love Alice, she would give him a child to love instead. Maybe I was wrong, but I doubted it.

"I was stupid," Zach said.

I shook my head. "You were young, and wonderful."

His eyes were sad. "I should have known what would happen. I saw the signs, her desperation to make me happy when she knew she couldn't. But she kept talking about a baby, like that would fix everything."

I reached across the table and placed my finger across his lips.

"I'm gonna pull the first date card," I said. "I asked about Alice. I wanted to know, and I can tell it was good for you to tell me. But I don't want to ruin this night with the bad parts of your past. I wanted to know about your wife, not about how you lost her. And I love that you told me, trusted me that much. But I want to talk about something else. Something happy. I don't like seeing that sadness in your eyes. Has anyone ever told you that you have beautiful eyes?"

He smiled at me, the sadness I had been referring to retreating. "No. Men aren't beautiful. Least of all me."

Damn, was he wrong. He was beautiful in all the best ways, but I didn't correct him.

"You don't see it, do you?" I asked.

"See what?"

"How handsome you are."

He grunted and shoved some food into his mouth. "I'm a caveman."

"You are not."

He wiped at the melted cheese from his chicken parm that had stuck in his beard and looked at me pointedly.

"A caveman would have left it to eat later," I suggested.

He laughed. "You're the one who doesn't realize how beautiful you are."

I blushed. "Don't compliment me. It scares me."

"Scares you?"

"Whenever my brothers compliment me it's because they did something that is going to make me mad and they want to soften me up."

"I don't think I've done anything that'll make you mad. You're just beautiful."

I fidgeted. "Stop it."

He grinned at me. "Yes, ma'am."

CHAPTER 16

I WASN'T READY to go home as I buckled my seatbelt and Zach started the truck. I wanted the night to go on a while longer before we had the awkward moment when we arrived back home and had to figure out where to go from there.

"Turn left," I said as he pulled up to Rt. 6.

He shrugged and turned. I was surprised he didn't argue or ask why. He was relaxed in his seat, awaiting my next direction.

"Turn left again, at the lights. I want to go to Campground Beach."

"Why?"

"Because it's a place I love and I want to share it with you."

He smiled but didn't say anything else. He followed my directions until we pulled into the large empty parking lot. The single street light lit the mountain of sand the town built up to protect the parking lot from ice. I unbuckled my seatbelt and pulled my leather jacket around me before stepping out into the wind. The wind always blew off the water, so hard that sometimes I could lean forward and not fall.

I walked around the sand piles and down onto the beach. It was low tide and the sandbars lined up one after the other with their bands of water between. The nearly full moon lit the sand and the water so that I could see everything perfectly. The lights from Provincetown shone on the horizon.

Zach followed me down, moving more slowly because he wasn't familiar with the beach as I was. He stood beside me and took a deep breath.

"It's freezing out here," he said. I looked over at him in his Carhartt jacket, hat and gloves. It was a balmy thirty-five degrees, fine weather for January. The fake leather jacket I wore was sexy but it wasn't warm. I was shivering but tried to hide it.

"You are such a southern gentleman," I said, taking shelter from the wind beside his large frame. "Anything else you want to say about my favorite place?"

He looked around. The dunes were steep and high, with summer homes in the process of falling off on the top. A rock wall had been built to the right of the parking lot to save the homes there. The homes to the left were at the mercy of hopeful plantings of beach grass.

"It's a beach," he said, looking at the large chunks of ice that littered the sand, left behind by the receding tide.

I sighed. I looked up at the cloudless sky. I found the Big Dipper and Orion's Belt, the only constellations I knew. Standing there on the beach with nothing but sky and horizon, I had an overwhelming feeling of the Earth being round.

"Why do you love this place?" he asked.

"Because it reminds me that the world is huge, I am small, and so are my problems."

He took a deep breath. "It is peaceful."

I shivered and he put an arm around my shoulders, pulling me against his warmth.

"Do you come here often?" he asked.

"When I'm upset about something. Or sad. Do you have a place you go when you need to feel small?"

He laughed, pulling me closer and resting his chin in my hair. "I've never felt small, babe. I was six feet tall in sixth grade."

"You know what I mean."

"I know. And I don't have a place. Or I didn't."

"You do now?"

"Sort of."

I turned so that I was facing him. "Sort of?"

His eyes were warm as he looked down at me. "When I'm upset or having a really bad day, I find you. And you do something or say something that makes me smile."

I dropped my eyes as my face flushed in embarrassment. His hand settled on my cheek and he flinched.

"You're freezing, honey." He unzipped his jacket and pulled me against him, wrapping the jacket and his arms around me. I snuggled into him, getting the chance to feel the muscles of his chest. His heart hammered in my ear and I let out a contented sigh. It felt like home being in his arms.

"You Yankees are crazy. It's cold as sin out here and you want to stand around and look at the waves," he said into my hair.

"I never thought of sin as cold. I always thought it was more of a hot thing." And I wanted to sin tonight with Zach. I wanted to make love to him and sleep cradled against this wonderful welcoming warmth.

"Depends on the kind of sinning, I guess," Zach said. I tilted my head so I could look up into his face.

"Can I be blunt?"

He laughed and dropped a kiss on my nose. "You're always blunt, babe. It's one of the things I love about you. It's up there with your beautiful gray eyes. Or maybe it's just the way you look at me with them."

I was blushing furiously. "Stop it. You're doing it again."

"Doing what?"

"Being adorable and charming and too damn perfect. It scares me."

"No one has ever called me adorable before," he mused. "But what were you going to be blunt about?"

"Are you going to bring me home and be a gentleman?"

"Ah, define gentleman?"

"Are you going to give me a kiss on the cheek and send me off to my own room? Or are you going to carry me into your bed?"

He answered me with a kiss. It was a slow seduction of lips and tongue, a definite promise of more.

"The southern gentleman is taking the night off, I assure you." He trailed his lips across my cheek. His beard brushed against my skin as he decorated my neck with small gentle kisses. But he stopped, straightening. He pulled me more firmly against him, wrapping his jacket around me. He rested his head in my hair.

"I think this beach has become one of my favorite places," he said.

"I'm glad. But I want to discover my own new favorite place."

"Oh?"

"Your bed. Take me home."

He laughed, the sound vibrating through my body and making me shiver in anticipation.

"As you humbly request, ma'am."

"You call me babe and honey but you can't say my name?"

"I will tonight. It's a promise."

CHAPTER 17

IT OCCURRED TO ME that James would likely be hovering in the living room waiting to pounce and give us a hard time. If he did, I was going to kill him. Zach sat back in his seat while he drove and looked completely relaxed. My body was trembling in anticipation, and sitting still was driving me crazy.

I dove out of the truck in the driveway and trotted up the steps. I opened the front door and looked around. James was nowhere in sight. Mop roused himself from the couch and lumbered slowly over; arriving at the same time Zach stepped into the room. Mop greeted him with an exuberant head-butt to the crotch. Zach's breath came out in a grunt and he hunched over, closing his eyes.

"Bad dog." I pulled Mop away. "I need that in working order."

Zach shook his head. "Rosey would wash your mouth out with soap."

"You like it."

He grinned at me and caught my shoulders, pushing me backward onto the stairs. Straddling me, he sealed my mouth with his. I was too surprised and turned on to be uncomfortable.

"Zach," I gasped, trying to free myself from under him. "James . . ."

"James is in his room and won't be coming out if he knows what's good for him," Zach said against my neck.

"OK, but, on the stairs?"

He chuckled and pulled me to my feet. "Fine. But you better hurry. If you go too slow I'll take you where I catch you."

Where the hell had the quiet reserved Zach gone? I dashed up the stairs with him hot on my heels. I almost ran into my room from habit but remembered at the last moment and passed it. I pushed inside Zach's room and had enough time to note he cleaned before he joined me. He grabbed me and used my body to shut the door.

"You have a thing for pinning me against walls," I observed.

"Maybe." He was nibbling on my neck, his hands pulling at my shirt. He pulled his head back, looking serious. "If it bothers you I won't."

"I didn't say I didn't like it."

"Good." He pulled my shirt over my head and I felt self-conscious. He didn't seem to notice. His hand snaked around my back to unclip my bra. He paused, looking down at me.

"What's wrong?"

"Nothing."

"Just tell me. I can make it right."

"You can make me magically lose ten pounds?"

He shook his head. "You're perfect. You have a beautiful body." He surprised me by dropping to his knees and nuzzling my stomach. His beard tickled over my skin and I let my hands sink into his hair.

He stood, pulling my bra off as he rose. My breasts weren't in view long before his hands covered them. His touch was lighting my skin on fire and making me feel beautiful. I relaxed against him, enjoying the play of his long sure fingers.

"This isn't fair," I said.

He made a sexy sound against my jawbone, his mouth moving down my neck toward my breasts.

"You have too many clothes on," I said in a whisper as his thumbs stroked over my nipples. I grabbed the bottom of his shirt and pulled it up. He helped me, bending down so I could drag it over his head. He returned to my body, warm and hard and sexy. His necklace brushed against my breasts, the wedding ring and cross heated from being close to his skin.

"Zach?"

"What?"

"Would you take the necklace off?"

He looked down at it.

"Why?"

"It's stupid; never mind." I reached for his shoulders to pull him back against me but he resisted.

"Tell me why," he repeated.

"Because the necklace is about Alice. I don't want her between us. I want this to be about you and me. See, I told you it was stupid."

He caught my face between his hands. "It's not stupid. I don't want the past between us either." He pulled the necklace over his head and set it on the bedside table. He held his arms out. "Just me, babe. Just us."

I fell into his arms, knocking him backward onto the bed. His hands unsnapped my jeans and shoved them down my legs despite my straddling him, but he got stuck at mid-thigh and tossed me off him. I landed on my back and he pulled off my heeled boots and the jeans followed. He made a very primal growl of appreciation at my lacy black thong before pulling it down my legs.

I watched him by the light shining through the window from the moon. I thought about turning on the light to see him better while he stripped out of his jeans and boxers. I stared at him and gulped. This was too much man for me. He was too much shoulder, muscle, bone, and strength.

He pushed a knee between my legs and settled that gigantic body over me. I felt incredibly small. But the slight unease I felt vanished as he kissed me. His hands were tender as they teased my body, sliding between my legs. Pleasure forced my eyes shut and I explored him with my hands. He leaned over me and opened the drawer on the bedside table. I listened to the package rip and felt him shift his weight. Then he caught my wrists in his hands and trapped them against the bed over my head.

"Is this OK?" he asked against my lips.

I could only moan. It was more than OK. It felt amazing to have him be so totally in control. He entered me slowly, so slowly I dug my nails into my palms. He bit at my neck and laughed at my frustration. He swallowed my scream when he settled fully inside me. I was afraid to move. He wasn't.

He began to rock inside of me, forcing the breath from my lungs. He transferred my wrists to one hand and slid the other hand down my body. He lifted me; shifting the angle and making my head nearly explode from the sensation.

"You like that, huh?" He chuckled knowingly, bending his head to lick my breasts. He was moving rhythmically but slowly. Too slowly.

"Faster," I gasped.

"Greedy girl."

He didn't move faster. It felt so amazing that I was brainless to do anything but experience it. But my brain never took that long of a vacation. I was a belly dancer, and I had some moves that could rock his world. I shifted my hips in a practiced move. He lost his rhythm, growling deep in his throat in approval.

"You like that?" I purred at him.

"Hell, yes. Keep going."

We drove each other crazy. He settled into the rhythm I chose, giving me everything I gave him. He slid his hand down my belly and into my short curls. He began to stroke me as he finally picked up his slow pace. I felt the orgasm building and wrapped my legs around him. I wanted him harder and deeper and hotter. He gave it to me. I bit down on my lip to keep from screaming as I came. He finally let go of my wrists and pulled my body against his chest. He yelled my name for the first time as he came hard inside me.

He collapsed on top of me, his weight crushing me deliciously into the bed. I wrapped my arms and legs around him, holding him against me. He was breathing hard into the pillow. It didn't last because he was so heavy I couldn't breathe.

"Zach?"

He pulled away, rolling onto his back with a groan of contentment. "Sorry. Didn't mean to crush you. You just… well. Damn."

Damn was right. I had never felt like that before. I curled against his side, running my fingers through his chest hair. "I'll second your damn and raise you a holy shit."

He kissed my forehead. "That mouth is gonna get you in trouble."

"Always."

He chuckled and tilted my chin up so he could kiss me. The kiss was soft and gentle. I had so many things I wanted to say to him, but I yawned instead. It was too right to ruin with words. I settled into his warmth, pulled the blanket over me, and fell asleep.

CHAPTER 18

I WOKE UP to the sound of Mop barking. I moaned and snuggled closer into Zach's shoulder. He shifted a little, pulling me so that I was draped half across his chest. He was warm and comfortable. I didn't care why Mop was barking.

"Morning," I said into his neck.

"I'm not awake," he said.

I smiled and traced his lips with my fingers. He kissed them but didn't open his eyes. I heard James's voice and the front door opening. I ignored any other sound as Zach's hand cupped my ass and pulled me closer against him. But I heard hard angry footsteps on the stairs over Zach's heartbeat. I raised my head as the bedroom door swung open.

"Zachary Ethan Cutter, you had best have a good excuse for still being in bed," an elderly woman with a familiar unwelcome voice barked as she stormed into the room. She stopped in her tracks as she took in the scene. I pulled the blanket up against my breasts and attempted to become invisible. Zach kept his eyes closed and muttered something not even I could hear.

"Sweet Jesus! Lord have mercy!" Zach's grandmother gasped, grasping the large cross that hung around her neck. She ran out of the room, slamming the door. Zach let out a gigantic sigh.

"Did I murder puppies in a past life?" he asked without opening his eyes.

"What?" The odd comment broke me out of my embarrassment paralysis. I had to get out of bed. I needed clothing and composure. I jumped up.

"Where's the fire?" Zach asked, sitting up.

"I need to get out of here, get dressed. I am so embarrassed." I gathered up my clothes.

"You're not stepping out of this room without me," he said, getting up.

"What?"

"If you go out alone she'll be waiting to hit you with a Bible."

"She'll have a hard time finding one in this house."

"She travels with one."

I groaned. He pulled on boxers and was buttoning his jeans. He pulled me into his arms.

"It's OK, Bo. She was going to hate you no matter what."

"That's comforting," I muttered sarcastically. "What the hell is she doing here?"

"Ruining my life," he said. "Let's go find out. Get dressed."

I rolled my eyes. I was too afraid Evilgranny was waiting outside the door with her Bible to go to my room to get clean underwear. I pulled on my jeans from the night before. I found my bra hanging from the edge of the dresser and put it and my shirt back on. I ran my hands through my hair and wished for a mirror. Zach didn't have one.

"Do I look OK?" I asked.

"She just walked in on you in bed with me. Do you really think it matters?"

I punched his shoulder. "It matters to me."

"You look beautiful."

"Good. Now put a shirt on and let's go face the beast."

"Please, just smile and be quiet. Let me do the talking."

* * *

James was sitting at the kitchen table looking miserable as his grandmother paced the kitchen. He looked at me and tried for a smile but didn't quite pull it off. Roberta turned to face us as we walked into the room.

"Good morning, Grandmother," Zach said.

"Good?" It came out practically a screech. "I find you in bed with trash and you say it's a good morning?"

I bit my tongue, literally. Zach wanted me to let him handle her. James was staring at his grandmother in disbelief, leading me to believe she was being unusually hostile. Zach was holding my hand and his grip tightened painfully. I glanced up at his face. If I hadn't lived with him for four months I would have thought he was calm. But the rage in his eyes scared me.

"Grandmother, while you are a guest in my house, an *unexpected, uninvited* guest," he emphasized the two words. "I request that you be polite." He spoke with his teeth gritted, his voice so hostile I wanted to cringe. His grandmother looked surprised.

"I apologize," she said, but I didn't believe she was sorry for a second. "I just thought you were smarter."

"Smarter?" Zach's tone had dropped even lower in warning.

"Yes. This woman is playing you. She'll get pregnant and force you into marrying her to get your money."

I couldn't stop myself. I knew that silence was what Zach needed from me, but there was only so much I could take. I realized only after I had said it that, "Fuck you!" was likely the worst possible thing I could have said.

Zach's grandmother stared at me in open-mouthed shock. James was doing the same. Zach had let go of my hand to rub vigorously at his temple as if he had a sudden horrible headache.

I stepped toward the old woman. "I don't give a shit about his money. I wanted his body and the generous, wonderful mind inside it. You wouldn't have to pay me to sleep with him. I'll do it for free." I knew it was beyond time for me to leave. I was too afraid to look at Zach and see just how pissed off he was. I saw Mop huddled under the table and seized my escape.

"I need to take Mop for a walk," I said to no one in particular. "I'll leave so you can spend some quality time together." I whistled at Mop, terrified the old dog would refuse to cooperate. But Mop seemed as repelled by Evilgranny as I was. He jumped to his feet like a dog half his age and ran to me. I snatched at his collar and trotted out, not bothering to grab a jacket or leash as I slammed the front door behind me.

I looked down at Mop.

"So," I said to his disapproving old eyes. "That went well."

CHAPTER 19

I WASN'T ABOUT to actually take Mop for a walk. Mop was old and I was lazy and that arrangement worked well for us. But I did need to get away from the house for a while, so I helped the giant dog climb into my truck.

"A drive is still exercise," I reasoned with my furry companion. "I'm moving my feet." But where was I going? I pulled out of the driveway and started for Mason's house but changed my mind. I pulled my cell phone out of my pocket, glad it was still in there from the night before.

It felt unnatural to call my brother before dropping in, but Maxine found our habit of popping in unannounced disquieting.

"Hi, Bo," she answered in her normal cheery voice.

"Hi. Would you mind if I came by? I need a place to hide for a bit. And someone to listen."

"Of course. Axel is in the kitchen making me pancakes. I'll have him make some for you too."

"Thanks. I'll be there in a few."

I hung up. Maxine surprised me. She hadn't asked me to explain why I was coming or what I wanted to talk about. In the year she had been married to my brother I never dropped in to talk. Mason was my go-to brother for bitching. But Axel had in-laws, and he might have some good advice for dealing with the grandmother from hell.

I pulled into Axel's driveway, marveling that my younger brother managed to buy the place. It was two stories, but the second hadn't been completed. The previous owners were working on an addition but divorced and sold the house before completing it. Axel bought it cheap, with the second floor still in the framing stage with plywood floors.

He, Mason, and my father spent most weekends working on it when there wasn't football.

I pulled Mop out of the truck and he watered the small decorative bushes Maxine had planted by the stone front steps. I didn't knock on the door; I just walked in. I may have learned to call, but knocking on my brother's door before entering wasn't second nature yet.

Maxine was stretched out on the couch, extremely pregnant. She was due any day and looked more than ready to be done with it. Her shoulder-length blonde hair was styled and accented with lady bug barrettes that matched the maternity shirt she wore. She looked adorable and completely at home being a pregnant wife. The idea of myself in her position made me ill.

She smiled at me, reaching out her hand. "Hey, Bo. You brought Mop."

I took my sister-in-law's hand briefly and sat down on the chair beside the couch. "I used him as an escape."

"You get in a fight with Zach?" Axel asked, walking out of the kitchen with a tray. He was wearing a pink apron and I burst out laughing. He sighed as he realized what I was looking at.

"I put it on as a joke," he said. "Forgot I was wearing it."

I watched my macho brother set down the tray of pancakes in his pink apron. I had to hand it to Maxine, she had domesticated him. I hadn't thought it was possible. Only two years ago he was living with Mason in their bachelor pad of filth and take-out food.

"I dressed up as a bug," Maxine said, indicating her lady bug shirt stretched tight over her belly.

"And you're the most beautiful lady bug I've ever seen," he said, bending down and kissing the top of her head. He picked up a plate and handed it to her. She set it casually on her belly as if it were a table. She smiled at the look on my face.

"Hey, I've had to carry this sucker around for nine months. I take all the perks I can get."

"My son is not a table," Axel said. He settled on the floor beside the coffee table because I was taking up the only other piece of furniture in the room. I settled on the floor beside him, not wanting to try and eat with my food balanced on my lap. Mop sat beside me, nose in my ear, begging.

"So," Maxine said around a bite of pancake. "What brings you here this morning?"

I sighed. "I went on a date with Zach."

"It's about time," Axel said, shocking me. "The two of you have been making eyes at each other for months. It was making me sick."

"So I slept with him," I continued.

"Good for you," Maxine said. "How was it?"

Axel held up a hand, his eyes closed. "Don't you dare answer that." I gave Maxine a look and she grinned. I was female enough to convey the answer without words.

"And this morning, Zach's grandmother walked in on us in bed," I said.

Axel burst out laughing, as I knew he would. Maxine looked horrified on my behalf and for a moment I wished I had at least one female friend. And when she reached out and placed her hand on mine, I realized that I did.

"Oh, honey," she said.

"Did I mention his grandmother is a Southern Baptist? A strict one."

Axel was still laughing and Maxine used the hand she had placed on mine to slap his arm.

"Stop that," she ordered.

Axel shook his head but stopped laughing. "So, how did Granny take it?" he asked.

"I believe her exact words were 'Sweet Jesus! Lord have mercy' then she slammed the door." This time I laughed with my brother. It really was funny.

"Were you wearing anything?" Maxine asked.

"Don't answer that," Axel begged.

"No." I sighed. "But I did manage to pull the sheet up and cover myself before she got a show. I think."

"What was she doing there?"

"I have no idea. She wasn't there last night when we got home. She wasn't expected. She must have gotten an early morning flight. She just showed up at the door." I took a minute to eat and Maxine did the same. Axel was more interested in the story than the food.

"So what happened?" he asked.

"We got dressed and went downstairs. Then she called me trash and accused me of trying to get pregnant so I could trap Zach into marrying me so I could get his money."

"Bitch," Maxine and Axel said at the same time.

I smiled. "My sentiment exactly. But in retrospect, perhaps telling her to fuck off was not the greatest idea."

"You did what?" Axel gasped.

"Well, my exact words were, 'Fuck you.' Then I proceeded to tell her I was more than happy to sleep with Zach for free."

Maxine shook her head in amazement. "You go girl."

Axel rubbed at his eyes. "Is Zach close with this woman?"

"No. He calls her a harpy."

"No worries then," Maxine said, resuming eating.

"No?" I asked.

"If he cared about what she thought, you'd be in trouble." She chewed a moment, pointing at Axel with her fork. "For example, I knew that I needed your parents' approval, because Axel needed it. If Zach doesn't care what she thinks, then you don't need her to like you."

I hadn't thought of that. I ate a few more bites of food.

"Why didn't you go talk to Mason?" Axel asked. "Don't get me wrong, I'm happy you came here, but this is usually the kind of thing you'd go to him with." I heard a shadow of jealousy in his voice that surprised me.

"Mason was only going to laugh at me," I said.

"I laughed at you," he pointed out.

"But you can give me good advice when you're done laughing."

"Why's that?"

"Because you have in-laws. You had to convince Maxine's family to like you, or at least accept you."

Axel leaned away from me. The look of shock on his face distracted me from my food and Mop snatched the bite of pancake off my fork. I shrugged and cut another bite for myself.

"You're serious about Zach? That serious?" he asked.

The idea made me uncomfortable.

"Cause you're never serious, Bo," Axel continued. "Hell, the longest relationship you've ever had lasted three weeks."

I didn't like him referring to my commitment phobia. I ate more food to avoid responding until I knew what to say.

"I'm not sure how I feel," I admitted. "But it wasn't just sex with Zach. I've lived with him for months. I'm his friend. I want to be his friend for the rest of my life. But I don't know about more than that."

"Fair enough," Axel said.

"He's serious about you," Maxine said.

"What makes you say that?" I asked.

"The way he looks at you. I have only met Zach twice, but he's obviously the kind of man who does something all the way or not at all."

That idea made me feed the last two bites of my pancake to Mop.

"Well, regardless of what's between you and Zach, you have an irate grandmother to deal with," Maxine said. "Want some advice?"

"I'd love some."

"Well, if her own grandchild, who is as polite as Zach, calls her a harpy, then she must be nasty. I bet she's used to everyone letting her have her way, backing down."

"I'd assume the same. James looked like a beaten puppy. Zach seems to have some backbone when she's around, but nothing impressive." I thought about how he'd reacted to her calling me trash. I appreciated his rage on my behalf, but he hadn't defended me in as blusterous or obvious a way as I would have liked.

"So." Maxine wiped her hands on a napkin. "Don't let her win. You can't make her like you, but you don't have to. The best you can hope to earn is respect. And you're only going to get that by fighting back."

"How?"

"Don't back down. If you want Zach, which I know you do, lay it out for her. Let her know you're not going to simply vanish because she isn't happy about it. Stand up to her. She'll still hate you, but if I'm right about the kind of woman she is, she'll respect you."

It made sense. And I had a feeling that Zach's grandmother would present one hell of a fight.

"Thanks," I said.

"Did you just encourage my sister to pick a fight with an old lady?" Axel asked his wife.

"Yes I did."

He leaned across the table and kissed her. "Love you," he said.

"Love you too."

I was jealous of them. They had been blissfully happy together for a year. I was afraid of that kind of happiness. I was terrified that I thought I had a chance of it with Zach. I would just concentrate on fighting with his evil grandmother for now.

Maxine winced and rolled her eyes. "This kid is going to play soccer." She took the plate off her belly and rubbed at the round red mass.

"Football," Axel corrected. "No kid of mine is gonna play soccer."

Maxine laughed and reached for my hand. "Want to feel him kick?"

I put my hand against her belly. I felt my nephew moving and smiled. I couldn't wait to hold him.

"Have you picked a name yet?" I asked.

"Daniel Alexander, after our grandfathers," Maxine said.

I rested my hand against her belly. "Hi, Danny."

For the rest of the morning, I forgot about my problems and enjoyed my brother's family.

CHAPTER 20

I KILLED THE MORNING at Axel's but it went against my nature to hide for long. I noticed that there was no rental car in the driveway as I walked up to the front door. Maybe she was gone. I opened the door to find James sitting on the couch. He gave me a comforting smile.

"Hey, Bo. Don't worry, she's gone. But she's coming back for dinner."

Zach appeared in the doorway to the kitchen. He didn't look happy. "She has requested your presence at dinner," he added in a flat tone. "And I request your presence in the kitchen. I need to have a word with you. Several, in fact."

I thought about running for the door, but Zach liked to chase me. I stepped past him into the kitchen. James turned up the TV, pretending he couldn't overhear us. I walked across the kitchen, passing the kitchen table. I was not going to sit down and have him towering over me while he yelled at me. I walked to the counter and turned around, intending to jump up and sit on it, but Zach followed me. His hands gripped the counter on either side of me.

"First, I need this," he said. He lowered his head and kissed me. It took me completely by surprise, but in a good way. I settled against his chest, allowing myself to relax. He wasn't that angry. Angry men did not kiss that gently. He rested his forehead against mine after breaking the kiss.

"That is what I should have been able to do this morning. What I've wanted to do all day," he said with his eyes closed.

"Sorry I kept you waiting."

He sighed and pulled his head back so he could look me in the eye.

"You could have handled my grandmother a little more diplomatically."

I bit my lip. "She called me trash. She said . . ."

"I know, and I'm sorry. You're not trash, babe."

"Why didn't you say that to her?" I asked, allowing the hurt to show in my voice. I hadn't realized how badly it bothered me that he hadn't defended me earlier.

"I've been handling my grandmother for years," he said.

"And you let her talk to all your girlfriends like that?"

"I've never had a girlfriend for her to hate."

"What about Alice?"

"Grandmother liked Alice."

I sighed. "I don't care. You should have said something."

"You kinda beat me to it. Part of me loved hearing you tell her you'd sleep with me for free." He was smiling, but I wasn't going to be that easily brushed off.

"You're missing the point." I was horrified to realize I was on the verge of tears. I didn't cry, especially not over something like this. Zach looked concerned, tilting my chin up.

"You're really upset," he stated the obvious. "If it makes you feel better I did defend you, after you left. And if she starts in on you tonight, I'll put a stop to it. I promise. I won't let her hurt you. You're too important to me."

I sniffed and blinked back the last threatening tear. "OK."

He kissed my nose. "I don't want her here. She decided to take offense that Walter left the house to us and not her. She's trying to convince me to sell it right away. I'm not going to, so don't worry. I booked her a flight back home tomorrow. She doesn't know it yet."

"Why did Walter marry her?" I asked, leaning against his warmth. He settled his arms around me.

"That's a long story," he said. I listened to his steady heartbeat and felt the last of my unease wash away. He began to make a humming sound deep in his chest and it made me laugh.

"You purr," I accused.

"Excuse me?" He sounded genuinely insulted.

"You heard me. You're like a giant cat."

He narrowed his eyes. "Cat? Really?"

"Well, I'd say bear but I've never heard of a bear purring. So maybe a lion, if the word cat offends you so much."

He laughed and kissed me, nipping at my bottom lip. "I'm sorry this morning couldn't be what it should have been. I didn't get to say the things I wanted to say."

"I didn't either."

"Mind if I speak first?"

"By all means." My hands had found their way under his T-shirt. I traced the muscles of his chest while he spoke.

"That is really distracting." He closed his eyes as I dragged my fingernails gently across his skin.

"What do you want to say?" I prompted, taking pity and resting my roving hands.

"That last night was amazing." He punctuated the words with a kiss on my cheek. "That I have never felt like this before, not with Alice, not with anyone." He kissed my other cheek. "I don't want to scare you. I am not promising anything. But I don't want to sleep alone. I want you as much as I can have you."

I felt my body tense despite trying to relax. My commitment phobia was rearing its ugly head. But he said the right thing. He wasn't demanding anything, he wasn't promising forever. He just wanted me right now. I could handle right now.

"I want as much of you as I can get too," I admitted. I kissed him, enjoying the relaxed way he held me. In my past relationships I had never known the man long enough to be comfortable. I acted on sexual attraction and fed off the lust for a week or two before moving on. Not that there were that many men. I had mostly male friends and had a hard time moving beyond that friend zone and into real intimacy. Zach hauled me right into intimate and I was happy as a clam about it.

"So," I said when he was done kissing me. "I have to be nice to your grandmother tonight?"

"Yes, if you can. At least subtly offending. If you can manage that."

"I can be subtle. I think Granny has met her match."

Zach looked at the ceiling in a habitual gesture I assumed he had learned from his religious background.

"If I still believed in the church, you'd drive me to pray," he said.

I kissed his chin, the best I could reach with his head tilted back. "I'll be good."

I took stock of my kitchen. If I was going to cook for the beast tonight I had to clean up and do some dishes.

"Tell me the story about Walter and Evilgranny," I said, moving to the sink.

Zach helped me clean the kitchen while he talked.

Zach's grandmother, Roberta, was born into a wealthy society family in Georgia. She married Timothy Cutter, a man she thought was upstanding and as wealthy as she was. They had their son, John, early in the marriage. It wasn't until John was six that Roberta discovered the truth about her husband. On their annual vacation to their Cape Cod house, Timothy went out for ice cream and never returned.

"What do you mean?" I asked.

"My grandfather had a gambling problem," Zach said. He continued the story as he scrubbed the kitchen counters. Timothy gambled away every penny they had. Eventually, he made the wrong bet with the wrong kind of people. Shortly after abandoning Roberta and John penniless on the Cape, his body was found in Boston.

"She didn't have any money?" I asked. "Didn't her family have money?"

"Her parents died in a car accident a year after she married Timothy. So she inherited all of the money, which she handed over to him."

"Which he lost."

"Yeah."

"So she had nothing?"

"Nothing. He had brought them to the summer house the day before the bank took the house in Georgia. And the house here was already sold—he just hadn't told her."

I found myself pitying her despite my hatred. No woman deserved that kind of betrayal and abandonment.

"So how does Walter come in?" I asked.

"My father told me that they met at the grocery store. Roberta was trying to buy food but the cashier wouldn't take a check because she had bounced two others. She started crying and Walter was in line behind her."

I nodded. "And being Walter, he paid for her food."

"Yes. Then he took her home after she told him her situation. My father loved Walter. To this day he speaks well of him. But Roberta never cared for him."

"But she was desperate so she married him," I said, sitting in the chair across from Zach. I rested my feet in his lap. He slipped off my shoes and began to rub.

"She stayed for five years," Zach said. "Then she divorced him."

"Wait." I held up a hand. "Southern Baptists believe in divorce?"

He sighed. "Not really. She just never talks about Walter, pretends she was never married."

I moaned as his hands rubbed a particular spot on my foot.

"So she left him and went back to Georgia?" I asked. "Why?"

"She had a great uncle who died with no heirs, so she inherited a house and a decent bank account. She didn't need Walter anymore. So she left him."

"I felt bad for her for about a minute there, but now I just hate her," I said.

Zach's hands squeezed my feet a final time and he sat back with a heavy sigh.

"Dinner's gonna be a nightmare," he said.

I pulled my feet from his lap. "I said I'd be on my best behavior."

"That's what I'm afraid of."

CHAPTER 21

I FRIED CHICKEN, mashed potatoes, steamed vegetables, and prepared strawberry shortcake for dinner. Zach told me his grandmother's favorite things and I made them. It was my peace offering. I knew she was going to throw it back in my face, but I was determined to be the better woman. Knowing I had Zach either way made it easier.

I was finishing cooking when she arrived. She was twenty minutes early, but I was prepared for that. She struck me as the kind to be early. I wiped my hands on the dishtowel that was threaded through the belt loop of my jeans and turned to face her when Zach and James led her into the kitchen.

I put a huge smile on my face. It hurt.

"We didn't really have time this morning to properly introduce you," Zach said, his tone amazingly neutral. "Grandmother, this is Bodel Tavish. Bo, my grandmother, Roberta Cutter."

I held out my hand and she shook it, looking like she wanted to slap it instead.

"Nice to meet you," I lied. "I'll have dinner ready in five minutes."

Roberta was a small woman, a few inches shorter than my five six. Her hair was gray and in a tight bun. She had small blue eyes and a semi-permanent scowl. She looked to be in her late fifties but I knew she was much older. She wore an ankle length black dress that was as flattering as a nun's habit.

"Thank you for cooking," she said. "I'll set the table; just point me to the dishes."

"We can do that," James said.

"Nonsense. You two go sit in the living room. I want some time alone with Bodel."

James looked at me apologetically before running. He really had no spine. Zach waited until I nodded at him that I was fine before he left.

"Plates are in there." I pointed to the cabinet.

She surprised me by actually getting them. She didn't speak a word except to ask where things were until the table was fully set. I ignored her impolite sniff when I informed her we didn't own any cloth napkins and she'd have to make do with paper. She stood directly behind me. I turned to face her.

"I don't care what Zach says," she began.

"I don't think you care what anyone says," I interrupted. "And it doesn't matter. What you think doesn't matter. I don't need you to like me, Roberta. I don't need you to approve of me. Zach and I are adults. We're in a relationship. And there is absolutely nothing you can do about it. So you can pout and act like a child or we can agree to hate each other and be civil."

Roberta glared at me. This was a woman who loved a fight. I would give her one, but one that wouldn't be noticed by the men. We wouldn't want to upset their delicate sensibilities.

"You're wrong for him. And I still think you're using him."

"Your opinion has been noted. I think you're pushy and overbearing and judgmental. Would you like red wine or white with dinner?"

"I don't drink."

"Fine. I have some seltzer and juice."

"Do you have any tea?"

I held up a metal tin containing the red tea I preferred. She nodded at me.

"I still don't like you," she said.

"I don't like you either. You take honey in your tea?"

"Yes. I'll get the boys for dinner."

I dished out the food as everyone sat down. James looked about as comfortable as a mouse staked out in an open field. Zach was calm and composed, but when he grasped my hand under the table his grip hurt.

Roberta insisted on saying grace and I lowered my head and went through a list of my bills while she talked. I realized I muttered, "Did I pay my cell phone bill?" aloud when Zach stepped on my foot. I glanced up at Roberta who was holding the cross around her neck and glaring at me. I was glad she didn't have the power to set me alight with malice alone.

"So, the boys tell me you are not a religious person," Roberta said.

"Grandmother," Zach said quietly.

"Don't *Grandmother* me." Roberta took a bite of her chicken. She chewed thoughtfully for a moment. "This is very good." She sounded too surprised for it to be meant as a real compliment. I smiled at her anyway.

"Thank you. Zach told me what you liked."

"He's a good boy. He's always taking care of people." She looked pointedly at me as she spoke. "He has this need to try and save lost causes."

James choked on his food.

I chose to ignore the comment entirely. "I made strawberry shortcake for later."

"Lovely."

She was winning the battle. James and Zach picked at their food while I plotted my next attack.

"Do you find waitressing to be a fulfilling career?" Roberta asked after a few minutes of strained silence.

"Sometimes." I shrugged. "I make good money, at least during the summer. I get to meet lots of people and sleep in. I'm not a morning person."

"Zach has always been the first one up. Even as a little boy he would be up with the sun. He used to make Francesca, his maternal grandmother, breakfast in bed." I could hear the jealousy in her tone. Attacking me was one thing. If she went after Zach I was going to get nasty.

"I like sleeping in, actually," Zach said. "I just never had the opportunity before."

Roberta shook her head. "I'm worried about you. You've always been so motivated. And here you are, puttering around this deserted island, wasting your time." She glanced at me again when she spoke.

"I'm happier here than I've been in years," Zach said.

"I do see that. But I fear you'll grow bored. There's nothing here to interest someone of your intelligence and education for long."

"You'd be surprised," Zach said, his tone dropping dangerously. His grip on my hand indicated he was losing his patience.

"Perhaps. Well." She sipped her tea. "You know I want what's best for you. And you seem happy here."

"I am."

"I'm glad. You deserve it. This is a wonderful meal, Bodel. I really must ask how you come to have such a unique name?"

"My great grandmother was Norwegian."

"Oh. I wouldn't have guessed that with your coloring." There was a boatload of disapproval in her tone but I forced myself to ignore it.

"I'm also Portuguese and Thai, and a few others mixed in."

"Interesting. I am of English descent, of course, as was my late husband."

I had the feeling I was being judged as a mongrel dog compared to a purebred.

"I'm a mutt." I shrugged. "I've heard we live longer. And we don't have as many genetic defects due to inbreeding."

This time it was Zach who choked on his dinner.

I smiled sweetly at Roberta. "Would you like more tea?"

"No thank you."

I resumed eating, petting Mop under the table with my bare foot. He hadn't moved in hours and I doubted Roberta knew he was down there because of the tablecloth. I wouldn't use Mop as a weapon unless she pushed me.

"How is your work coming along?" Roberta asked James.

"Great," was his terrified reply.

"I can't see how working part-time taking care of dying people can be great."

"It's very rewarding. And I'm being promoted next month to full-time when Abby retires."

"Will you be making at least decent money with the promotion?"

"It's not like I need it," James said. "Zach invested for me."

Roberta reached across the table and patted Zach's hand. "I have no idea why you gave up being an accountant. You could be running your own firm by now."

"I got bored," Zach said.

There were a few minutes of silence while the men shifted uncomfortably on their chairs and Roberta and I plotted our next verbal jab.

"So, what do you plan to do?" Roberta asked me.

"Do?" I asked.

"After the renovation is finished and Zach sells the house."

"We discussed this earlier today," Zach cut in. "I'm not sure I am going to sell it. James likes it here. He's got a good job. I like it here."

Roberta glared at him. "You can't mean to stay here."

"Why not?" Zach asked.

"Don't be ridiculous, Zachary. You'll grow bored of this little project and come back home where you belong."

Zach was vibrating with tension and anger but he said nothing. He chewed his food with a violence that worried me. I was glad that the food was almost gone. I was going to end this dinner as soon as humanly possible.

"I booked you a flight home tomorrow," Zach said.

Roberta set her fork down hard. "Without consulting me?"

"You didn't bother asking me before you came here."

"That is an entirely different matter. This house should have been mine. I had to live with that miserable man for five years. The least he could have done is left me the house."

I was done being nice. I nudged Mop awake, feeling only slightly bad about it. The giant dog twitched, his long legs tangling in Roberta's dress. She shrieked as Mop stuck his head directly into her crotch and woofed.

Zach looked down at me, disapproval in his green eyes.

Roberta jumped out of her seat and Mop took it as a game. It was luck alone that his age prevented him from jumping up on her. He did lean his entire weight against her and wag his tail like it was a baseball bat. Roberta was knocked backward a few steps. I grabbed Mop by the collar. "It's OK, boy."

"What is that monstrous thing?" Roberta screeched.

"This is Mop. He's just an old dog. I'm sorry he startled you." I patted my partner in crime and went to the cabinet to get him a treat.

"You let him sit under the table?"

"He sits where he wants. He's harmless."

Roberta settled hard back in the chair, her face flushed, eyes furious. "I hate dogs."

"I figured as much."

The rest of the meal was eaten in stony silence. I cleared the plates and dished out dessert. James vomited up a nervous bout of chatter about his work that got us through the shortcake alive. Zach, after calming down enough to unclench his teeth, went into detail about his plans for the renovation.

"I wish you hadn't booked me a flight so soon. I would have liked to stay a few days," Roberta said, delicately wiping her hands on a napkin.

"I figured you hated the hotel and wouldn't want to stay," Zach said.

"I do hate it. But you have room here."

"We're using all three bedrooms," Zach said through his teeth that were back to being clenched.

"You weren't last night." The comment was said with such condemnation I was tempted to glance up and make sure I wasn't about to be struck by lightning.

I smiled sweetly at her and opened my mouth to say something I was positive was a bad idea. Zach grabbed my hand and squeezed so hard I actually shut my mouth.

"Thank you for coming to dinner, Grandmother. It's late. You'll be wanting to get back to the hotel."

"I am a bit tired. Thank you for a lovely meal, Bodel."

I was too angry to speak so I forced myself to smile at the harpy. Zach and James stood and lead Roberta to the door. I rubbed at my hand where Zach had squeezed it. It didn't really hurt, not physically anyway. I set the dessert plates on the floor so Mop could lick up the crumbs and leftover whipped cream.

I had just finished wrapping the leftovers when James and Zach returned. I didn't turn to look at them.

"That went OK," James said.

"You two should go away. Now." I muttered some profanity and seriously considered breaking a few plates.

CHAPTER 22

I HEARD one of them leave the room and figured it was James.

"Are you OK?" Zach asked.

"No."

He took a few steps toward me.

"Just leave me alone."

He ignored me as I knew he would. He stood behind me, so close I could feel his breath in my hair. I looked down at my soapy hand, remembering how his grip had tightened. I rubbed at my fingers.

"Did I hurt you?" he asked, reaching for my hand.

"Of course not," I said, trying to jerk my hand free.

"I'm sorry." He brought my hand to his lips and kissed me gently.

"I was going to say something extremely inappropriate and embarrassing. You did us both a favor. And it didn't hurt."

"I shouldn't have done that. I'm sorry my grandmother was so, well, herself. You handled her beautifully."

I sighed. "I hate her."

I heard the front door open and turned. From where I was standing I had to lean sideways to have a view of the door. James saluted me.

"I'm headed out to get drunk and lucky," he said.

"You realize it's Cape Cod in the winter right?" I asked, but he had already shut the door behind himself. "He'll find a drink, but much more than that I wouldn't bet on."

I turned and noticed the whipped cream and sugared strawberries were still on the table. I picked up the bowl and the can and went to the fridge but Zach stopped me. "I'm not done with that," he said.

"You want another piece?" I asked, looking at the shortcake sitting on the counter.

"Not of that."

He lowered his head and kissed me happy. It was more my nature to stew over my anger for a good long while until I had an excuse to overreact and be dramatic, but Zach's touch worked wonders on my disposition.

He used his body to shift me around and out of the kitchen. I took one quick glance at the dirty dishes and dismissed them. They could wait. Hell, I didn't care if I left the stove on and the fridge door wide open. I wanted to pick up where we had left off that morning.

I would have gone into Zach's room but he pushed me into mine. Mop tried to follow us but Zach shut the door in his disgruntled face. Zach hadn't said anything aside from some extremely sexy male sounds while he nibbled at me during our walk to the bedroom.

He stripped me and picked me up to set me on my bed on my stomach. I looked over my shoulder at him as he pulled off his own shirt and jeans. I went to roll over but he caught my hips in his large warm hands and held me down.

"You are such a control freak," I teased. But there was a shadow in his eyes at my words and his hands released me.

"I'm sorry," he began.

"Why?" I rolled partly over so I could look at his face easier. "You're a dominant guy."

"I shouldn't push you around. I . . . never mind."

"Say it."

"It scared Alice. The way I like . . ." He stopped again.

I reached my hand to stroke his face. "I'm not Alice. And I like being dominated. I like that you're in charge. If you haven't noticed, I'm pretty bossy normally. I take care of things. It's nice to be taken care of, to be bossed around, in bed."

"Really?" There was so much hope and excitement in his eyes I had to pull him down for a kiss.

"Absolutely. Do what comes naturally to you, Zach. If anything makes me uncomfortable, I'll let you know."

He kissed me, using his teeth to scrape at my lips. It made my body shiver as he shoved me back onto my stomach. He slid his hands along my arms, spreading them out over my head. I left them where he put them as his lips explored the back of my neck and shoulders. I jumped a little as he poured some of the sugared strawberry sauce in a line down my back.

"We are going to get so sticky," I said in a moan as he began to lick it off. His response was a deep growl of approval. I closed my eyes and let everything but what he was doing to my body disappear. I had never had a man focus so completely on me before. Even the best sex I'd had before Zach hadn't been good enough to keep random I *need to do* chores from popping into my head. There was nothing in my head now but Zach.

I felt like a pagan goddess as he covered my body in whipped cream, strawberries, and his tongue. The few times I tried to move he easily held me in place where he wanted me. I should have hated it. I should have wanted to control him. But I rolled in the feeling of helplessness and pleasure.

Much later, with him collapsed over my back pinning me to my sticky sheets, I reached behind me and stroked his hair. His face was nuzzled against my neck and he kissed me there.

"Am I crushing you?" he asked, his voice still breathless.

"A bit, but I like it."

"I can't move yet. I will when I can."

"Take your time."

I fidgeted under his weight as little as I was able. Despite Zach's rapt attention with his tongue, we were both sticky. My sheets were practically edible.

"Shower?" I suggested, though I was so sexually satisfied and content I didn't think I could move that far. Zach shifted off me and held out a hand to help me up. I checked the hall to make sure James wasn't there to see the show of the two of us dashing across the hallway naked. Mop woofed at me woefully and sulked.

"Voyeur," I accused.

Showering with Zach was surprisingly intimate. I had never had a man wash my hair before and the feeling was almost as good as sex. And there was definitely something to be said of having someone to wash your back. The hot water ran out quickly as it was prone to do and we reluctantly left the steamy comfort of the bathroom. I went into my room to get something to sleep in. I put on panties and the shirt Zach had discarded on my floor. I wanted my legs bare to rub against him while we slept.

Zach stepped into the room wearing boxers.

"That's a good look for you," he said.

"Back at you, stud."

He looked down at himself doubtfully, his hand rubbing at the imperfection of his slight gut. I laughed. He really had no idea how handsome he was and how edible his body. I tried to convey my thoughts in a kiss. I won a smile and a pat on my ass.

"Go dry your hair," he said, catching a handful of it. "I know women hate going to bed with wet hair."

"I need to get these sheets off the bed," I began.

"I'll do it. Go dry your hair."

"Don't think that because I let you boss me around in bed I'll let you do it everywhere."

He smiled and kissed my nose. "I want you in my bed, the sooner the better. So if you let me do this we can both be settled in my bed sooner."

"Fine. I'll do it. But only because I would have anyway."

His beautiful laughter followed me to the bathroom.

CHAPTER 23

SLEEPING WITH ZACH was so natural that none of us seemed to notice that anything had changed. James never said a word or teased us. We alternated which bedroom we slept in based on our mood. Mop learned to sleep with James instead of me and Zach. There wasn't room for both dog and man in the bed, and I refused to feel guilty about my choice.

I wasn't sure how to go about bringing the relationship up to my brothers. Axel and Maxine knew, but they were unlikely to have informed Mason or Gage. Zach solved my dilemma on Sunday during the football game. He settled in one of the big chairs and I planned on walking by but he grabbed me and hauled me backward onto his lap. My brothers all glanced at us while Zach put a very obvious and possessive arm around me and grasped my hip.

"Bout damn time," Mason said. And that was the end of it.

I expected Zach to open up and talk more as time passed, but he didn't. I realized it really was his nature to be quiet. When he did speak it was always carefully thought out. I didn't mind his quiet. I talked a lot and mostly without expecting anyone to listen. My brothers learned long ago to tune me out and nod at semi-appropriate times. Zach constantly surprised me by mentioning some random thing I had spoken of. He actually listened to me and that was scary because I rarely listened to myself.

My parents were happy for me and had Zach and me over for dinner. My father did his best to intimidate Zach but didn't accomplish anything. I baked him cookies to soothe his ruffled ego. Trace Tavish wasn't used to being smaller than his daughter's dates.

That night after dinner I asked Zach about his parents but he didn't have much to say.

"We're not close." He shrugged. "I love them. They are good people. Hard working. My father is one of the best cardiologists in the country. My mother specializes in spinal surgery. They are both very respected in their fields."

"I get that," I said, resting my cheek against his bare chest and shifting under the blanket. "But what are they like? As people?"

"My mother is a bit uptight," he admitted. "If she's not in scrubs she's in a suit. She's a no-nonsense kind of person, extremely organized. She's not really the mothering kind." He shifted a little and pulled my body over his. "I remember she used to come in after her shift when I was in bed and kiss me goodnight. But other than that brief moment, she was more of a disciplinarian. She asked about school and homework and what we did for fun. She made sure we had what we needed and weren't getting into trouble."

"What about your Dad?"

"My father?" Zach's hand had settled on my butt. "Do you really want to talk about this now?"

I propped my elbow on his chest and he winced. "Yes."

"Fine, just stop that. You're boney." He continued once I settled down on top of him. "My father is just as distant as my mother. He was home even less than she was. He took a little interest in sports. I played football in high school; so did James. He came to the games when he wasn't in surgery. But he's nothing like your father."

"Don't you like my Dad?"

"Trace is great," Zach said, kissing my shoulder. "He's a dad. I had a father. There's a difference."

"Are you jealous?" I asked seriously.

He didn't answer right away. I wasn't surprised. Zach never rushed answers to important questions. He nibbled at my shoulder while he thought.

"Sometimes," he said at length. "Your family is great. They love each other so openly. Y'all are there for each other. But on the downside, the companionship is there even if it's unwanted. I like that I grew up with privacy."

I laughed at the idea. "I have never had privacy. I used to have to brace my feet on the bathroom door to ensure the boys didn't barge in."

"No lock?"

"They broke it, and the door, numerous times."

"I wish I had stories like that. But I was always so well-behaved."

"You didn't have someone like me there influencing you."

"It's a shame."

"Well, you have me now. And I work on corrupting you one day at a time. I'll get you swearing and belching yet."

"Keep dreaming, babe."

Later that night I woke up from a bad dream. I didn't remember anything about it. Zach had pulled away from me in his sleep and was settled on his stomach. I had fallen asleep with the blinds open and moonlight striped the bed. The light settled perfectly on the tattoo on Zach's neck. I traced the numbers and bit my lip. February 18th was rapidly approaching.

I kissed the tattoo and Zach shifted in his sleep. I hadn't asked him anything else about Alice or what happened ten years ago on that date. I didn't know if he had a hard time on the anniversary or not. How could I ask him? And what about Valentine's Day? I was so excited to have a boyfriend for the first time on Valentine's Day I hadn't considered the fact that Zach's wife died four days after it. Would he want to celebrate with me? Would he go to Georgia? Would he want me to go with him? He hadn't said anything.

I settled against him, running my fingers across his broad back. After a few minutes, he shifted his face on the pillow so I could see one eye.

"What's the matter?" he asked.

"Nothing."

He yawned into the pillow.

"I'm too tired to call you on that lie. We'll talk about it in the morning." He rolled onto his side and pulled me against him. He forgot about it in the morning and I didn't bring it up.

CHAPTER 24

MY CELL PHONE rang on the kitchen table. Mop had been peacefully sleeping under it and forgot that he was faking hearing loss to avoid listening to my commands and jumped up, hitting his head.

"Idiot," I said. I picked up the phone. "Hey, Axel. What's up?"

"She's having the baby!" my brother screamed into my ear. I pulled my phone away in shock and pain for a moment.

"Right now?" I asked.

"Mason just dropped us off. He's parking the car."

"You're at the hospital?"

"Yes."

"Then calm down. Everything is going to be fine."

"Everything is not fine. I'm going to fuck this kid up. I know it."

"Axel, he hasn't even been born yet. Take a deep breath for me."

My brother ignored me and continued hyperventilating. I felt bad for poor Maxine. Axel wasn't going to be much good for her until he calmed down.

I assumed the tone of voice my mother always used on us. I inherited it, which unnerved me, but it was effective. "Axel Tavish, cut it out. You're wife is having this baby. She needs you there to help her. Now calm down and be useful and stop being an idiot."

There was a long moment of silence. "OK. Can you come here and say that? I can't do this, Bo. I'm so nervous I'm making Maxine want to hit me."

"Please Bo. If you don't come I'm going to kill him," I heard Maxine yell in the background.

"I'm on my way."

I hung up the phone and walked right into Zach.

"I need to go to the hospital," I said.

"I overheard. I'll drive."

I didn't argue. I spent the drive making phone calls. Mason and Axel had beaten me to most of them, but not all. My parents were in Maine for a short vacation and were driving back to the Cape at illegal speeds. Maxine's parents were driving from Maryland. That worried me. Maxine needed a Mom and there wasn't going to be one for hours.

Zach dropped me off at the door of the hospital and I asked my way to the maternity ward. It wasn't hard to find. Mason was sitting in the closest waiting room, looking pale.

"How is she?" I asked.

"She's in a damn hurry," Mason said. "Doctors said it won't be long. They didn't want to give her any drugs because they weren't sure there was time. But she slugged one of the nurses and they changed their minds."

I laughed and looked at the closed door. I heard a heavy thud from inside that worried me. A moment later, a stressed nurse emerged.

"Which one of you is Bo?" she asked.

"I am."

"Maxine is asking for you."

"Me?" I gasped. "I can't go in there." The idea terrified me.

"Well, Daddy-to-be just passed out cold on the floor, and Mom-to-be is demanding to see her sister."

I blinked. "She's an only child."

"You're her sister, you idiot." Mason pointed toward the door.

"You're just happy she isn't asking for you."

"Hell yes."

Mason shoved me inside the room, which was the only way I was getting in there. Maxine was on the bed, covered in a sheet with her legs in stirrups. I was glad I couldn't see anything around the doctor crouched in front of her. I had never seen Maxine without her make-up and hair done. She looked possessed as she glared at the unconscious body of my brother on the floor.

I stepped over Axel, giving him a slight kick for putting me in this position. I took the hand that Maxine stretched out to me.

"Thank God you're here." Some of the strain left her pretty face as she lay back. Her grip on my hand was surprisingly strong.

"How are you?" I asked lamely.

"The drugs are starting to work a little," she said in a sigh. "That idiot passed out when they gave me the epidural."

I looked down at my brother.

"What a wuss," I said.

She smiled and closed her eyes. I knew how she hated to have her hair out of place so I took a moment to run my fingers through it and straighten the worst of the tangle. I didn't know how to be a sister. It was largely why I avoided Maxine since Axel told me he was marrying her. But I didn't feel awkward as I fixed her hair and helped her try and get as comfortable as possible.

"OK, Maxine," the doctor said. "I need you to push for me now."

"No!" Maxine shook her head. "I need Axel. I will not deliver this baby with him unconscious on the damn floor!"

I kicked my brother without letting go of Maxine's hand and used the tone again. "Axel Tavish, get your sorry ass up off the floor. Your baby is being born and I will personally beat you to death if you miss it. Now get up."

Axel opened one eye. "What happened?" he asked.

"You passed out. Now get up so Maxine can have this baby."

"I didn't pass out," Axel said, opening his other eye. He had the grace to look embarrassed as he realized he was lying on the floor.

"Get your ass up here now!" I yelled at him.

Axel jumped to his feet despite being unsteady once he gained them. I went to move away but Maxine didn't let go of me. It looked like I was there for the long haul. I swore under my breath. Axel took up position on Maxine's other side and kissed her forehead.

"Push now," the doctor said.

I had to close my eyes. I did not want to be in the room. I had never thought about having a baby and I was fairly certain this experience was going to convince me to adopt. But Maxine needed me. She needed another woman and I wasn't going to leave her. So I held her hand and listened to her struggles and swearing and effort. And then I heard my nephew scream. The sound forced my eyes open.

I only had a second to look at the baby before Axel falling to the floor in a dramatic heap distracted me. Maxine was too exhausted to notice. The nurses took the baby aside to clean him. I watched their backs, eager to get a real look at him. A moan from Maxine drew my attention and I looked just in time to see the placenta. That image ruined the beautiful experience for me. I tore my hand from Maxine's and ran into the attached bathroom to puke into the toilet. But at least I didn't pass out.

CHAPTER 25

THE MORNING AFTER Daniel was born, both sets of grandparents and all the aunt and uncles were gathered in the hallway for their turn to hold the baby. Zach came with me but James was at work.

We let the grandparents go in first because the room was small and we couldn't all fit. Gage, Mason, Zach and I waited impatiently for our turn. I noticed that Zach seemed just as eager to see the baby as the rest of us. I was going to ask him about how he felt but the grandparents emerged.

"Your turn," my mother said. "The doctors said she is free to go home. They're bringing a wheelchair for her."

We entered the warm little room. Maxine looked beautiful in her hospital gown, her hair flat and messy. She looked beautiful as only a woman holding her newborn could. I shoved ahead of my brothers and looked down at Daniel.

"He looks a lot cuter now that he's not all bloody," I said.

Maxine rolled her eyes at me. "Want to hold him?"

"You break it you buy it," Axel chimed in. Maxine would have hit him if she wasn't occupied transferring the baby into my arms. I cradled his tiny head and was amazed how light he was. He had a small thatch of hair and the most perfect little fingers. His eyes were closed in sleep. I expected him to wake up but he didn't.

"Hi, Danny," I said, realizing I was rocking unconsciously.

"You made a good looking kid, Maxine," Mason said, looking over my shoulder.

"I helped," Axel said.

"You passed out on the floor. Twice," Maxine said, but she stroked his hand where it lay on her shoulder.

I looked at Mason and Gage. "You want to hold him?" Both men paled and stepped back. I laughed at them and looked back down at Daniel. "They're scared of you," I said to him.

Axel walked to my side. "You look good holding one of those," he said.

"Only because I'm borrowing it." I laughed and transferred the baby into his anxious arms. I stepped back and looked at Zach. The look in his eyes took my breath away. He was looking at the baby with such obvious longing. There wasn't a doubt in my mind that Zach wanted a baby of his own. The only reason I didn't panic and run was that his eyes stayed on Daniel and didn't travel to me.

Axel looked at Zach. "You want to hold him?" he asked.

I smiled at my brother. Out of the three of them, Axel would have been the one to notice the look in Zach's eyes.

"I'd love to," Zach said.

I watched Axel carefully hand Daniel to Zach. Zach held him confidently, as if he had held a newborn before. Daniel let out a chirp and looked up at Zach with wide dark eyes. Zach smiled down at the baby.

"He looks like you," Zach said, looking at Maxine. "But I think he'll have Axel's eyes."

I watched Zach with the baby. He was perfectly at home with the little life in his arms. I loved it but was terrified at the same time. There was no fear in Zach. No hesitation. He would be a wonderful father, and he was obviously ready to be one. I hadn't thought that six years was that great a difference in age, but in this respect it was. I still thought of myself as a kid. I had never considered the idea of having a baby of my own. Looking at Zach with the baby made me question everything. I wasn't ready for that kind of thing.

Zach handed Daniel back to Axel.

"He's beautiful," Zach said.

I smiled. Zach was beautiful. He was everything a woman could hope for in a man. But I hadn't been looking for my ever-after. I wasn't ready to be an adult. And I had the unsettling feeling that Zach would want things from me that I just couldn't give.

"Bo?" Zach was touching my shoulder. "What's wrong?"

"Nothing."

His eyebrows dipped down in concern. "Not going to tell me, are you?"

"Nothing's wrong."

"We'll talk about it later."

I let myself be distracted as the doctor came in with the wheelchair for Maxine. We could all go home. The idea of going home with Zach wasn't as wonderful as it had been that morning.

CHAPTER 26

FOR THE REST of January everything moved along seamlessly. Zach finished the basement and decided to take a month or so off before deciding to renovate the kitchen. He said I was monopolizing his time and I was unapologetic.

There wasn't much to do on Cape Cod in the winter, and after pestering Axel and Maxine for the first week of Daniel's life, they asked for some privacy. Zach and I went for cold walks on the beach. I brought Mop to the National Seashore because the sign said No Dogs Allowed. The idea that I couldn't take my dog for a walk in the woods irritated me to the point of rebellion. No one was around to notice or care in the winter anyway. The sign was there for the uppity summer tourists who wanted their quiet quaint vacation.

Roberta called regularly to inquire about the progress on the renovation and the plans to sell the house. We all learned to check the caller ID before picking up the phone. She tricked us a few times by using her bridge partners' cell phones, but mostly we avoided her.

Valentine's Day and the anniversary of Alice's death were rapidly approaching. I knew I should talk directly to Zach about it, but I chose to ask James instead. If it was a really bad time, James could let me know and I wouldn't mention it to Zach at all.

James was eating lunch in the kitchen and I sat at the table with him.

"I need to ask you something serious," I said.

James reached across the table. "No. I won't marry you. Zach would kill me."

I sighed and rolled my eyes. "Very funny."

"I try. What's up?"

"Valentine's Day is in four days. I haven't said a word about it to Zach. I didn't know if it was a bad day for him."

James stopped eating, which wasn't a good sign. "It's not a good day." He looked like he would have continued but his eyes moved over my shoulder into the living room and he shut up. I didn't have to turn around to know Zach was standing there. I really needed to put a bell on him.

"Why didn't you just talk to me?" Zach asked, his tone far more hostile than I thought I deserved. I turned in the chair so I could look at him. "I'm not a child," he continued bitterly.

"You're acting like one," James said. "She was trying to avoid hurting you and you're being a jerk."

Zach grunted and pointed upstairs. To my astonishment, James picked up his food and left. Zach stayed in the doorway, glaring at me.

"Cut that out," I snapped. "I didn't do anything wrong and you know it. You're not really mad at me. You're just taking out your anger on me." I hoped I was right. I must have been because his shoulders went from stiffly angry to slumped in cowed apology.

He sighed. "I'm sorry, Bo. You're right. I'm not mad at you. Alice wanted to get married on Valentine's Day, and I never could say no to her. So we did. I have a hard time with the day. A really hard time."

I stood up and hugged him. "It's OK. We don't have to do anything."

"No." He pushed me back a few steps but kept his hands on my shoulders. "I want to do something. I want to take you to a nice dinner, or whatever you want. I just don't think I'll be up for it."

"Well, I have two ideas," I said, playing with the hem of his shirt. "Idea one: I throw a big Valentine's Day party." I could tell by the look on his face that wasn't going to work. "OK, no. Option two: We sleep in and make love until noon. Then I want to go for a walk on the National Seashore, to that place where the benches overlook the water. Maybe I can teach you to feel small for a while. Then I'll go to work and you get a few hours to feel shitty and sad. I'll have Angelica make the two of us a nice dinner after we close. You can come in and share it with me in the empty restaurant out of take-out containers. How does that sound?"

He framed my face with his hands and kissed me. He rested his forehead against mine. "I love you, Bo."

If he hadn't just kissed the air from my lungs I would have screamed. He caught me firmly as I tried to run away.

"Easy," he said, pulling me against his chest. "I knew it would scare you, but I had to say it. I don't expect you to say it back. Please don't run away." I fought back my instinctive fear and listened to his heart beating against my cheek. I was scaring him. I put my arms around him.

"I'm sorry," I began.

"Don't." He lifted my chin with his hand and kissed me. "You have nothing to be sorry for."

"I don't know what to say to you."

"You don't have to say anything. I'm not pushing you. I'm not demanding anything. I feel the way I feel but that doesn't change anything."

"I'm a freak."

"What?"

"You're perfect. You're wonderful. And you love me. What kind of stupid moron runs like a fucking idiot from that?"

He chuckled and kissed my hair. "It was a reflex. Besides, I caught you."

I rested my cheek against his chest. Had he caught me? All of me? What did I feel for him? I was too afraid to even think about it. So I didn't.

"So you liked the second option?" I said.

"What?"

"For Valentine's Day."

"Oh. Yes. It sounds like the perfect day."

He kissed me again. I let him make me forget my fear in the physical bliss that I always found with him. I knew that it was more than physical, but for now that was all I could let myself feel. I was so fucked up.

CHAPTER 27

MAXINE ANSWERED THE PHONE on the first ring. "Hello?"

"Hey, Maxine. It's me," I said.

"Oh, hi. Axel's at work right now, if you were looking for him."

"No, I actually wanted to talk to you. Mind if I come by?"

"Of course not. Danny is sleeping. At least I pray he stays that way for at least a few hours. Bring me coffee. Please. I beg you."

"Sure thing."

I stopped at the Hole in One, across the street from the big chain coffee shop. The coffee was good and the staff knew my name. Everything was cooked in the kitchen instead of trucked in. I got coffee and some gingerbread muffins with raisins.

Maxine looked tired but beautiful when she opened the door. Her blonde hair was pulled back and she had dark circles under her eyes, but she'd put on some makeup and a smile. I held out the bag of food and coffee.

"You are amazing," Maxine snatched the coffee and sipped at it. "I know it's decaf, but it still makes me feel awake." I handed her the bag and she looked inside. "Scratch amazing, you're a goddess."

We sat on the couch with the baby monitor buzzing at us.

"So, what's wrong?" Maxine asked.

"Why do you think something's wrong?"

"It's all over your face. And you aren't really in the habit of coming over just to say hi to me."

I bit my lip. "I'm sorry about that. I don't want you to think I only talk to you when I need something. I've never had a sister or any female friends. I'm not very good at it."

Maxine smiled and patted my hand. "It's fine. I'll call and invite you over to hang out until you get the hang of doing it yourself."

"I'm glad you married my brother."

"That is probably the highest compliment I could ever get from you. Thank you, Bo. I know how you are about your brothers. I'm lucky to have Axel. Now, tell me what's wrong."

I took a bite of my muffin and followed it up with the hot coffee.

"Zach told me he loved me, and my reaction was to literally try and run screaming."

She smiled. "It's a bit of an extreme reaction, but not entirely surprising. I assume you didn't actually run screaming?"

"No. Because he caught me when I tried to run. Seriously, Maxine, what's wrong with me? What kind of a woman does that?"

"You do, apparently. What scares you so much about a man loving you?"

"It's not any man. It's Zach."

"So, what scares you about Zach?"

I sighed. "He's too good for me."

"That's crap and you know it. What's really wrong?"

"He knows what he wants," I admitted. "He always has. He picks something and goes for it and gets it. He is the most motivated man I have ever met. And I'm a loser."

"You are not."

"Really? I dropped out of community college. I have no career plans. I work as a waitress, have no savings and no plans for the future. I am in exactly the same place I was when I graduated from high school. And I have no idea what I want to do when I grow up." I paused but Maxine seemed to sense I wasn't finished. I continued, "Zach is only a few years older, but they are important ones. He wants kids. He wants a wife and a family and a white picket fence."

"And you don't?"

"Me? Have a kid? I am a kid."

"You're older than me, sweetie."

And she was married with a baby. And blissfully happy with it. It baffled me.

"I just never thought about that kind of thing. I never planned out a wedding, never picked out baby names or dreamed of Mr. Right."

"Does this have anything to do with your parents?"

I stared at her. "What?"

"Your mom got pregnant in high school. They got married and had the four of you and are happy as clams together. But I know they had both planned on going to college. And because they got married and had babies they ended up working for their parents' businesses instead. Your father loves his work, and so does your mother, but I know that your Mom wanted to be a teacher. So maybe you associated marriage with losing your opportunities."

I sat back on the couch and considered it. It wasn't a new thought. Mason and I had discussed it a few times. Mason was the accident that caused the marriage. My parents would slap us if they heard us call him that, but it was the truth. And I was born only ten months after he was. The two of us decided to share responsibility for taking away college from my parents. Axel came along three years after me, and Gage two years after that. By that point my parents were both busy and settled in their lives and careers. I always wondered if they regretted any of it.

"I see what you mean," I said. "But it doesn't make sense. I don't have dreams, or goals. I wouldn't be giving anything up. In fact, he has the money to let me do anything I wanted."

Maxine held up a hand. "Money. He has a lot. That bothers you."

"Yes." I sighed. "I don't want to be a charity case. I'm afraid he sees me as one of his projects. Take something that's shabby and not quite perfect, and make it better."

"You think he's trying to fix you?"

"Sounds stupid when you say it."

"No. It's not. Have you talked to him about this? He's a rescuer. It's in his nature. I don't think that's how he sees you, but if it's on your mind you should ask."

I took a healthy bite of gingerbread muffin. "Now is a bad time."

"Why?"

"You know that Zach was married, right?"

"Axel mentioned that he's a widower."

"Well, he married his childhood best friend on Valentine's Day and she died a year later on the eighteenth."

Maxine sat back, frowning. "Is he OK?"

"I can't tell. He seems fine but it's still a few days away. I don't know how he is going to be. I tried to ask James but Zach came in and got mad at me. Then he calmed down, we talked and he got all lovey on me. Classic Zach mixed signals."

"How long ago did she die?"

"It'll be ten years. But it's more complicated than that." I finished my coffee.

"How did she die?"

"I don't know," I admitted. "But I think she killed herself. And based on the look in Zach's eyes sometimes, he found her."

Maxine sat back. "Poor guy."

"I know. He was twenty-two years old. So was she. And I can't ask. I don't want him to tell me if he doesn't want to. But I can tell he's still messed up about it. And without knowing what happened I can't help. Not that I think I could anyway." I sighed. "And none of this helps me figure out how I feel about Zach."

Maxine shifted her empty coffee cup. "Maybe I should have had you get some vodka."

CHAPTER 28

ZACH WOKE ME on Valentine's Day at six but made love to me so thoroughly I couldn't complain. I fell back to sleep draped across his broad chest until he woke me again at nine with similar results. We didn't get out of bed until eleven. James was out at work so we had the house to ourselves. I made breakfast and Zach followed me around the kitchen, kissing my neck and distracting me.

After we ate we loaded Mop into my truck. Zach's truck was higher and Mop couldn't jump into it. I had a feeling even my truck was going to be too much eventually. I pushed the sad thought aside as I drove to the National Seashore. I loved that Zach didn't mind when I drove. I knew it irritated him, but he never complained.

We walked around Salt Pond and into the woods. The trail was too skinny to walk side by side and he walked behind me, so close he nearly stepped on my heels. We stopped at my favorite tree. It was to the right of the path and had grown into a natural low slope like a vertical hammock. There were names in hearts carved all over the old smooth trunk. I called it the Love Tree. Zach sat down on its broad flat section and pulled me onto his lap.

"I like this tree," he said, resting his chin on my shoulder. His beard brushed against my cheek.

"My parents used to take me here all the time. Their initials are over there." I pointed up a branch. "My dad carved them when they got married."

I thought about one day having my initials on the tree. With Zach holding me snugly against him, the idea wasn't as terrifying as it had been a few days ago. But it still made me queasy.

"Come on, I want to go look at the water," I said.

Zach followed me up the path to the top of the hill. Two benches were positioned to have an amazing view of the cove and the ocean beyond. The wind whipped off the water despite it being a mild warm day for February. Cape Cod was always windy. I shivered a little in my old jacket and Zach pulled me against him again.

"What is your obsession with standing by the ocean getting blasted by the wind? Crazy Yankee," he said, but he was nuzzling my hair.

"I told you. It makes me feel small. Look at all that water. It goes on for thousands of miles. The world is so big. There are so many people, so many things. I am unnoticeable."

"You like that feeling? Which I disagree with. You demand notice, babe."

I smiled. "If I am so small that the world doesn't notice me, my problems must be even smaller. Which makes it easy to forget them."

He sighed. "I wish I could do that."

I turned to face him and tried to kiss the sadness from his eyes. It almost worked but the shadow remained.

"This is not wallowing time," I scolded him. "This is part of you and me Valentine's Day. When I go to work you can wallow and get it out of your system before dinner."

He tried to smile for me but it didn't reach his eyes. "I'm sorry, Bo."

"Don't be. Come on, it's cold. We'll go back home."

I looked down at Mop, who was collapsed beside the bench. This was a long walk for him with too many hills. Next time I would only go around Salt Pond to the bridge and back. He was too old to drag through the woods.

"Come on, Old Man," I said, bending down to ruffle the fluffy fur on his head. "I'm sorry I dragged you this far from your warm kitchen floor."

Mop woofed at me and jumped up with surprising energy.

"How old is Mop?" Zach asked.

"He's twelve." I didn't like the number. It made me worry about my best friend. Now I was depressed. I turned to the ocean again. I sighed as I let the world work its magic on me. Mop was getting old, but he had lived a wonderful happy life and I would make sure the rest of his was just as great. And while I had him I wouldn't waste my time being sad because I would lose him.

"Let's go home and make you some bacon," I said to my dog.

I looked at Zach. The ocean didn't work a miracle and make me able to admit how I felt. But it did make me realize that running was stupid. Zach would wait patiently for me to come to terms with myself. He wouldn't push me. And no matter what I decided I felt for him, it wasn't something to be afraid of.

I took his hand when the path widened enough for us to walk side by side, and I didn't let it go.

* * *

Everyone decided to take their significant other out for Valentine's Day and my feet were killing me, but my apron was full of cash. Zach showed up five minutes after the kitchen closed and I begged Angelica to make us dinner. She gave me a hard time but cooked the special for us.

I told the other waitress to go home to her husband and kids and leave the closing to me. I had to wait for food anyway. Zach helped me wipe down tables, put up chairs, and restock for the next day. He acted like he had worked in a restaurant before. I didn't ask.

We sat down at a small table with our food in plastic containers because the dishwasher would kill me if I added to his work. I lit the candle with the lighter I always had in my apron.

"How was your night?" he asked.

"Good. I'm tired, though. My feet hurt."

"I'll rub them when we get home."

I moaned at the idea and he smiled.

"How are you feeling?" I asked.

"Better than I ever have on Valentine's Day. Thank you for giving me some time to be miserable. I got it out of my system, I promise."

"I had to work anyway," I said.

"Why can't you just accept a compliment?"

"Because."

The food was wonderful and I yelled my thanks to Angelica as she headed out the door. She came over and Zach charmed her with his southern drawl and manners. I watched him, wondering how it would feel to be that comfortable in my own skin. Zach never seemed nervous or hesitant. The only time he was self-conscious at all was when he was naked, which was when he had the least reason. When Angelica left, he looked back at me.

"What?" he asked.

"Nothing."

He smiled and reached across the table to take my hand. "If I tell you I love you will you run screaming again?"

I rolled my eyes. "I got that out of my system. I think."

"I love you, Bo. Thank you for making this a perfect day for me."

I bit my lip. I wanted to say it back to him but I couldn't. "Thank you for being with me." Wow, that sounded lamer out loud than it had in my head. But he only leaned across the table and kissed me.

"Let's bring the rest of this home. I owe you a foot rub," he said.

We ate the last of our dinner in bed and he rubbed my feet. We watched Fried Green Tomatoes and he didn't even complain. It was the perfect day.

CHAPTER 29

I WASN'T SURE what woke me, but I found myself looking at my alarm clock blaring three a.m. at me. I felt wetness on my hair and neck and groaned as I realized that Zach's face was nuzzled there. He was drooling on me. I shifted to wake him up and growl at him but I stopped when I saw his face. The wetness on my hair and neck were tears. He was crying in his sleep.

I froze and stared at him. He had been quiet for the past two days. It was the seventeenth; tomorrow was the anniversary of Alice's death. I tried to distract him but had been unable to make him laugh. And now he was crying in his sleep. What should I do? If I woke him he would only be embarrassed. So I dried his face with the sheet and kissed his forehead. He shifted a little, pulling me closer. I settled against him and he nuzzled his face against my neck again. I fell back asleep, wishing there was something more I could do than soak up his tears.

I woke later to hear Zach's soft footsteps moving around the room. I felt cold without him pressed against me. I opened my eyes and glared at the clock as it told me cheerily that it was four thirty. I pushed the covers away and looked around the room. Zach was dressed in jeans and was buttoning a collared white shirt. My eyes went to the suitcase that was sitting on the dresser.

"Oh," I said dumbly. "Where are you going?"

"Home to Georgia," he said, buttoning the last button on his shirt.

I came fully awake and sat up. "When? For how long?"

"My plane leaves at seven. I'll be back in a few days."

"Why didn't you tell me you were going?"

"It has nothing to do with you."

I stared at him. "Nothing to do with me?" I didn't like the squeaky hurt sound of my voice. "Nothing to do with me?"

He frowned. "I just have to go home. I'll be back."

"You should have told me you were going."

"I don't have time for this. I'm running late as it is."

I was not going to be dismissed that easily. I jumped out of bed, thankful I was wearing Mason's shirt and silk pants instead of being naked. Yelling at him naked would change the whole conversation.

"You didn't tell me for a reason," I accused.

"What?"

"If it wasn't a big deal you would have mentioned it. But you kept it from me."

He leaned against the wall and glared at me. "This is not about you. It has nothing to do with you."

"Like hell it doesn't."

"How I mourn Alice is my business," he said through gritted teeth.

"No. It's ours."

"We're not having this conversation right now." He reached for his suitcase but I knocked it to the floor.

"Like hell we're not!" I shouted at him. "If you were going to go down to Georgia to remember your wife, to put flowers on her grave and miss her that would be different."

"How do you know that's not what I'm going to do?"

"Because I know you, Zach. There is a huge difference between going to pay your respects to your wife and drinking yourself into a coma to punish yourself for something that wasn't your fault."

"You have no idea what you're talking about." His body was tense with anger, his hands fisted.

"I don't need to know. I know you. You would have done anything for her. Whatever happened was outside your control. And you need to stop dragging the guilt around."

He didn't say anything. I had never seen him so angry before.

"Zach," I sighed, and reached for his arm but he stepped away from me. I let my hand drop. "You've been punishing yourself for ten years. It's time to let it go."

"So I should just forget about Alice?" he said bitterly.

"Of course not." I moved a step closer and he didn't back away. "You loved her. She was your best friend. She will always be in your heart, and that's the way it should be. What you need to forget is the guilt, this feeling you have that you were responsible."

Some of the anger left his body. He looked down at his boots. "I was responsible. You don't know what happened."

I stepped closer so I was only inches from him. "I don't need to know. I know you. You would have saved her if you could have." I touched his chest. His heart was beating too fast.

"You should honor her memory instead of hurting yourself with it," I said.

The anger returned but he didn't move away from me. "This has nothing to do with you."

I glared at him. "That's insulting. You're in love with me. That makes your pain my business."

"How I feel about you is my problem to deal with," he said.

I flinched. "Being in love with me is a problem?"

He bit his lip. "I'm sorry, Bo. I didn't mean it like that."

"Well, you said it." I took my hand away from his chest. "I won't play second fiddle."

He frowned at me. "What?" He paused and then glared at me. "You're mad because I was married before?"

"No!" I yelled, tired of being misunderstood. "I don't have any problem that you were married. I have a problem that you're using Alice to push me away."

"She was my wife," he said. "I loved her. I lost her. I'm allowed to deal with that however I want to."

I reached under his shirt and pulled the necklace with his wedding ring free. It hung on the end of the chain between us.

"This is what's keeping me away," I said. "Not that you were married, but the blame you carry around. You can't really be with me. Not if so much of you is still in the past, trying to save her."

I regretted it the moment the words were out of my mouth. But I folded my arms and stood my ground. He looked at me for a long time without moving. I couldn't even tell if he was breathing.

"Well?" I asked at length.

"Well what?" he growled. I felt the tears threatening and blinked a few times. He looked at the clock. "Dammit, you're gonna make me miss my flight." He reached around me and picked up the suitcase without touching me. He left without another word, slamming the door.

I sat on his bed and burst into tears.

CHAPTER 30

I HEARD raised male voices over my sobbing but I burrowed my face into the pillows and ignored it. I wasn't even sure why I was crying. I hated crying, and getting angry at myself only made me cry harder. There was a knock on the door.

"Go away!" I yelled.

"It's me, Bo," James said. "Can I come in?"

"No. Go away."

"Are you crying?" James sounded surprised. I heard the door open. "I should have punched the sorry son of a bitch."

I forced myself to raise my head from the pillow. He sat on the bed and pulled me up so I was leaning against his shoulder.

"My brother is a jerk," he said, kissing my temple. "I didn't realize he was an idiot too, though."

"What?" I asked, rubbing at my eyes.

"I never thought he would be stupid enough to make you cry. Are you OK?"

I sighed as the last of my tears and sobs subsided. "Not really."

"What did he say to you?

I leaned against James and gave him the highlights of the fight. When I was finished, I felt miserable.

"He was right. It is none of my business," I said. "He said I was a problem. That loving me was a problem."

"Oh honey, he didn't mean that." He stroked my back. "He was just upset. It's hard for him. He's found the perfect girl and she literally tried to run away when he said he loved her."

I closed my eyes. "He told you that?"

"I caught him at a weak moment."

I tried to pull away but he didn't let me go. I didn't try to escape his comfort very hard. I slumped against him. "He wishes I wasn't such a stupid kid."

"I'm positive he didn't say that."

"No, that's how I feel I guess. What kind of woman runs from 'I love you?'"

"You, apparently." He smiled and patted my head. "Zach has an advantage over you."

"How?"

"Zach has been looking for you for his entire life. He always wanted to settle down and have a family. He was looking for you, but you weren't looking for him. You were looking for fun. And he fell madly in love with you, like any sane man would." He chucked me lightly on the chin. "And it's hell on him waiting for you to catch up. He made himself extremely vulnerable to you without any confirmation that you wouldn't hurt him."

I sighed. "I wish I knew how I felt about him."

"I think you know how you feel; you're just not ready to admit it."

"Shut up." I sighed. "What is Zach going to do in Georgia?"

"He'll go to a hotel room, then to a liquor store. He'll drive to the cemetery and drink himself unconscious. That's what he's done the last nine years. I've tried every year to get him to leave the cemetery but he won't until sunrise. Then he allows me to drag him to the hotel to puke and shower. He visits his in-laws and then goes home. And he acts like none of it happened the next day."

I hated being right. "I figured. If it was something healthy he wouldn't have hidden it from me."

We cuddled together in companionable silence for a few minutes. The question hummed around my brain until it turned into a scream and I had to ask.

"What happened to Alice?"

James stiffened and stopped breathing. His eyes lost focus and I had a horrible feeling that he was seeing it again. I did some quick math and realized that he had been fourteen when she died. What had he seen to put that look in his eyes?

"They had taken her down by the time I got there," he said, his voice eerily quiet and distant. "She was on the couch. It looked like she was sleeping. She was in her nightgown, but she only had one of her bunny slippers on. The other was in the middle of the floor. Zach was sitting on the coffee table, holding her hand. They kept trying to make him let go because they wanted to take the body away. But he wouldn't let her go."

"James?" I waved my hand in his face.

He blinked and looked at me. "Sorry. I can't really talk about it. I'm sorry."

"Don't be. I'm sorry I asked." Now I was absolutely positive I did not want to know the whole story. "What time is your flight?" I asked to change the subject.

"My flight?" he asked, still a little lost in the horror of his memory.

"You're going to fly down and drag him out of the cemetery. Or at least sit with him. Right?"

He muttered a little under his breath. "I went online to book a flight and the next available isn't until late tonight." He looked at me and a light flickered in his eyes. "And you're going to be on it."

I blinked. "Me?"

"Yes, you." He jumped up off the bed with enthusiasm. "He needs you. He's too stupid to admit it. He should have brought you with him. He needs to trust you with this. Because if he blocks you out you will never forgive him, and he'll lose you. He may be stupid enough to let that happen, but I am not going to let him lose the best thing that ever happened to him."

I stared at him. "Me? The best thing that has ever happened to him?"

"Duh." He rolled his eyes. "Where have you been the last six months?"

With Zach, I thought. And James was right. If Zach shut me out of this, I would never forgive him. It would give me the excuse to run, and I didn't want to run.

"I can't afford the ticket," I said.

"It's already paid for. And I have a rental car ready. I'll give you directions to the graveyard. He'll be there by the time you land."

"I'll pay you back."

"If you get my brother out of that cemetery, out of the past, I'll owe you for the rest of my life."

*   *   *

I sat on the beach with Mop panting obliviously beside me. The tide was high and the waves were dancing up the sand. I looked up at the gray winter sky and thought about Zach. I thought about his smile and the pure joy in his laughter. I thought of the way he always touched me when he walked into the room. I thought about the feel of his beard on my neck as he pulled me close against him in his sleep. And I thought about losing him.

What would I do without him? How would I feel? Would I be OK? The answers to those questions scared me. I wanted to be with Zach. I needed to have his love in my life. I still couldn't admit that I loved him, but needing him was a big step. I wasn't going to simply walk away. I was going to fly down to Georgia and drag his sorry ass out of the cemetery and into my arms, where he belonged. I was going to have him tell me everything so it wouldn't be between us anymore. I wanted all of him. I was willing to share him with a memory of a lost loved one, but I was not willing to share him with a ghost. He would either leave Alice fondly in the past and move into the future with me, or . . . what? The or what scared me. He would just have to see it my way.

With that thought I got up and drove back to the house.

CHAPTER 31

JAMES DROVE ME to the airport, fidgeting in his seat with emotions he wasn't interested in talking about. I had my small carry-on bag with two changes of clothes and some toiletries. Zach's cell phone had been off all day. The normal business message was changed to say that he would be unreachable until the twenty-first. I didn't leave a message because I had no idea what to say. I had no idea what I would say to him when I found him either.

"Do planes make you nervous?" James asked as we snaked our way through the various roads of Logan Airport.

"I don't know," I shrugged.

He looked at me longer than was prudent due to the traffic we were in. "You've never been on a plane before?" He sounded astonished and I was reminded of the differences that growing up with or without money create.

"No. I've been to Maine and New Hampshire. But other than a handful of camping trips, I've never left Cape Cod."

James was stunned into silence for a while. I fiddled with my cell phone, wanting to call Zach but knowing he wouldn't answer. I was worried about him. He'd had hours to do himself all kinds of bad.

"Where are some of the places you've been?" I asked, hoping to distract us.

"My parents went on two vacations a year. One they went on alone, the other they took us. I loved Hawaii, but Zach preferred Italy."

And my parents took a long weekend in a dingy rented house in Maine once a year if they could. I realized as we pulled up to the curb that if I stayed with Zach, I could go to the places I had always dreamed of. I pushed the thought aside. I didn't want him for money. I wasn't getting on an airplane for the first time so I could get a trip to Italy out of him. I was worried about Zach, my lover, my friend, and I was going to help him.

"Do you need help getting to the gate?" James asked as I slung my backpack over my shoulder.

"I can figure it out. I'm a pretty girl; I can just look cute and confused and someone will help me. Don't get a parking ticket." I leaned into the car and kissed his cheek. "I'll go get Zach. Don't worry. I'll take care of him."

"Thank you, Bo. Call me when you find him. Please?"

"I will."

Getting through the airport was an experience I could have done without. It seemed like a lot of fuss over nothing. But I was seated on the plane forty minutes later. I discovered that flying did bother me, but not so much that I was panicking. I just gripped my chair and closed my eyes and wished I had Zach there to hold my hand.

* * *

I followed James' directions through Savannah in the rental car. It was dark and I had a terrible sense of direction, but I was motivated. The graveyard where Alice was buried was outside of the city. It was already eleven and I was worried about getting lost. It was a lot colder than I thought Georgia had a right to be. This was supposed to be the south.

As the GPS barked at me I looked around at the southern landscape and almost had to pull over as it occurred to me for the first time that maybe Zach wouldn't welcome me here. Maybe he would be angry. What if we fought? I couldn't get back home, I didn't have any money. I pushed those thoughts away and swore creatively at the GPS to calm my nerves.

I found the cemetery at midnight and parked next to a rental car very similar to my own. It was the only one there. I pulled my jacket tighter around me and swore as I looked into the darkness. I had no idea where Alice's grave was or how big the cemetery was. I hadn't thought to bring a flashlight.

I used the tiny flashlight on my cell phone but it didn't help much. I tripped on a short gravestone and bruised my shin and scraped my palm. While I was sitting on the ground cursing under my breath I heard the distinct sound of glass bottles clinking together.

I brushed myself off and headed for the sound. I found Zach sitting on the ground with his back against a tombstone. His face was in his hands, his legs drawn up against his chest. He looked broken and small. The wind finally blew the clouds away from the moon, highlighting him in his grief. Two empty bottles were lying beside him in the grass.

I knelt down between his knees and pulled his hands away from his face. There were dried tracks of tears on his face and his eyes were swollen and red. He reeked of whiskey but I barely noticed. He looked at me and I tried to smile for him.

He was shaking. He stared at me for a moment as if he wasn't sure I was really there. I put my hands on his face. His big arms wrapped around me and pulled me forward against his chest. I lay my cheek against him, shifting so I was curled against him lying on one hip between his legs. I was insanely uncomfortable but there wasn't anything in the world that could have made me move.

"Are you really here?" he asked into my hair.

"Yes. I got here as soon as I could."

"Bo, I'm sorry. Those things I said . . ."

I covered his mouth with my fingers. "Don't. You were upset. You didn't mean to be a jerk. It's OK. I'm here now."

He let out his breath in a shuddering sigh and held me closer. He was wearing jeans and a sweatshirt but his skin felt like ice. He had obviously been sitting there for a long time. I shared my warmth and made soothing sounds. Eventually my hip demanded that I move. I tried to sit up but his arms didn't release me.

"Zach, my spine is not enjoying being bent like this. I'm not going to leave you, just let me move around."

He shifted me around like I was a toy instead of a person. I found myself sitting on my butt with my back braced against his chest, his legs hugged on either side of me. His arms settled around my torso and pulled me back against him. I sighed and sat back, resting my head on his shoulder and jaw.

"I know it's a stupid question," I said. "But are you OK?"

"No. But I'm better now that you're here." He kissed my temple. "I should have brought you with me."

"Yeah, you should have. Luckily, your brother has more sense than you and he sent me after you."

The sound he made was almost a laugh but came out more of a grunt.

"This is a really unhealthy ritual," I told him.

"I know."

"Then why do it?"

"It's complicated."

"No, it's not. She died. You feel responsible although I'm sure you weren't. So you spent the last ten years being so busy you couldn't think about it. But once a year you stop running to torment yourself and come sit here."

"Sounds worse when you say it."

"Alice would be disappointed in you." I knew it was a low blow but I had to say it. His body stiffened around me but he didn't push me away.

"Why do you say that?" he asked.

"Because she loved you. The last thing she would want is for you to hurt yourself like this."

"I didn't hurt myself."

"You sabotaged your relationship with me, got shitfaced drunk and tried to freeze to death."

"Did I mess us up?" he sounded so wounded I had to blink back tears.

"Almost. But I'm here, aren't I? And Alice would be horrified that you remember her by doing this to yourself. You should honor her memory. Come here on her birthday instead of the day she died. Bring flowers instead of a bottle of whiskey. Remember her for the woman you loved instead of the woman you lost."

"You don't understand."

"No. I don't. I've never lost someone I loved. But I do know that if something happened to me, I wouldn't want anyone blaming themselves and spending the rest of their life punishing themselves for it."

"I can't get it out of my head," he said, his body shivering from the memory and not the cold. "How could she have done that to me? She knew I would be the one to find her."

I pushed my back more firmly against him and rubbed my cheek against his jaw.

"I think you need to tell me about it. All of it."

He started crying softly. I waited quietly while he lost control. I soaked up his grief as much as I could, but I wanted out of the graveyard. I was cold and exhausted.

"I haven't talked about it," he said when he could speak again. "Not to anyone but the police, and they don't know all of it."

"Well, you're going to tell me. But not here. We're going to get up and go to the hotel. We're going to get you warm and have you eat something."

"I can't leave yet," he said.

"Why not?"

"I don't know."

I started to get up but he tightened his hold.

"Zach, let go of me." I said it slowly and firmly. His hands slowly relaxed but he didn't let me go.

"I'm getting up," I said. "I'm cold and tired and I found out today that flying scares the hell out of me. So I've had a pretty shitty day and I'm not going to spend any more of it in this graveyard."

I pulled out of his grasp and stood up. My body creaked and my shin throbbed from where I had smacked it on the tombstone. I looked down at Zach and felt petty for even noticing the slight pain.

He looked up at me forlornly. "You won't stay with me?" he asked.

"Yes, I will. In a warm lighted hotel room. Stop being a martyr and get up. You're coming with me if I have to start screaming and get the cops here." I held my hand down to him. The moonlight glinted on the blood from my scraped palm.

Zach's eyes went to the blood. "What happened?"

I glanced at my hand. I hadn't realized it was that bad. And I thanked the tombstone I tripped over. Zach would never let me limp out of the cemetery without him while I was hurt.

"I tripped in the dark. I didn't think it was that bad."

He stood up, showing me just how drunk he was by swaying like a sapling in a windstorm. I slid under his shoulder and grunted as his weight shifted my way. He caught his head in his hand and swore.

"Let me see your hand," he said.

"It's too dark out here."

"Are you hurt anywhere else?"

"I hit my shin really hard. It's how I cut my hand. I tripped over a gravestone and fell." Zach took my hand and held it in the faint moonlight. He gently kissed my palm on the undamaged section.

"Let's go to the hotel so I can fix this."

I let out a sigh of relief as we hobbled together toward the cars. I was getting him out of the graveyard, and all I had to do was maim myself. Step one was complete. Now I had to get him to talk about why he had planned on sitting there all night. I was not looking forward to hearing the story, but I knew I had to.

CHAPTER 32

I DROVE US to the hotel and helped Zach into the room. We cleaned my palm of dirt and blood but Zach started throwing up in the toilet while I put band-aids on my hand. I left him hugging the toilet to get the bag of food that I picked up at an all-night gas station out of the car. Zach was in the shower by the time I got back. I peeked around the shower curtain to see his forehead and arms braced against the wall. He opened his eyes and glanced over at me.

"I'll be out in a second. I won't pass out and fall, I promise," he said.

I wanted to climb into the shower with him but I figured he was asking for a few minutes alone. I went back into the main room. His bag was sitting open on the bed. I picked out one of his shirts and changed into it. I paired it with red cotton pants and settled on the bed to wait for him.

He emerged from the bathroom holding the too-small hotel towel around his hips. He looked ridiculous and it made me laugh. He looked at me and managed a small smile. Normally I had a hard time concentrating when he was naked, but for once I wasn't distracted. I held out boxers and the polar bear pj pants I bought him for Christmas. He almost fell over trying to get them on and I laughed again. He didn't.

He rubbed the towel through his hair and tossed it carelessly onto the floor in the general direction of the bathroom. He leaned back against the headboard, looking far sexier than a grieving man should have.

I settled against his side and tangled my legs with his. His hand rested on my hip and he sighed.

"We don't have to talk about this right now," I said. "It can wait till tomorrow."

"Can it wait forever?" he asked, closing his eyes.

"No. I need to know what happened."

"Why?"

"Because you need to tell me."

He nodded. "This isn't going to be easy to say. Please just let me struggle through it, OK? Don't interrupt. Don't rush me."

"I won't."

He was silent for a long time, and it took all of my willpower not to prompt him. I ran my hand across the planes of his chest. He was warm now and smelled of soap instead of booze.

"I should have known that morning when I left for work," he said, startling me. "Every day I would leave for work and she'd kiss me and say, 'I'll see you later.' But that morning when I left, she said goodbye." He paused for a few heartbeats. "I didn't think anything of it at the time. It wasn't until later that I noticed.

"I went to work, at the accounting firm. I had class that night. I was taking night classes, working toward my degree in architecture. Alice hated how much I was gone. She had started crying every day. I dropped out of two of my classes so I would have more time with her. She had been growing more and more detached and depressed but I didn't know what to do. So I just pretended it was OK.

"She looked so sad that morning that I decided to take a long lunch. I headed back to the house to surprise her. I stopped and bought her roses."

He stopped talking again. He pulled me closer against him. I was staring at the wall but I looked up at his face. Fresh tears tracked down his cheeks. I didn't try and wipe them away.

He continued, "She picked out the house we lived in. She loved the exposed beams in the living room. The master bedroom was the only room on the second floor and there was a balcony that overlooked the living room. The beams were easy to reach from there. Maybe that was what she had been thinking of when she picked the house. I'll never know."

I wanted so badly to tell him to stop but I couldn't. I let my tears join his and cuddled against him.

"I walked in the front door and saw her hanging there," he said, his voice without any intonation. "She was in her pink nightgown and the bunny slippers I bought her for her eighteenth birthday. One had fallen off when she jumped off the balcony. It was on the floor under her. She was just hanging there." He was barely breathing. I shifted so that I was kneeling beside him. I framed his face with my hands and looked into his eyes.

He took a deep breath and nodded. "I'm OK. I just can't stop seeing her. They told me that her neck broke when she jumped, so she didn't die slowly by suffocating. I don't remember what happened very well. The neighbors heard me screaming. They found me standing in the living room staring up at her. I don't remember. I guess I started insisting that I take her down. Carl climbed out onto the beam and cut the rope while Maria called the police. The cops were angry at me for moving her. But I couldn't leave her like that. I couldn't."

He stopped to cry for a while and I crawled onto his lap. He held me and cried for a long time. I cried with him.

When he could talk again he continued. "I caught her when Carl cut her down. She seemed weightless. I set her on the couch and it looked like she was sleeping. I sat down on the coffee table and held her hand. I was in shock. I don't remember the police getting there. Eventually one managed to get my attention. He tried to get me to let go of her. I hit him. I don't remember doing it. Carl told me I didn't even let go of Alice's hand; I just hit the cop with my free one. The next cop was smarter. Everyone was telling me I had to let her go. They needed to take her way. But if I let her go it would be real. So I didn't. Until James got there. The high school was only a few blocks away. James used to skip out during lunch to eat with Alice. If I hadn't come home early, James would have been the one to find her.

"He saw the police cars and ran in. Then he saw her on the couch. He didn't scream. He just froze and went gray. It snapped me out of it. I had to get him out of there. So I let Alice go and took James outside."

"I'm sorry, Zach. So sorry."

He sighed. "That's what everyone knows. But there's more. There's something I have never told anyone."

I closed my eyes. How could it get worse?

"Are you sure you want to hear this?"

"I need to. You need to tell me this or you wouldn't have mentioned it. Tell me everything."

He was quiet for a long time and I hoped he had fallen asleep. But he shifted me on his lap and I knew I was going to hear the rest. "I stayed with my parents that night. And the next day. My mother gave me some pills and I passed out. I wasn't functioning really well. They were worried about leaving me alone. But I wanted to go back to the house. I wanted to be home, at our home. I wanted to touch her things, to smell her. So I waited till they were all asleep and I drove home. I saw the answering machine light blinking and hit it automatically. The first message was from Alice's doctor. She had gone for a physical a few days before. He said." Zach stopped. His whole body shook for a moment.

The silence lasted so long that I touched his face. "What did he say?"

"Alice was pregnant when she killed herself."

I curled around him, feeling a horrible wrenching pain in my chest. I started crying but he didn't seem to notice. He cradled me against him.

"We'd been trying to have a baby. Her doctor repeated his opinion that stopping her medications was unnecessary and dangerous. He said that it wouldn't hurt the baby like she was afraid of. I guess she stopped taking her antidepressants." He stroked my hair. "I don't know if she knew she was pregnant. She must have known. But she never would have killed herself if she knew. Would she?" His voice sounded lost and afraid.

"She didn't know," I said, needing to believe it.

"Why do you think that?"

"Because she wanted to give you a baby. She wanted to give you something to love because you couldn't love her. She never would have taken that away from you."

He let out a shuddering sigh. "She's still gone. And my baby died with her."

I thought of the way he looked at Danny in the hospital; the way he held the infant in his arms. He lost his child and never told a soul about it.

"I'm so sorry, Zach." I knew the words were stupid but I said them anyway. "Why didn't you tell anyone?"

"Because it would only make it worse. I had to fight with the minister to get permission to bury Alice in the graveyard."

"Why?"

"She killed herself. Southern Baptists frown on that. I had never been very close with the church, but after fighting with the minister for Alice's resting place, I swore never to go back. Her funeral was the last time I was in a church. I don't believe there is a God that would put a beautiful spirit like hers into such a broken vessel."

I stroked his cheek and stayed quiet, because there really wasn't anything to say.

CHAPTER 33

ZACH WAS GONE when I woke up but there was a note letting me know he was getting coffee and food. I rolled over onto his side of the bed, going over everything he told me the night before. He told me he loved me as I drifted off to sleep but I waited too long to respond and he kissed me quiet. He bared his soul to me and I still couldn't say three words.

He was back by the time I got out of the shower. He looked tired and worn, but not as broken as the day before. He managed a full smile for me as I gave up on the tiny hotel towel and wrapped it around my hair instead of my body.

"I think you should be naked all the time," he said.

"I don't think that's quite the impression I wanted to make on your family."

He laughed and I relaxed.

I got dressed and sat on the bed with my coffee. Zach was eating some gooey form of pastry.

"Where's mine?" I asked.

"I got you something else."

"But that looks good." I leaned over and took a bite, licking one of his fingers before sitting back. He rolled his eyes at me.

"Thief," he muttered.

I leaned forward for another bite but he pulled it away. "Hey, give me some more."

A very mischievous look entered his eyes and I started to move back. I ended up pinned beneath him, his fingers coating my arm in gooey syrup. His other hand still held the pastry. He kissed me and I licked the sugar off his lips. We ended up naked, sweaty, and in need of another shower. He fed me the last of the pastry while we lay in bed.

After our shower, we got dressed and he changed his plane reservation to include me. We wouldn't be able to leave till the following morning, but I was happy about it. I had a friend covering my shift at work and I wanted this day to see Zach's home and family.

"I'm running late," he said as he finished buttoning his jeans. "You have that effect on me."

"It's good for you. Where are we going?"

He tripped over the 'we' for only a moment. "I, ah, *we* are going to go see Charlotte and Carter Blaize for brunch. Then we'll swing by and you can meet Rosey."

"What about your parents?"

Based on the look on his face I guessed he hadn't thought of them at all. It made me sad.

"They're busy."

"Are you trying to keep me away from them?" I couldn't stop myself from asking. "Because they wouldn't approve?"

He laughed at the idea and kissed my nose. "No, not at all. If I was worried about that you wouldn't be meeting Charlotte, Carter and Rosey. My parents would be polite to you no matter what. My mother would ask if you had good genes, my father if you had a good heart, and they would both be content knowing you made me happy. They are surgeons. Their bedside manner sucks, even out of the hospital. But they are good people and I love them. If it's important to you, I'll see if we can stop by the hospital for a quick hello."

I thought about it for a minute. "I'd like to at least say hello, have a face to put with them. Walter talked about John all the time, but I don't even know your mother's name." It seemed so wrong that he was so distant from his parents.

"My mother's name is Patricia. Now, let's go. Charlotte makes the best brunch in Georgia."

* * *

Alice had been a carbon copy of her mother. Charlotte was a beautiful southern belle, from her artfully wavy blonde hair to her pink dress and sensible heels. She smiled warmly and hugged Zach the way my mother hugged my brothers.

"There's my boy," she said in a heavy Georgia drawl. "I was getting worried about my baby. You're never late."

I was standing behind Zach so she hadn't seen me. I refused to admit I stepped behind him when the door opened because I was a coward. Zach pulled me forward when she released him.

"Mama, this is Bodel Tavish. She's the reason I'm late. She says it's good for me. Bodel, this is Charlotte Blaize."

He called her *Mama* with such open affection it nearly brought tears to my eyes. If it weren't for the love of this woman, Zach would have been a very different person. He would have been a good man, but not a warm loving one.

I extended my hand but she pulled me into a hug. She was a few inches shorter than me, even in heels. It was like hugging a doll. And like a doll, she seemed to be created solely for the enjoyment of others. She radiated warmth and energy.

"Welcome, Bodel. What a pretty name."

"Thank you. I was named after my great grandmother. Most people call me Bo."

"Come on in. I'll get another setting for the table. Go on into the family room and see Carter. She's so pretty, he's gonna just eat her up."

I blushed and grasped Zach's hand. The southern hospitality was creeping out my northern jaded sensibilities. The house was gigantic and old, the kind with big columns in front. I had never seen *Gone with the Wind* but I had a feeling I was standing on the set. The inside looked to be professionally decorated, but the overall effect wasn't polished, but warm and welcoming.

Carter Blaize was sitting in a big overstuffed chair. He was at least a decade older than Charlotte, his dark hair liberally spattered with gray. I would have put him in his early sixties. He was a narrow man, decently tall but without much more dimension. He had a kind face and he stood up when Zach led me into the room.

"Well, well, well," he said, grasping Zach's hand for only a moment before turning his attention to me. "Look what you brought me."

"Good to see you too. Bodel, this is Carter."

I shook the offered hand. "Do you call him Papa?" I asked.

Zach blushed and Carter laughed.

"Pops, actually." Carter beamed at me. "I like her," he said to Zach. "Welcome to my home, Miss Bodel."

"Thank you."

"Zach's never brought anyone with him before."

"He tried to leave me behind, but I'm like a bad cold and I followed him."

Carter laughed and put an arm around my shoulders, pulling me away from Zach.

"If you're not gonna keep her, I will."

"*You* are happily married," Zach muttered. "Give her back." He looked so cute I started laughing. And after pouting for a moment, Zach laughed with me. I felt Carter's reaction to Zach's laughter because his arm was around me. He pulled me closer and walked us toward the dining room.

"I have never been happier to meet someone in my life," he whispered in my ear.

CHAPTER 34

"SO," CHARLOTTE SAID after we passed most of the meal with small talk and general information about me. "Now I don't have to worry about finding Zach a date for Peter's wedding."

I plastered a smile on my face to hide my fear at the word *wedding*.

"They set a date?" Zach asked, oblivious to my reaction.

"June fourteenth. Peter tried to keep Michelle under control, but she wants a big white wedding and her daddy is fronting the bill happily."

"I think the guest list is up around three hundred now. I don't know how she even knows that many people." Carter rolled his eyes and forked up more French toast.

Three hundred people? Three hundred wealthy educated southern hospitality dripping people? And me. The idea had me nearly throwing up my breakfast. Zach picked up on my discomfort when he pried my fingernails out of his thigh and held my hand firmly instead.

"You think I could get away with not going?" Zach asked.

"He's your cousin." Charlotte looked offended.

"Not a chance. If there was, I'd be hiding with you," Carter said.

"Bo? Are you feeling well?" Charlotte asked.

"Fine. Peachy. This food is excellent, Charlotte. You put my French toast to shame."

Zach squeezed my hand and stroked my wrist with his thumb. It helped me calm down.

"I can give you the recipe, though I don't think you have Georgia peaches growing in your yard."

We finished the meal and had coffee afterward in the living room. They were wonderful people whose love for Zach was obvious. None of them mentioned Alice and I had a feeling it was because of me.

There were pictures of her everywhere. The largest was a framed shot hanging above the mantel in the living room. There were two smaller ones I couldn't see clearly from my seat. I stood up and brought my coffee cup to the kitchen despite Charlotte protesting she was the host. I took the opportunity and walked to the mantel instead of the couch. A silence fell on the room while I studied the pictures.

Zach looked handsome in a tuxedo. His clean shaven face made him seem even younger. Alice stood beside him in a frilly white dress. They were the perfect image of happiness. Good looking bride and groom full of hope and expectations. In a year she would be dead and Zach heartbroken. But I pushed that aside and really looked at the picture.

"Alice was really beautiful," I said carefully. "She looks just like you, Charlotte."

There was a long silence and I took the coward's way out and kept looking at the picture to avoid seeing the family's reaction.

"Thank you," Charlotte said quietly. "We miss her."

The silence continued and I searched for some way to break the tension. I looked over my shoulder at Zach.

"You look like James without your beard," I said as lightly as I could.

Zach stood and walked up to me. He looked at the picture.

"I'm older. James is the one that looks like me."

I didn't know if it was a bad idea, but I was going to go for it. "Are there other pictures I could see?"

Charlotte stood up. She looked nervous. "I have a few albums."

"I'd love to see some embarrassing baby pictures," I said.

The uncertainty left her eyes and she smiled. "I have some of those."

Zach turned to her. "No. Please, have mercy."

We spent the next hour looking through old photographs. Alice was in almost every one. She clung to Zach, literally most of the time. He always had an arm around her or was holding her hand. I loved seeing the pictures of him as a child. There was so much happiness in those pictures. I recognized the look in his eyes that I had only recently been seeing. I think Charlotte and Carter saw the same thing.

While Zach went outside to make a phone call, Charlotte and Carter hugged the breath out of me.

"I can't tell you how happy we are that Zach found someone like you," Charlotte said. "After we lost Alice, I thought we were going to lose him too. And we did, for years. But the part that was gone is coming back. And I know it's because of you. Thank you, Bo."

I would have fidgeted under the praise but she hugged me again.

"I just happened to be living in the house he inherited. And I was too stubborn to leave."

Charlotte wiped a tear from her eye.

"I hope you'll come visit again, soon."

"I hope so too."

*   *   *

"I'm sorry they sprung the wedding thing on you," Zach said when we were alone in the car. I had forgotten about it but the feeling came rushing back.

"It's not your fault I'm an overreactive psycho."

Zach took my hand while he drove, resting it on his thigh.

"My cousin has been engaged for over a year. She kept moving the date. I hadn't thought to mention it to you. I know you don't want to go. You don't have to."

But I did have to. If I was going to be with him, it was going to be all the way. And that meant learning to mingle with his kind of people. I didn't know if I could do it.

"Bo?" His thumb stroked my wrist again.

"I'm fine. Where are we going?"

"Why do you always do that?"

"Do what?"

"Lie to me."

I tried to pull my hand away but he didn't let go. I let him keep it rather than getting into a childish tug of war.

"I don't lie," I snapped at him.

"Every time something bothers you, you say you're fine. You don't want to talk about it."

"That's not lying."

"You're not fine. You're upset, babe. Why won't you let me help? Why won't you talk to me?"

I shifted my body away from him and looked out the window. He let out a long sigh.

"We're going to the hospital. My father is busy in surgery but my mother is free for another half hour."

I felt childish and stupid. I turned back toward him and stroked his thigh with the hand he had trapped. He didn't look happy and it made me feel worse.

"I'll talk to you about it when I know what's wrong," I said.

He raised my hand to his lips and kissed it but didn't say anything else.

CHAPTER 35

PATRICIA CUTTER WAS DRESSED in surgical scrubs but still managed to look elegant and beautiful. Zach had her eyes but his were warm where hers were ice. She shook my hand stiffly and formally.

"Hello, Miss Tavish," she said.

"It's nice to meet you, Mrs. Cutter." The formality felt odd on my tongue.

There was a long silence and I realized I had no idea what I should say to this woman. She was a mountain lake, beautiful and inviting until you dipped your foot into the frigid water.

"How is the progress on the Phearson project?" Patricia asked Zach.

"It's still hitting some roadblocks but I'll have it figured out soon."

"You'll iron out all the problems and make it look easy. You always do," she said with confidence and a touch of pride. It made me like her a little. She turned her green eyes on me. "I wasn't expecting my son to bring you along."

I wasn't sure how best to respond.

"She followed me," Zach said, taking my hand. "She has a mind of her own. She doesn't listen to me at all."

Patricia smiled and the ice cracked a little. "Good. You need a strong woman who won't simply whimper at your feet."

"I don't whimper," I assured her.

"She snarls until she gets her way," Zach said.

This time Patricia's smile reminded me of Zach's. It was almost warm.

"Did you have breakfast with Charlotte and Carter?" she asked.

"Yes," Zach said.

"She is an amazing cook," I said.

"That she is. I'm lucky I have her as a friend, as a second mother to my sons. I don't do domestic well," she said it casually. "Zach tells me your mother is a mechanic?"

"Yes. We never complained when dinner tasted faintly of diesel oil."

"He told me you have brothers but I forget how many."

"I have three."

"I respect your mother. I have no idea how women work a full time job and have children. I couldn't have done it without Charlotte and Rosey."

I smiled at the praise of my hard-working, trash-talking mother. "We all pitched in to help. And my dad wasn't allowed to sit on the couch and watch."

"I sometimes wish that Zach had more of that kind of childhood. He grew up to be so independent I worry about him being able to work as a team."

"I'm in the room, Mother."

She smiled at him dismissively. "Of course you are. I've said the same to you many times. You like being the boss too much. I think Bodel is good for you. Something tells me she won't let you boss her around."

"As I said, she doesn't listen to me." Zach surprised me by kissing the top of my head.

"It's good for you." She checked her watch. "I'm due in surgery in a few minutes. I have to go, but it was nice to meet you, Bodel."

She shook my hand and her smile was actually warm. Zach hugged her and kissed her cheek.

"Love you," he said.

"I love you too."

*   *   *

I wanted to see the house Zach grew up in. Once I saw it I almost wished I hadn't. It was a huge monstrosity of a house, and I realized I hadn't left the set of *Gone with the Wind*. The landscaping alone was too much to take in. I paused on the porch, leaning against one of the shining white columns.

"What's wrong?" Zach asked.

"Most of the time I forget how much money you have. These reminders take me by surprise."

Zach shrugged. "It's just money. Come on, I want you to meet Rosey."

Zach's dismissal of wealth and privilege disturbed me. He couldn't possibly understand how I felt. I grew up in a family where sometimes we would eat bluefish for days because there wasn't money for anything else and my father fished after work. We wore hand-me-down clothes and Salvation Army specials. The four of us shared a half-dead Jeep Cherokee for years and we were amazed our parents managed to afford a car for us at all.

I walked through the house and felt like a beggar taken off the street. Everything was clean, organized, and grand. There were no scuff marks, cracks, spiderwebs, or second-hand furniture. It was like walking through a magazine.

Zach led me into the kitchen and I stared in envy. There were miles of granite countertops, two stoves, a fridge you could easily hide a body in, and flowers in a vase on the island. A short heavyset woman was bent over the stove and I smelled pie. Rosey stood up.

She looked to be about sixty. Her hair was graying at the temples and braided into tight corn rows. Her face was lined with wrinkles that only enhanced her beauty. She had dark eyes that seemed to smile as much as her generous mouth. She let out a whoop and moved with the energy and grace of someone much younger.

Zach caught her when she approached and picked her up in a hug. When he set her down I realized how small she was. She probably didn't clear five feet. What was it with these southern women and being short? I looked down at her and would have said hello but she threw her arms around me and squeezed the breath out.

"I didn't think he was going to bring you," Rosey said. "I told him to, but he never listens."

"I don't listen to him," I said when she released me.

"That's a good girl. I'm so excited to finally meet you. Zach and James have told me so much about you. Why don't we all sit down and have some coffee while we wait for this pie to cool."

I sat down at the huge polished wooden table and watched her make coffee. She wore a simple gray dress with a white apron that was spotless.

For the next forty minutes she buzzed with questions about my home and family. Her personality was so warm and inviting that I found myself talking without any restraint or discomfort. She told me embarrassing details of Zach's childhood while he blushed and muttered under his breath. The coffee was delicious and the pie was amazing. I never had the patience to make pie crust from scratch. After the coffee and pie were gone, Rosey walked to the trash can and made a huge fuss of how heavy it was and could Zach please take it out for her.

"Of course," Zach said.

"And while you're out there you might as well start the car and warm it up. It's freezing out."

Zach smiled good-naturedly and rolled his eyes. "I'll stay gone long enough for you to talk about me."

"That's a good boy." Rosey patted his arm. When Zach was gone she sat down at the table with me again.

"Learn to do that," she suggested. "Play on his good manners. I ground them in good and solid."

I smiled. "I'll remember that."

"So, how is he really doing? I know he comes down here and drinks himself stupid at poor Alice's grave. He didn't drag you along for that, did he?"

"No. He picked a fight with me back home and left me there. So James got a ticket for me and I flew down last night. I found him in the cemetery. I managed to trip and cut my hand so that motivated him to bring me to the hotel."

"Let me see," Rosey demanded, reaching for my hand. It was an automatic mothering gesture and I didn't stop her. I showed her my bruised and cut palm and she muttered over it like mothers do.

"Not so bad. But a good thing you did it. Not sure how you'd get Zach out of the cemetery without it. I went down two years in a row trying to get him out but I couldn't. None of us could. We all tried one year. It wasn't pretty. He and James nearly came to blows." She sipped at her nearly empty coffee cup.

"I don't understand why he comes down here on the anniversary of her death. Why not their wedding anniversary? Or her birthday? Why this day?"

"He's never answered me when I asked."

"Maybe I should ask him."

"Best way to get an answer from a man is a straight question. Ask when you're naked. That may help."

I laughed with her and we finished our coffee.

CHAPTER 36

"SO, WHAT DID you two ladies talk about?" Zach asked as we drove to a restaurant for dinner.

"You."

"Not gonna tell me, huh?"

"When I know the right words I will. Why aren't we having dinner with your family?"

"Because my mother is in surgery for an indeterminate amount of time and my father is having dinner at the hospital with her."

"What about Rosey?"

"She has a date tonight."

"Seriously?"

"She's dating a man she knew in high school. He lost his wife a few years ago."

"Was she ever married?"

"No. She'd never admit it but she's been in love with Tim forever. He got married right out of college and she became our housekeeper. I don't remember her dating much. Not until Tim started coming around again."

"That's sad for her."

"Not now. She's got him now."

"But he loved his wife first."

Zach frowned and glanced over at me while he drove. "Are we still talking about Rosey?"

I rolled my eyes at him. "Yes. Really, Zach, you're too sensitive about this. I've told you over and over I am not jealous of Alice. It's sad for Rosey because Tim knew her first but chose someone else."

We went to a small restaurant for dinner. It was dimly lit and warm and full of southern charm. The food was good and the local beer interesting. We called James after the meal to check on Mop and tell him when we were getting back.

As we drove home my mind kept going back to the sparse flowers that had decorated our table during dinner. A cherished memory deserved flowers, not drunkenness and tears. I saw a grocery store and asked Zach to stop.

"Why?" he asked.

"Because."

He insisted on coming in with me but didn't say anything as I bought a bouquet of flowers. He tried to pay for them but was too dignified to engage in the fight I started in public. He muttered something as we got back in the car.

"Stop muttering like that. If you have something on your mind, say it," I said.

He glared at me in response.

"Fine. Be that way. I want to go to the cemetery."

"I don't."

"Then point me in the right direction. I'll walk."

He sat back in his seat and closed his eyes. "You are the most stubborn pain-in-the-ass I have ever met."

"Thank you. Now either drive or I'm gonna start walking."

He started the car and drove in silence. We were the only people in the cemetery parking lot. I got out with the flowers and glared into the dark. Zach pulled out his industrial strength cell phone and turned on the flashlight built into it.

"Why are we here?" he asked.

"So you can apologize."

"Apologize? For what? I haven't done anything to you to apologize for."

"Not me. We're here to apologize to Alice."

"What?"

I was probably out of line, but I rarely let that stop me. "You should come down here on happy anniversaries, her birthday, for instance. But instead, you come on the day she died and hurt yourself. It's no way to remember someone who loved you. I am not religious, you know that. But if there is an afterlife or something, you are making her cry remembering her like this. So I came to bring her flowers and tell her how sorry I am that I didn't get to meet her."

Zach stared at me and I couldn't read his emotion. I snatched the cell phone from his hand and used the flashlight to retrace my steps from the night before. I found myself alone at Alice's grave. I set the flowers down and wondered what I was doing. I wasn't a spiritual person, and most of me scoffed at the idea of talking to a stone. But it couldn't hurt.

"Hi," I said lamely. "I'm taking care of Zach now, when he lets me. I hope it's OK with you. He's told me about you. I'll be honest, I'm not sure if we would have been friends. I'm not good and kind like you were. I'm a bit more rough around the edges. But everyone says I'm good for him. I just hope you approve. That's all." I rested my fingers on the stone. There was no sign or message from the heavens. It was just a cold night in February.

Zach's arms wrapped around my waist and he pulled me against him, resting his chin on my shoulder. I jumped a little because I hadn't heard him coming.

"Did you hear that?" I asked, embarrassed.

"Maybe." He kissed my hair. "You're right."

"What?"

"You're right. Alice would be furious with me. People have been telling me that for years but I never heard them until you." He looked at the gravestone. "I'm sorry, Alice. You deserve better from me. I'll come see you on our birthday this year. And I won't come on the seventeenth again. I promise."

He held me close against him and we stood looking at the grave for a long time. I started to shiver because as usual, I wasn't dressed warmly enough. Zach shook his head where it rested on mine.

"Let's get you back to the hotel where it's warm. Thank you for making me come here. For making me come here in the right spirit."

I twisted in his arms so I could see his eyes.

"I'm good for you, remember?"

He laughed and shifted me under his shoulder and walked beside me back to the car.

CHAPTER 37

I WAS GLAD to be off the plane and that I wouldn't have to be on one again in the near future. I was distracted enough during the flight down that I handled it beautifully. On the return trip I was no longer worried about Zach and I delved deep into my discovered fear of flying. There were bruises on his arm where I gripped it but he hadn't complained.

I noticed that my truck had been moved as we pulled into the driveway. It had also been cleaned. I could tell because a few large chunks of the frame were missing where vigorous scrubbing had been more than the rust could handle. The hood wasn't shut. It was impossible to shut if you didn't know the trick. The trick was a lot of swearing and jiggling of the lever and a good slam if all else failed.

I took a moment to fight with my failing rust bucket as Zach carried our things inside. Slamming the hood worked on the second try and the whole truck shook and I heard a clunk as something fell off. I turned my back on it and ran into the house to greet Mop.

Mop had the decency to muster up some enthusiasm for me and that made up for the misbehaving truck. James was cooking, which was not a plus. He left the stove and hugged me. I noticed that his hand was bandaged.

I rolled my eyes. "What did you do to my truck?" I asked.

"Me?" He glared out the window with real malice. "That thing bites."

"That she does. What were you doing messing with my truck anyway?"

"I just wanted to clean it. I clean things when I'm anxious. Cars usually."

"Well, thanks for the thought, but you'd be better off leaving my truck alone. She really is a nasty old bitch and she likes the way she looks."

"Well." James shifted his weight and glanced at Zach, who turned off the stove and was dumping the eggs into the trash. "There was nothing wrong with those," he said.

Zach only grunted.

James returned his attention to me. "How long has the check engine light been on?"

I tried to look innocent.

"Cause while I was cleaning I found this weird piece of paper taped to the dash. Right over the light."

I didn't want to answer him. I didn't like the look on Zach's face.

James continued. "So I started the truck and it started smoking. And I mean like bonfire smoking. That's when I cut my hand, trying to open the damn hood."

"She's been more moody lately than usual," I admitted.

"Your mother is a mechanic," Zach pointed out. "Why didn't you take it to her?"

"Because I can't afford to fix it and if I bring it to my Mom she'll insist on paying for it and I know they can't afford it so I'm just ignoring it."

"How much could it be?" Zach asked dismissively. I clenched my jaw and fought back my temper. His nonchalance with money was maddening.

"A lot. If I bring my truck to the garage they might tell me to take her out back and shoot her to put her out of her misery. I can't afford a new truck."

"I'll just get you one," Zach said.

I knew he was going to say it but I still had to fight to keep from screaming at him. James was looking at Zach like he was an idiot.

"No," I said. "I'll figure it out myself."

"Don't be stupid," Zach said. "I have the money. I'll fix it."

James was making frantic hand motions at his brother but Zach wasn't noticing. He also wasn't noticing the smoke billowing out of my ears.

"What?" he asked, finally taking in my expression.

"Fuck you, Zach."

He stared at me in complete bafflement. The house phone started ringing. We all ignored it. The ringer was the only sound. Then my cell phone rang and I pulled it out and checked it. I hit the silencer as I noted it was the credit card company that was hounding me.

"Who was that?" Zach asked.

"No one."

"You've silenced your phone three times since we got off the plane."

I was not going to tell him I was behind a few payments on my credit card. He would only offer to pay that off as well and I would have to kill him. The house phone stopped ringing for a moment only to start again. I glared at it.

"Why are you angry at me?" Zach asked.

"Because I'm not a hooker."

"What?"

"You're grandmother accused me of going after your money and you're trying to make her right."

"That's not . . ." he began.

"Don't. I don't want to hear it right now. And don't ever call me stupid again."

"I didn't mean it like that."

"Well then don't say it, jackass."

He stared at me with his hands out in a peaceful gesture that did absolutely nothing to calm me. The phone kept ringing. I couldn't take it anymore. I grabbed the phone and snarled, "What!" into it.

"I see your manners haven't improved," Roberta said demurely.

I pressed the phone against my thigh. "Fuck my life," I said quietly. James and Zach were staring at me. I ignored them and raised the phone back to my mouth. "I'm sorry, Roberta. I thought it was a telemarketer."

"I'm surprised you answered. For three people who only work part-time you seem to be awfully busy."

"That's us. Busy as bees. What can I do for you?"

"I just wanted to let you know that I will be visiting soon. I learned from last time, so don't worry, I am staying at the Sheraton. I'm bringing a friend with me as well. She's an old friend of Zach's, actually. Poor thing just went through a divorce and I figured she could use a vacation, and Zach wouldn't mind showing her around. He's always been fond of her."

I glared at the phone. She was bringing my replacement. This day had gone from bad to shit.

"I'm sure he'll be glad to see her. When will you be here?" I was amazed my voice sounded so normal.

"The twenty-fourth."

"What's her name?"

"Lacey Goodwin."

I bit my tongue to keep from making a comment. "I look forward to seeing both of you. I'll pass the word on to the boys."

"Thank you."

I hung up the phone with her smug victorious tone ringing in my ears.

"What was that about?" James asked.

"Your grandmother is coming for a visit. She's bringing Lacey Goodwin along."

Zach rubbed at his temple.

"So, I get to cook dinner for your grandmother who hates me, and the woman she's bringing along to replace me. That'll be oh so much fun," I said with sarcastic cheer.

"Bo," Zach began, but I shoved him.

"Don't say anything," I snapped. "You don't fucking get it. You don't fucking get anything." I headed for the door and he caught my arm.

"Bo, wait."

I turned to him ready to bite his head off but I saw the fear in his eyes. It allowed me to rein in my temper.

"Zach, I am storming out in a rage. It is truly in your best interest to let me do so. I'll be back when I'm calm."

He visibly relaxed as I said the words *I'll be back.*

I turned and headed out the door. It nearly made me smile when I heard James say, "You are such an idiot," as I closed the front door behind me.

CHAPTER 38

I WAS OVERREACTING, but I figured it was a woman's privilege to do so from time to time. My truck had the sense to start for me and not smoke as I drove to the beach. I stepped out of my truck and slammed the door and heard another metallic clang as something fell off the undercarriage.

I took off in a dead run down the beach. Rage poured out of my feet as they slammed into the wet sand. I ran under the cloudy gray New England winter sky with the waves far off past the sandbars. The icy cold wind pulled the tears across my face and dried them. I ran for what seemed like forever but it was probably no more than three minutes. I stumbled to a halt and started walking back. I wiped at my tears and gasped in the frigid air. I was only wearing a sweatshirt and it was freezing. I stuffed my hands in the pocket and rubbed them together to restore feeling.

I sat in the cab of my truck for a long time listening to the wind rage against the glass. I let my thoughts swim around my brain while I watched the tide come in. I didn't pay any attention to what I was thinking. If I tried to figure it out I would just get angry again. So I watched the water and breathed and listened to the wind.

I started my truck and instantly realized what part had fallen off this time as the giant hole in the muffler made itself known. My mom welded on the third patch six months ago and glared at me that I needed to replace the damn thing instead of patching it. The engine started smoking as I drove to Mason's house. I could barely see by the time I pulled into the driveway.

My dad was sitting in the cab of his work truck talking to Mason in the driveway. They must have just gotten off of work. I swore and turned off my truck. Dad eyed the smoke pluming from the hood and shook his head at me. My mom would know about my truck-neglect within the hour. I groaned.

"Hey," Mason said.

"How's my girl?" Dad asked. It must have showed that I had been crying because my brother and father went into protective mode.

"What did Zach do?" Mason demanded.

"Why do you assume it's Zach?" I snapped.

They both watched me warily for a moment.

"She's mad as a snake," Dad commented. "She's all yours, Mase."

"Thanks," Mason rolled his eyes.

"One question before I go home and sex up your Mama," Dad said, turning his eyes to me. "Do I need to get my shotgun and visit your boyfriend?"

"No. I'm going to hit him with a baseball bat for being such a dumbass."

"That's my girl."

I leaned in the window and kissed his cheek. "I'll be OK. Don't kill Zach. I want him in working order."

"Anything for you," Dad said, and drove off.

Mason put an arm around my shoulder and I smelled sawdust and sweat and thought about Zach.

"So, what did Zach do?" Mason asked as we walked inside. "And what is wrong with your truck?"

*   *   *

I hadn't answered Mason's questions until he showered and ordered us a pizza. I refused to go pick it up because my eyes were still red from crying so he begrudgingly drove to get it. I sat back on his creaking torn couch with my meat-lover's pizza and my fifth beer.

"So," Mason prompted.

"Zach offered to buy me a new truck," I said flatly.

"And this pissed you off? You're a practical girl. He's got the money."

"If he had offered to get it for me as a present, as something amazingly nice he could do for me, it would be different. But that's not how he said it."

"What did he say?"

"James tried to clean my truck while I was gone and he noticed the check engine light and the fact that it's doubling as a barbeque at the moment. I said I couldn't afford to fix it. And Zach shrugged and said, 'I'll just get you a new one.'" I paused to chew moodily on my pizza and finish my beer. "He brushed it off. It was a problem and he'd just throw some money at it and be done with it. He didn't want to get me a new truck because I need one and it's something he can do for me."

"I see where you're coming from, but I'd still take the free truck."

I laughed and went to get another beer.

"What did you say when he said he'd get you a truck?" Mason asked when I sat back down.

"I said no, that I could figure it out myself. Then he called me stupid."

"Is he still breathing?"

I leaned back on the lumpy couch. "Yes. Because at that moment his grandmother called and informed me she would be visiting. And she is bringing a recently divorced southern belle with her to dangle in front of Zach's face so he'll forget all about me."

"I know you're pissed at him right now, but you could dangle ten naked supermodels in front of Zach and he would look past them at you."

I choked on my beer. Mason patted my back.

"Don't say shit like that. It scares me," I said.

"It's just a fact. Has he asked you to marry him yet?"

I nearly threw up my pizza and beer.

"No! Thank God."

"OK." Mason held up a placating hand. "So what's wrong with him?"

I sat back and drank more beer to settle my stomach. I was done eating. Possibly forever. I glared at my belly, which was not as slender as I wished it were. I imagined that Lacey Goodwin had a perfect flat stomach. I bet she did yoga and Pilates and had a gap between her thighs.

"Earth to Bo?" My brother shook my knee.

"Sorry. Just feeling fat and ugly. It's a result of overreacting and raging then crying."

"For the love of all that's unholy don't cry on me. And you're not fat, or ugly. Now, tell me what's wrong."

I finished my beer and missed the table when I went to put it down.

"Zach's rich," I said.

"Yeah? So?"

"So he doesn't get it. He has no idea what it's like to struggle. He's never worn hand-me-down clothes or gone hungry because there wasn't enough money for food. His attitude about money scares me. Every time he dismisses it, it's dismissing how hard I've struggled just to get by. It's dismissing Mom and Dad working their asses off to give us food and a roof over our heads."

Mason nodded and chewed on pizza. "It's not something he does intentionally," he suggested. "He's not a snob."

"No. But that doesn't change anything. I'm afraid he sees me as just another broke-down truck. A project."

"I'm not following."

"I met some of his family. And I don't fit. I won't fit. He grew up cultured and rich. His friends, his family, they aren't our kind of people, Mase. They're suit and tie, golfing, fine wine drinking people. They'll smile at my face then laugh behind my back.

"I'm not cultured like that. Zach's cousin is getting married in June. Three hundred people plus at the wedding. I can't afford the kind of dress I'll need and I'll hate the damn thing. So he'll buy me a dress so I can fit in. But as soon as I open my mouth I'll stick out again so he'll coach me what to say, who to talk to, who to avoid. And I'll be stuck clinging to his arm having everyone look at me like I'm the poor street urchin that Zach found up north."

"You're being a bit dramatic," Mason said. "But not entirely. They won't be our kind of people, but that doesn't make them bad. Zach's their kind of people and we get on with him fine."

I sighed and went to stand to get another beer but lost my balance and sat back down. Mason watched me skeptically.

"Six beers and you're falling down? What have you eaten today?"

I looked at the single piece of pizza I had eaten half of. "That."

"Dumbass."

"Hey, I came here to be consoled."

Mason sighed. "So you think Zach doesn't really want you, he wants what he can turn you into?"

I blinked. "No. Yes. Maybe. I have no idea."

"You are drunk."

"I think so."

"Have you talked to Zach about any of this?" Mason asked.

"No. I just got mad and left."

"Perfectly reasonable."

"Shut up."

CHAPTER 39

I WAS VAGUELY AWARE that there were men talking close by. I opened my eyes and figured out after a full minute of dizzy speculation that I was still on Mason's couch. It was dark outside and the movie we had been watching was over. And I was horribly drunk and feeling like I was going to throw up. I huddled miserably under the blanket someone had tossed over me.

"You sure she won't bite me or something?"

I smiled a little at the sound of Zach's voice.

"No guarantees, but she was pretty calm when she fell asleep," Mason said.

I glanced up through my haze of alcohol and saw Zach's face over me.

"You awake, babe?" he asked.

"Nope," I said.

"You still mad at me?"

"Yep."

"OK. Are you gonna be madder if I pick you up and bring you home?"

"Nope."

Mason's couch was lumpy and had teeth in the form of old springs. I did not want to sleep on it. And if I stayed at Mason's I would have to cook him breakfast. So I wrapped my arms around Zach's neck when he bent to pick me up.

"Bye, Mase," I muttered into Zach's chest.

He settled me in his truck and I slumped against the window and hoped I wasn't drooling. I gave my truck the finger as we left the driveway.

I didn't protest when Zach picked me up and carried me into the house, upstairs, and deposited me on my bed. I lay on my back as he took off my shoes and pulled my jeans down my legs. I got tangled in my shirt and bra but he didn't comment. He pulled off his shirt and slipped it over my head. I cuddled into the warmth and smell of him, remembering that I was mad at him but not really caring.

"You gonna throw up?" he asked.

"Don't think so."

He pulled the blanket back and settled me under it. He stopped in the doorway.

"Bo?"

"Mmm?"

"I know you're mad at me, but." He paused. I forced my eyes open to look at him. He stood in his jeans in the doorway, his hands stuffed into the pockets like an embarrassed kid.

"What?" I asked.

"I want to make it better," he said. "Can I sleep with you tonight? Just to hold you? Please?"

His tone nearly made me cry. The poor man was terrified I was going to up and leave him as soon as I was sober enough to stand on my own. I reached for him.

"Get in here. I'm cold."

* * *

Zach's arms were around me when I woke up. I had a mercifully slight hangover that nipped at me without drawing blood. I shifted and realized that Zach was awake. I looked up at his chin.

"Hi," I said.

He stayed perfectly still, as if afraid I was going to snap at any moment and start snarling at him. If he didn't look so good shirtless I may have succumbed to the bitchy tendency, but it was hard to be mad at a man who looked that sexy.

"I'm not going to bite, I promise," I said.

"You're not mad anymore?" he asked hopefully.

I sat up, sad when he didn't try and stop me. He propped his broad back against the headboard and watched me. The sheet settled on his hips just below the band of his boxers. He looked amazing. He needed to put some clothes on so I could work up a proper mad.

"I'm still mad," I said.

"Damn."

I sighed. I wasn't mad at him. I was disappointed. I was scared. I was pathetic. I sat cross-legged beside him, resting my arms on my legs and my chin on my arms. He watched me warily and stayed quiet.

"Do you know why I'm upset?" I asked.

"No. I'm really sorry, Bo. I wish I knew what I'd done. It's about the truck, right?"

"Kind of. It's about a lot of things."

"Like the thousand things you should tell me every time you get that look in your eyes and tell me *nothing* when I ask what's wrong?"

"Yeah. Those things."

"So tell me, babe. I can't do anything to make it better if I don't know what's wrong."

I didn't know where to start. I latched onto the truck. My issue with it would be a way to lead into the bigger stuff.

"I need a new truck," I said. "This is common knowledge."

"I offered to get you a new one. Should I not have? I know you like being independent."

"It's not about my independence. You couldn't leash me if you tried, which you don't."

I watched his tentative smile and continued. "It's the way you said it. Do you have any idea how much it would mean to me if I came home one day and there was this shiny new truck there? A present from you because I need it and it's something wonderful you can do for me? But that's not what you said. You just shrugged and said you'd replace it. It wasn't about me, it was just about being practical because it was an old piece of shit and you have the money to replace it."

He looked at me for a few breaths without speaking.

"It is just a truck," he said. "I didn't think anything of it."

"There!" I reached out and tapped his bare chest. "That is what pisses me off."

"What?"

"The way you think about money. The way you just dismiss it."

"It's not important."

I snorted. "To you. Because you grew up with it. Because you've always had it. Do you have any idea how it makes me feel when you dismiss money like you do? I have struggled so much just to buy that truck and keep it running. You've never gone hungry because there wasn't any food in the house. I wore a pair of shoes for three years. By the end they were duct-taped together and I hid them from my parents because I knew there was no money to replace them and they would try anyway. To you it's just a truck. Just a couple disposable thousand dollars. But to me, it's my life. It's my way to get to work. It's monumental. And the way you dismiss it is insulting."

He rested his hand on my knee.

"I'm sorry, Bo. I don't mean it like that."

"I know you don't but it still hurts. We come from very different backgrounds, Zach. You grew up with everything. I grew up with the bare essentials and sometimes not even that. You've never had to struggle for money in your life. You don't know what it's like to be hunted by credit card companies. Or have your cell phone turned off and not have the money to pay the bill."

"Am I supposed to apologize for that? For the money?" There was an edge to his voice.

"No. You're lucky to have all that you do. And you've worked really hard for it. I just wish you realized it. Appreciated it. Try to see things from my perspective. Don't see it as just a truck, because that's not what it is to me. It's freedom. It's being able to drive to the hospital when Danny was born. It's my ride to work. I used to ride my bike to Orleans to work. My legs were in much better shape because of it but damn, did it make me appreciate my truck when I finally scraped up enough money to buy her."

Zach sat back and considered what I was saying.

"I'm not sure what I can do differently. I could give away all my money but I don't think that's the point you're trying to make."

"No. I'd kick your ass if you did that. But realize that what you dismiss as trivial are the kind of things that keep the average person awake at night worrying. Appreciate what you have, I guess. And don't ever dismiss my struggles like that. If you want to buy me something because you love me I'm all for it. But don't just see something broken and fix it because you can. That is insulting."

"OK. I'll try not to take things for granted."

I could see he wasn't getting it.

"Here's a hypothetical," I said. "Say Rosey was in a car accident. What would you do?"

He frowned and shook his head. "I don't like this hypothetical."

"Again, you miss the point. Anyway, if something happened back home you would be on the first flight to Georgia. You'd rent a car and be at the hospital that same day."

"Of course."

I nodded and shifted my legs around more comfortably. "My cousin went on a cross-country motorcycle trip two years ago. He was hit by a car in Texas. And none of us had enough money to go to him. My uncle sold most of his furniture so he could afford the plane ticket and the hotel in Texas for the four weeks Ben was in the hospital."

"I'm sorry."

"Thanks. But my point is that you have no idea what it's like to know someone you love is hurt and be unable to help them because of money. I never would have been able to follow you to Georgia. I don't have the money for a ticket. Or a rental car. Just try and see that. Think of how hard most people struggle before you take your life for granted."

He was quiet for a long time.

"There's more," he said. "What else is bothering you?"

I took a minute to look at him; his broad shoulders, confident hands, generous mouth, deep green eyes. I ran my fingers gently through the dark hair on his chest, loving the feeling against my skin.

"Spit it out, Bo," he said, catching my hand.

"I'm afraid that you see me as a project."

"What?"

"I'm afraid you're trying to rescue me. Save me." He started to talk but I put a hand to his mouth to silence him. "No. Let me say this. I don't think it's something you're consciously doing. But let's face it, Zach. You like to save things. You like to take something that's broken or not very good and fix it. It's an honorable thing. But I'm afraid you see me that way. As something you need to fix. Please don't say anything. Just think about it. Really think about it."

I slowly lowered my hand from his mouth. He didn't say anything for a while. I looked down at my hands, wishing that he would touch me.

"I don't fit in your life, Zach." The words escaped me without thought or permission.

"What?"

"I'll embarrass you."

"What? When? How?" He was starting to look angry.

"At your cousin's wedding."

"You won't embarrass me."

"I own two dresses. One I got for my great uncle's funeral. The other is a simple cotton sundress I wore at Axel's wedding. If I wore it to this fancy wedding, you'd be embarrassed, trust me."

He didn't deny it, which made me feel better.

"My cousin is a snob," Zach admitted. "But I can get you a dress," he trailed off. "And that's just as bad as replacing your truck."

I was so happy I leaned forward and kissed him.

"You got it!" I smiled. "I don't want to have to change anything to be good enough for you. I need you to be sure that you love me for me, and not for some potential me you think you can make. Because I won't change, Zach. Not that much. I will not be with someone who is embarrassed by me. I know you aren't consciously, but I need you to really think about this. Would you really be comfortable bringing me, in my cheap cotton sundress, to your family's prissy high-class wedding?"

He closed his eyes. "I am not embarrassed by you."

"Here. In my home. With my kind of people. But back in Georgia, with your people, you might be. Just think about it. That's all."

He reached out and framed my face with his hands. "I love you, Bo. I hope you know that. I love *you*. The woman sitting in front of me."

I smiled and he visibly relaxed.

"To quote Han Solo," I said. "I know."

I saw a flash of hurt in his eyes.

"Are you ever going to say it?" he asked, so quietly he must not have meant for me to hear.

I pulled his hands away from my face and grasped them in mine.

"Take some time and really think about what I've said. And I'll take the same time and work through my insane fears so I can tell you what you need to hear."

CHAPTER 40

ZACH SPENT THE DAY out in his truck somewhere. My truck had been impounded by my mom, who was furious I kept driving it when it was obviously unsafe. I borrowed James's car and took Mop for a slow hill-less walk and berated myself for not thinking about how I felt. I knew that Zach was out there seriously mulling over all I said. I was such a hypocrite and a bitch.

I went grocery shopping and bought salmon to make a special guilt-ridden dinner. I could distract Zach with good food and sex in hopes he would forget what I promised to think about. Had I promised? I hadn't actually said the words, but I knew that was just a copout. I meant it as a promise and I was going to break it. I baked cookies and fought with phyllo dough to make the salmon cream cheese and spinach concoction as penance.

I managed to distract Zach with the food and James's company that night. When he opened his mouth to talk seriously to me in bed I stuck my tongue in it to distract him. His stubbornness was disconcerting because he continued to try and talk until I had put my mouth somewhere more inventive.

I barely slept because I felt so awful for avoiding my feelings. I crept from the bed before dawn and left in James's car. I was lucky enough to have a lunch shift at work so I only had to wander around aimlessly for a couple hours. The other waitress asked me to cover for her that night and I dove on the chance and stayed at work all day. I lingered to have drinks with the bartender and milked the evening until I was sure Zach would have gone to bed.

There were no lights on when I pulled into the driveway. I let out a sigh as I shut the door and Mop didn't come charging at me. He must have been asleep with James. Now I had to decide if I was going to crawl into bed with Zach or go to my own bed. If I didn't go to Zach and he woke alone, he would likely be scared something had happened to me. I normally called when I was staying at work late. So I had to go into his room and hope he didn't wake up when I got into bed.

The stairs creaked and I swore under my breath. I braced myself and opened the door to Zach's bedroom. The light was off but the TV illuminated the room and Zach sitting up in bed, his back braced against the headboard. He glanced over at me and didn't look happy.

"Done hiding?" he asked.

"I wasn't hiding. Sue asked me to cover for her and I had a drink with Ken."

"You didn't call."

"I was busy."

"You always call."

"Were you worried?"

"No. I knew you were avoiding me."

I was so not in the mood. "How's this for avoiding you?" I snapped, and left the room. I stomped into mine and shut the door. I stood there feeling like an idiot as I strained my ears to hear any movement. He didn't come after me. The fact that I had been hoping he would irritated me. I did not play games like that. I changed into pajamas and went to bed. I didn't sleep for the second night in a row. The bed felt huge and cold and wrong without Zach in it.

I stayed in bed long after I heard James and Zach get up. I hoped Zach would go out so I could have the house to myself. Eventually I gave up. I was too worn out from not sleeping to bother changing out of my rattiest sweat pants and tank top.

Zach was sitting at the kitchen table looking over some paperwork. He glanced up at me.

"Ready to talk now?" he asked. His tone hadn't changed from the previous night.

"No. I'm going . . ." I began.

He stood up so fast I jumped back. "Don't run from me again, Bo. Sit down." It was an order spoken so harshly I shivered. He pointed to the other chair.

"Don't talk to me like that," I said.

"Act like a child and I'll treat you like one."

"Fuck you."

He crossed his arms and looked at me calmly. I was damned if I would sit down on command.

"What do you want, Zach?" I demanded.

"I want to talk to you," he said. "I've spent the past few days thinking about what you said. And I figured you'd want to hear what I've come up with. But my opinion has changed since you started hiding from me."

"I was not hiding!"

"Bullshit."

I stared at him. He never swore around me. He might appear calm but he obviously wasn't.

"Sit in the chair," he said, drawing out the words.

He looked so angry that I slid into the chair before my knees collapsed.

"You said you thought I was trying to fix you. And I really did think about it, Bo. I did. I like saving things. I like improving things. But you are not a project to me. I won't get bored and move on once I buy you nice things. I could buy you beautiful flashy dresses, jewelry, trucks, anything, and it wouldn't change you. You would be the same. And that's what I love about you. I grew up with a lot of shallow people obsessed with things and appearances. You aren't like that. You throw all your cards on the table. And it's an unbeatable hand, babe."

I stared at him. His tone was far too cold to be saying the words I heard.

He continued, "I've wanted to tell you that since I got home from my drive the day before yesterday. But you avoided me."

"I did not avoid you. I made salmon and . . ."

"You shoved food and yourself in my mouth to keep me from talking. And I couldn't figure out why. Or I didn't want to. Now I get it."

The rage was gone from him, replaced by a daunting sadness that made me catch my breath.

"Zach, you don't understand," I began.

"I do. I finally understand what it was like for Alice all of those years."

I was stunned. "What?"

"Now I know how it feels to love someone who doesn't love you back."

I didn't try to blink back my tears. I wanted to drown myself in the kitchen sink.

"Zach," I began, but I had no idea what else to say. He didn't fill the silence for me. I took a deep breath. "I don't want to hurt you. I never meant to. Honestly. I just don't know."

He looked down at me and the cold had returned.

"You don't know?" he growled. "I handed my heart to you on a fucking platter. I told you I'd give you time. All the time you needed. But dammit, Bo, I can't live like this. I have no idea if I am going to wake up one day and you'll just be gone."

"What?"

"I have no idea how you feel about me!" he yelled, making me jump. "You've never said anything. Nothing. Do you have any idea how hard it was for me to trust you? To risk my heart again? But I did it. I just made the mistake of falling in love with a coward."

I choked on my self-loathing.

"I don't know how," I managed to croak out around the misery.

"Don't know how to what?" he demanded.

My words failed me and I just cried. He watched me for a long minute.

"What the hell are you so scared of?" he demanded.

"I'm not scared," I sniffed, wiping at my tears.

He glared at me. I tried to dig up anger to replace the pain and devastation.

"I knew this wouldn't work," I snapped, embracing the only defense I could find. "I do embarrass you. I'm just the sexy waitress, the failure college drop-out who has nothing to offer but a good meal and a good fuck."

His hands slapped down onto the arms of my chair loud enough that Mop came bounding in from the living room. Zach loomed over me, shaking.

"I," he said, pausing to take a long steadying breath. "Have never, ever, said anything like that. You." He grabbed my chin in one hand. I was surprised that his touch was still gentle despite his anger. "You are the one that thinks you're not good enough. The only one who is embarrassed of you in this room is you."

The air left my lungs in a horrible sob. Mop howled and ran from the room. I had to get out. I had to get away from Zach. His fingers were so gentle on my face. I was a waste-of-space loser and he still touched me like I was precious. I shoved him away from me, kicking at him in my panic to be free of his gentleness. He stepped back, hands held out.

"Bo, calm down," he said.

There was a horrible buzzing in my head. It drowned out the rest of his words. I had to get away from him. I ran. He tried to catch me but I slipped under his arm and slammed the front door behind me. I must have hit him with it because it slowed him down enough so I had time to get to the cars. I didn't have a car. James had driven his to work.

I jumped into Zach's truck and grabbed the keys off of the passenger seat. I was stealing his truck. What the hell was I doing? But I had to get away. I had to be gone and I was not going to go running down the road barefoot in holey sweatpants and a tank top in February.

I was crying so hard that Zach appeared only as a blur on the steps as I left.

CHAPTER 41

I WAS CRYING so hard it was difficult to see the road. I knew I was completely out of control and that I needed to get out of the truck. I wanted my mom. But my mom was working. If I went to the house to wait for her my Dad would likely come home first and upon seeing me in tears he would go right to Zach and hit him with a shovel. So my parents weren't an option. If I tried to go to Mason he would run from my tears and go after Zach in much the same fashion as my father. Gage was in Boston at school. Axel was working and going to him created the same problem as going to Mason. And I didn't want any of them. I didn't want a man. I wanted a woman so I could sob and be consoled. And I realized that for the first time in my life I had one aside from my mother.

I pulled into the driveway and let out a shuddering sigh of relief that I hadn't crashed Zach's truck in my hysterics. I wiped at my eyes as I walked up the stone walkway to Axel and Maxine's front door. It opened before I could knock.

"Come on in, honey." Maxine opened her arms to me and I fell into them. The gesture was so warm and perfect that I started crying harder. I was sobbing by that point and I hoped that Danny was asleep in some distant part of the house so I wouldn't scare him.

Maxine guided me to the couch and sat with her arms around me.

"Are you hurt?" she asked.

I shook my head, knowing she meant physically.

"OK. I just needed to be sure I didn't have to call Axel and have him go kill some worthless southern jackass."

Her tone was protective and it made me cry harder. Zach hadn't hurt me. I hurt him and he simply made me see it. He made me see myself and I didn't like what was there.

"Just cry for a while," she suggested, stroking my tangled hair.

I did what she said. I settled into her arms and sobbed my throat raw. I had no idea how much time passed. Eventually I became aware of the hum of the baby monitor sitting on the table and was thankful Danny was indeed asleep upstairs. When I had no more tears to shed and my trembling had subsided, I sat back on the couch.

"OK." Maxine took my hand. "Now tell me what happened."

The phone rang before I could speak. It made me jump. Maxine smiled reassuringly at me and checked the number. She glared at the phone but answered.

"Yes, she's here. She didn't crash the truck." She paused and listened to him a moment. "OK." She hung up.

I blinked miserably at her. "He asked about the damn truck?" I asked.

"No." She settled on the couch next to me. "I mentioned it to test him. I believe his words were, 'She can take a hammer to the damn thing as long as she's OK.'"

I sighed.

"I have never heard a man quite that scared before. What the hell happened?" she asked.

I told her and she provided me with Kleenex, soda, and cookies. She never let go of my hand and I swore I would never take having a sister-in-law for granted again.

"I wanted to be mad at him," I admitted. "I want to be mad at him now. But I can't. He didn't do anything wrong."

"That's debatable," Maxine said, chewing thoughtfully on a cookie. There was a loud cry through the baby monitor and she went to get Danny. Seeing my beautiful little nephew cuddled in her arms made it really hard to stay depressed. She handed him to me and he gurgled and started crying again.

"He's hungry," she said, taking him back. "You mind if I feed him? I can go in another room if you want."

"No, it's fine," I said, although I wasn't sure. She settled on the couch and opened her shirt. I watched the baby nursing and was strangely comforted and calmed by it.

"How did you know?" I asked.

"Know what?"

"That you loved Axel?"

Maxine stroked Danny's little brown-haired head. "It wasn't love at first sight or anything. I was staying at my parent's beach house for the summer and he crashed a party my sister had thrown. I found him passed out in my bed."

I laughed, having heard the story but still finding it funny.

She continued. "I knew pretty quickly that he was a special guy."

"But when did you know you loved him? How did you know for sure?"

She smiled at me. "I just knew. I felt it. I looked at him one day and couldn't stop smiling."

I sighed. "That's it?" I was disappointed. I wanted her to give me something, a concrete description so I would know how I felt.

She laughed at me. "I can't describe it, Bo. Love is one of those things that existed before words. You have to feel it, not smother it with words describing it."

I ate a cookie.

"OK, I'll try anyway," she said, adjusting Danny. "I imagined my life without Axel in it and the idea scared me. I needed him. I wanted him. Every time I woke up alone it felt so wrong. And it wasn't because I was alone; it was because he wasn't with me. I found myself thinking about him all the time, being unable to think of the future without him in it."

That I could understand. I took a moment to imagine driving back to the house and finding Zach gone, back to Georgia. The idea made me feel cold fear. I needed him. I wanted him in my life. The idea still scared the shit out of me.

"How did you take it?" I asked.

"Take what?"

"Knowing you were in love with him?"

"I don't understand."

"Weren't you scared?"

"A little." She shrugged and it unsettled Danny, who cried a minute. She switched breasts and I felt a little uncomfortable but Danny settled back against her and I relaxed again. "But I told him I loved him and he said it back and I knew it was true, so it stopped being scary. What about loving Zach scares you?"

"I have no idea." I ate another cookie.

"You come from a loving family, Bo. So what's so scary about Zach?"

"It's not Zach. It's me." I hated admitting it but I had to. "I know he loves me. He's told me often enough and shown me too. But I don't understand why. Why me? There are so many better people out there. Women that wouldn't need to change to keep from embarrassing him." I sat back. "Who am I kidding? I don't embarrass him. I embarrass myself."

"That's something you need to work on," Maxine said. "You have no reason to be embarrassed."

"I'm going to say something, and please be honest with your opinion."

"Sure."

"I think that what scares me about love has nothing to do with Zach at all. I have problems with him but I am calm enough now to know that we can work through them. He's not better than me or perfect or any of that crap. He's a good man. A solid man who's all about commitment and providing."

"What's wrong with that?"

"I think I grew up seeing my parents, and all they sacrificed to be together, to be parents. And I just linked falling in love with losing possibilities. Not only am I afraid of love, but I was so afraid of the possibility of not being able to achieve my goals that I never made any. And Zach is handing me possibility on a gold fucking, er, sorry Danny, platter. And it scares me. Because I'm an idiot."

Maxine watched me a moment and smiled. "You're not an idiot. I think you need to grow up."

That was it. I needed to stop acting like a kid and pretending that I could stay in my safe little unchallenged bubble forever. Zach made me want things that responsible adults had. All I had to do was get over myself and step into my new life as an adult.

I hugged Maxine carefully around Danny.

"Thanks. I can't tell you how much it helped to talk to you." She smiled at me and I found the courage to say what I had never said to anyone outside my family. "I love you."

She kissed my cheek. "I love you too, Bo. Now, are you ready to go home and tell Zach how you feel?"

I bit my lip. "Maybe after I have a few more cookies."

CHAPTER 42

DESPITE BEING ANXIOUS about the reception I would get from Zach, I was happy as I pulled up to the house. At least until I noticed the rental car. I parked the truck beside it and stared as my rage returned. Evilgranny and the Southern Belle were there. Did the beast of a woman have a divining rod that told her the exact worst moment to arrive?

I looked down at my dirty torn sweatpants and tank top. I was barefoot and my hair was unbrushed and tied back with a rubber band. My eyes were still red from crying. In short, I looked like hell. There was no chance I could sneak inside and avoid explaining my appearance. And what explanation could I give? Not the truth. The last thing I was going to tell Roberta was that Zach and I had fought.

After pulling a quick story out of my ass I headed up to the house. I opened the front door to see Zach standing in the living room with Roberta and an attractive thin blonde. I couldn't stop myself from looking at the woman. She was wearing a simple pale blue pleated dress and matching pumps. She made me think of Dorothy from *The Wizard of Oz* despite the blonde hair. All she needed was a wicker basket and a cute little dog. She oozed charm grace and femininity. I wasn't even wearing a bra.

The three of them turned to me. Zach looked relieved. Roberta looked smugly triumphant. The blonde looked stunned.

"Bo," Zach said. His tone said all of the things I was feeling. I forced a smile onto my face.

"Hi." What else was there to say?

"How is Maxine? I told Roberta and Lacey you left to see her before I woke up this morning," Zach said.

I could have kissed him for setting up my bullshit story so perfectly. "She's doing a little better. I'm sorry for my appearance," I said, offering a hand to the blonde. "My sister-in-law's friend died of cancer this morning. She called me, upset, and asked me to come help her with my nephew. I just ran right out the door. I'm Bodel Tavish."

"Lacey Goodwin." The perfect blonde rested her delicate hand in mine for a brief moment. "I'm so sorry to hear about your sister's friend."

"Thank you. It's nice to see you again, Roberta," I said, offering my hand. She shook it reluctantly. "I didn't think you were coming for another day or so."

"I guess it's easy to lose track of the days when you work so little," Roberta said with a bitter smile. I was fairly certain she told me the wrong date during our phone conversation but I kept that revelation to myself.

"Just give me a few minutes to clean myself up. I'll be right back."

I escaped upstairs as fast as was dignified. I was so angry I was shaking, the euphoria of realizing I was in love with Zach gone. I stalked into my bedroom and searched for the nicest cleanest clothes I had. I heard Zach on the stairs and ran into the bathroom in hopes of avoiding him. He saw me dash inside and followed me. He shut the door behind him, crowding me in the small room.

"Bo, I'm so sorry," he began.

I placed my fingers over his mouth to silence him.

"Don't apologize. We have a lot to talk about. I have a lot of things to say to you. But not right now. I can't tell you the things I need to while I'm this pissed off. It would ruin it." His eyes were still full of concern so I replaced my fingers with my lips and gave him a gentle kiss.

"We're OK, Zach. Or we're going to be. But first I have to clean myself up and go make nice with your evil grandmother and the skinny gap-thighed blonde down there."

"We're OK?" He sounded so relieved it nearly broke through my anger.

"We will be. Now get back down there and occupy our visitors while I shower."

He pulled me into his arms, hugging me so tightly that he forced the air from my lungs. I was preparing for the coming battle but I allowed myself a moment of pure contentment in his embrace. I struggled free.

"Now go and entertain my replacement," I said, slapping his butt.
He frowned. "She's not your replacement," he said.

"I don't think she knows that."

"We'll set her straight. Lacey is a friend of mine, Bo. But she's not a good friend."

"So I don't have to be nice to her?"

He smiled and kissed my nose. "Be yourself, babe. And as soon as we get rid of them, we'll talk."

I jumped into the shower and prepared for battle. I spent a few precious minutes blow drying my hair and putting on mascara and lip gloss. I pulled on my favorite pair of jeans and an elegant top that made me look thinner than I was. I checked the result in the steamy bathroom mirror. I wasn't the picture of feminine gentility that was downstairs. I didn't have the face or the attitude for it. But I did look sexy and confident, which I thought was better.

I headed back downstairs to find Zach, Lacey, and Roberta seated at the table over coffee and tea. I smiled at the shocked look on Lacey's face. She was sitting beside Zach, leaning close and brushing her arm against his. He didn't look happy about it.

"So, how was your flight?" I asked, grabbing a mug out of the cabinet and making myself some tea. Mop barked from outside and I paused a moment. How had he gotten out there?

"I put that dreadful dog outside," Roberta said. "He frightened poor Lacey."

Lacey looked embarrassed. "He startled me is all. You didn't have to put him outside."

I opened the back door to let him in. It took every ounce of my self-control not to pour my tea over Roberta's head for kicking *my* dog out of *my* house. Mop came in with a woeful woof and shoved his nose in my crotch. I scratched his shaggy head and muttered apologies to him.

I turned my attention to Lacey. "He's harmless. Trust me."

Lacey didn't look interested in Mop in the slightest. Mop had the good sense to leave the room with the evil in it and settled in the living room. I sat down in the chair across from Zach. He slid his foot across the floor to brush against mine and it made me smile.

"The flight was horrid," Roberta complained. "I swear the accommodations in first class are not what they should be. I heard from my daughter-in-law that you recently flew down to Georgia."

Zach looked uncomfortable and I had a bad feeling about the turn in conversation.

"I did. It was my first time flying. I found out I don't like it very much," I said, drinking my tea without tasting it.

"However did you afford the ticket on a waitress salary?" Roberta said with so much false concern I had to stare at her a moment.

"I paid for it," Zach said. "I wanted to show her my home."

"Generous of you."

"I was raised to be a gentleman," he said, a bit coldly. I rubbed my foot against his under the table.

"So, Lacey," I said, hoping that she would be less hostile. "What inspired this vacation?"

"Well, things have been hard for me recently," she said in her light, angelic voice. "My divorce was finalized a month ago." There were tears in her eyes but I didn't sense the depth of emotion in her to rationalize them. My suspicion that she was acting was cemented when she started sniffling and grasped Zach's arm pathetically. "I'm sorry. Could you get me a tissue? I keep falling apart."

I drank tea to keep from making a vomiting sound while Zach got up to get her some Kleenex. As soon as he sat back down he returned his foot to rest against mine.

"I'm sorry to hear that," I said, trying to mean it. "How long were you married?"

She looked to be a little older than me, closer to Zach's age.

"Eight years. Most of them were good, but I found out that Peter was having an affair."

"Disgraceful scandal," Roberta said, but she took Lacey's hand in a gentle gesture. "Poor dear."

Lacey did some impressive woebegone sniffing and leaned heavily against Zach's arm.

I didn't like Lacey, but I didn't think anyone deserved to be cheated on. I repressed my impulse to call Peter a jackass and considered something more tactful. I didn't need to give Roberta extra ammunition.

"I'm sorry. That's terrible," I said. Zach's foot tapped mine twice and I had the impression I was being petted.

Lacey wiped at her face with the Kleenex and finally straightened. I relaxed as she stopped draping herself on my man.

"So you decided to come up here on a vacation?" I suggested. "Change of scenery?"

"Yes. I've never been up north before. And Roberta mentioned that she was coming to visit James and Zach so I begged to tag along. I haven't been able to travel as much as I used to. I have to care for my son."

That information made my heart jump. She had a son? Just great. She was a beautiful recently divorced single mother. Dangling her in front of Zach the Savior was disgraceful behavior on Roberta's part.

"You have a son?" I asked.

"Yes." Lacey smiled and her hand settled possessively on Zach's arm again. "Benjamin—he's seven."

"How is he taking the divorce?" I asked.

She blinked at me, caught completely off guard. "He's in boarding school, so it's not affecting him directly."

I tried to absorb that. She said that she couldn't travel because she had to care for her son, but he was in boarding school? I found the grace inside myself not to bring that insight to light.

"We'll be happy to show you around while you're here," Zach said, neatly changing the subject. "There's not much to see this time of year, but there are a few spots worth a drive."

"Wonderful. I really need a distraction," Lacey said, looking at Zach with such obvious adoration I nearly gagged. He stepped on my foot under the table.

"I'm sure you do," I said, trying to sound polite instead of snarly. I indulged myself in the fantasy of diving across the table and tackling the skinny pretty blonde. Zach's foot pressed harder on mine and I stopped imagining smacking Lacey's head against the floor.

"You have plenty of time to show us around," Roberta cut in, looking at me. "But we wouldn't want you to take any time off. I'm sure you can't afford to miss any work. Zach can escort us around." She smiled evilly at me.

I counted silently backward from ten.

"Well, I'm sure you're hungry," I said. "Zach, why don't you go into the living room where it's more comfortable while I make us some dinner."

"You cook?" Lacey said. "I've never had the time to learn. I don't know what I would do without Marie; she's my cook." She looked at me and I knew she was seeing me as Zach's hired help. It made me feel justified in hating her.

"I'll just get dinner started," I said, standing. "It's so nice to have company." The lie tasted bitter and I dumped my tea in the sink. Zach surprised me by walking up behind me and kissing the back of my neck. Roberta turned red but kept her comment to herself. Lacey looked at me with thinly veiled distaste.

"Can't wait for dinner, babe," Zach said, nipping my ear. "She puts your cook to shame, Lacey."

I smiled at the praise and had to suppress a whoop of victory as Zach patted my ass affectionately before heading into the living room. Roberta gave me a death-glare before following him. I smiled sweetly at Lacey. She turned her nose up at me and walked out like an affronted ballerina. Mop dashed out of the living room to join me in the kitchen, and it was all I could do not to laugh out loud as I fed him scraps of food as I prepared dinner.

CHAPTER 43

DINNER WAS EXCRUCIATING. James arrived home from work and upon seeing his grandmother assumed his monosyllabic terrified mouse routine. Roberta spent the meal criticizing everyone and everything, but me in particular. I won a few rounds but Lacey was on Roberta's side and I had a feeling I lost the battle.

James walked them out to the rental car and I closed the door behind him and braced my back against it. Zach let out a heartfelt sigh.

"Thank fucking Christ that's over," I said, sagging against the door.

"You were amazing," he said, closing the distance between us but stopping a foot away. "You *are* amazing."

I lost myself in his eyes until James opened the door and knocked me forward with it. Zach caught me while James shut the door and locked it.

"Don't ever leave me alone with those two ever again." He shuddered.

Zach was rubbing the spot on my head where the door had clocked it. James noticed and smiled apologetically at me.

"Sorry, Bo."

"It's OK. I'd do more than hit someone with a door to escape from that."

"I need a drink after that torture. You two want to come out with me? I'm gonna go hit on that hot bartender, the little brunette."

"Leave Quinn alone," I said. "And I'm not up for going out."

"Your loss." James picked up his jacket but peeked around the door to make sure his grandmother and Lacey were gone before he left.

I turned to Zach. He looked solid, warm, and sexy in his jeans and blue T-shirt. But there was too much between us, so I slid my eyes around him and into the kitchen.

"Dishes." I sighed.

I walked past him and started loading the dishwasher with plates.

"Are we going to talk?" he asked.

"Not right now," I said, giving up on the task and abandoning the dishes in the sink. "I'm too damn tired. I haven't slept in two days. I spent a lot of today crying and I had to eat dinner with Satan and the perfect blonde. I can't handle any more emotion today."

"OK. No talking."

He pulled me against him and I settled into him with a sigh of contentment. My contentment was short-lived as he shifted and flipped me up into his arms. I was too tired to protest as he carried me upstairs. I let him take off my clothes and lay me on his bed. If he thought he was getting sex he had another thing coming. But instead of my breasts or ass his hands settled on my back and began to massage it. I groaned in appreciation as he rubbed the stress out of my body. I felt deliciously boneless as he removed his shirt and slipped it over my head. He stripped off his jeans and wrapped his big comforting body around me. I fell asleep with my face pressed into his neck.

* * *

Any doubts I had been struggling with vanished when I woke up in Zach's arms. I realized as I snuggled into him that I wanted to wake up next to him for the rest of my life. Admitting it to myself did not erase the fact that it terrified me, but I was making progress.

"Hey," he said.

"I'm still sleeping," I murmured into his chest. His chest hair tickled my nose and I had to pull my head away. He sat up and I gave up on the fantasy of feigning sleep. We had to talk and the time was now.

"I have a few things I want to say to you," he said.

I was relieved. I really didn't want to go first.

"OK," I said.

"I never meant to hurt you, Bo," he began.

"Don't you dare apologize," I interrupted. "Everything you said was true."

"But I shouldn't have said it like that. I hurt you."

"No. I hurt myself. I hurt you. I'm the one that's sorry."

He shook his head at me and closed his eyes. I didn't know what to say, so I didn't speak.

He opened his eyes and continued. "One of the things I love most about you is that you don't need me."

I stared at him in confusion.

"Everyone in my life has needed me for something," he said. "I've always had to take care of people. I don't have to do that with you. You don't need me like that."

I choked on a horrified sob. "But I do need you!"

He took my hand. "You don't understand, babe. Don't cry. What I mean is that you don't need me to take care of you, you just want me to."

I sniffed and watched his eyes. "That's a good thing?"

"You have never made me feel obligated. I have never worried that if I couldn't do something for you that you couldn't do it for yourself. Taking care of you is a pleasure because you don't take it for granted. You don't *expect* me to pay for things, to cater to your most trivial whim. With you, for the first time, I feel like I have a partner instead of a responsibility."

I tried to see myself as he did. It took a lot of effort.

"I have problems, Zach," I admitted. "I don't think very highly of myself and it's getting between us. You think I'm wonderful and I feel like I'm shit."

"You are wonderful."

"Don't do that." I sighed. "I need to do a lot of work on myself. I need to grow up."

"OK."

"But it's not going to happen overnight," I said, trying to read his expression. "I need to pick some goals and start working toward them. I figured you could help me. I don't mean pay for it." I slapped a hand on his chest and he grinned. "I mean help me emotionally while I try and convince myself that I can be more than a dumb waitress."

"You are not dumb. And I'll do anything you need. And I know you hate the idea of using my money, but it's there if you want it. If you want to go to school, or anything, it would mean the world to me if I could help make it happen."

I leaned forward and kissed him.

"Tell me you love me again," I said against his lips.

"I love you, Bo. With all I am."

I breathed in his breath and closed my eyes. "I love you too, Zach."

He pulled me against him so fast and hard it made me laugh. He kissed me; gentle warm kisses that made my body melt. I placed a finger on his lips.

"The fact that I love you still scares the hell out of me," I warned. "I may run screaming at any moment."

"I'll catch you," he said. "I'll always catch you."

CHAPTER 44

DESPITE HAVING THINGS PEACEFUL between Zach and me, Evilgranny and the skinny blonde gold-digger were still around. Lacey's intentions became increasingly clear as she hinted that she simply couldn't survive on the alimony her ex was providing. I snorted at the idea. God forbid she would have to fire one of her three maids.

I avoided spending time with Roberta and Lacey, but it made me nervous leaving Zach alone with them. It wasn't that I didn't trust Zach. I knew he had no interest in Lacey. But he was too polite to brush her off if she was overly friendly.

We hadn't talked about what I was going to do about replacing my truck, and I wasn't really comfortable taking Zach's all the time. I wasn't sure I wanted him to buy me a new one, but the idea was growing in appeal. I pulled into the driveway and saw the rental car. Would they never go back to Georgia? They had been visiting for a week.

I opened the front door and saw Zach and Lacey. Zach stood rigid and unhappily in Lacey's amorous embrace. She was trying to kiss him and he was resisting. He saw me and his eyes lit with panic. He was too much a gentleman to push her off. Luckily, I wasn't a lady.

I stalked across the living room grabbed Lacey by her hair and yanked her backward. She shrieked like a cat and flailed her arms to catch her balance. I shoved her against the wall to stop her from falling. None of what I did could have possibly hurt her. Well, maybe the hair pulling did a little. But she had no excuse to be carrying on like Scarlet O'Hara.

"Oh, shut up!" I snapped at her.

Her eyes went huge and she shut up.

"There." I stepped back from her. "That's better. Now, I've been pretty easygoing up to this point. I have welcomed you into my home, cooked food for you, and shown you around. But I'm done sharing, darling. Zach is mine. Keep your manicured southern belle hands off of him. Got it?"

She stared at me with her mouth open. It was the most unladylike thing I had seen her do and I loved being responsible for it. She looked at Zach. I glanced over too. He looked like he was seriously considering running out the back door.

"Are you going to let her treat me like this?" Lacey shrieked. I checked to see if my ears were bleeding.

Zach looked at me. He made up his mind and planted his feet, crossing his arms over his chest.

"You didn't listen when I said no," he said.

"You didn't mean it," she said, abandoning her fear and resuming her normal seductive coyness.

"I meant it, Lacey. I'm with Bo. I've made this extremely clear."

"You can't be serious, Zach. I mean, look at her." Lacey waved her hand airily in my direction. I looked down at the jeans and white button-up shirt I wore to work. I hadn't even spilled anything on the shirt. I thought I looked pretty sexy.

Lacey continued. "She's not nearly good enough for you. She's a waitress, for heaven's sake. She just wants you for your money. You're smart enough to see that."

Zach's jaw twitched. I knew that wasn't a good sign. He was one more nasty comment from losing his temper and I knew he would be angry at himself for it. So I decided to lose my temper instead.

"The only woman here that wants his money is you," I snapped. "You lost your meal-ticket and are shopping for a new one. Well fuck off, lady. This guy is mine."

"You can't talk to me like that." Lacey tried to look down at me but it didn't quite work seeing as she was five inches shorter.

"I can talk to you however I want. Or not at all. In fact, Lacey, it's time to go."

"I'm not leaving."

"It was so nice of you to stop in," I said, my voice dripping with honey. I grabbed Lacey by the hair again. I dragged her to the door and shoved her outside.

"This is assault!" Lacey yelled.

"Always good to see you, Lacey." I slammed the door in her lovely enraged face.

I turned back to Zach, expecting him to be angry. He collapsed into one of the overstuffed chairs and burst out laughing. It took me a moment to push my anger aside and join him. I settled on his lap. The sound of the rental car peeling out of the driveway was barely noticeable over our laughter.

"That was great," he said.

"You're not mad at me?"

"I thought you were gonna be mad at *me*. I was kissing her."

"No. She was trying to kiss you. You looked positively revolted."

"James will never believe you grabbed her by the hair and threw her out the door."

I looked around the living room. "Where is James? And Evilgranny?"

"James and Grandmother went out for a late lunch. They should be back soon."

I sighed. "Won't that be fun?"

"Are you gonna throw my grandmother out by the hair?"

The idea had me smiling, but I shook my head. "She'd fight back."

"My money is on you, babe."

*   *   *

I flinched instinctively when Roberta and James returned from lunch. She masked the look of vicious hatred with a fake smile when Zach walked up behind me to stand in the kitchen archway.

"I thought Lacey was here with you," she said with mock sweetness. James froze in the doorway. He took a step back so he was technically outside.

"Lacey had to go," I said with equally false sweetness.

Roberta's eyes narrowed.

"Why?"

"You'll have to ask her."

There was a long horrible minute of silence while the two of us tried to kill each other with our eyes.

"Zachary, dear, go outside with your brother. Bodel and I need a moment."

James was gone from the doorway before I could glance over. Zach watched both of us warily.

"I'm not sure," he began.

"Don't be silly." Roberta patted his arm. "I just want to say a few things to her. Girl things."

I knew it was a bad idea to be left alone with Roberta, but I didn't see a way out of it. I nodded at Zach and he left. But I doubted he went far.

Roberta turned to me with cold contempt and let the charade of polite behavior evaporate.

"You are going to ruin everything," she snapped.

"Under the circumstances, I think I should be proud of that."

She glared at me with renewed hatred. "I've tried being subtle. I figured you would take the hint. But you've got more backbone than I thought. It doesn't matter. Zachary is not going to waste any more of his life with trash like you." She made a face like she had smelled something rotten. "I will never understand what he sees in you. Disgraceful. But it doesn't matter. I'm prepared to deal with this. How much is it going to take?"

I stared at her. "What?"

"How much money will it take to make you go away?" She said it matter-of-factly and it stole my breath. I didn't have a nasty comeback for that one. Was she seriously offering me money to leave Zach? Did people really do that?

"What?" I repeated, too shocked to think.

"I'll pay you whatever you want. Ten thousand? Twenty? Whatever it takes to get you to pack up your meager belongings and that hideous dog and go."

"I'm not for sale," I snapped, finally overcoming the shock.

"Everyone has a price, dear." She sounded so reasonable it made me sick.

"I don't. I love Zach and I won't leave him. Not for money, not for anything."

"Don't be ridiculous." Roberta looked flustered. "Thirty thousand dollars is more than reasonable."

"I won't go. Not for you. The only thing that could possibly make me leave would be if Zach asked me to."

Instead of looking defeated, she looked smug. "Fine. You forced my hand. I didn't want to hurt Zachary, but you leave me no choice."

I stared at her. "I want you out of my house."

"It's not your house."

"Fine. I'll get Zach and he'll throw you out."

I tore out of the house to find Zach and James sitting on the tailgate of the truck.

"Go in there and throw that horrible bitch out of my house," I snapped.

James slid down from the tailgate and took a few steps back from me. Zach tried to touch me but I stepped away from him.

"Just get rid of her," I said, fighting tears.

"OK, babe. Don't cry. And don't break anything. I'll take her back to the hotel."

I was so angry it took me a minute to realize I was alone. James had literally slunk off down the street somewhere. I was going to have to find his backbone and surgically insert it.

When Zach didn't emerge from the house with Roberta right away, I lost my patience. I went back up to the front door but stopped before opening it. I could hear them talking. I was glad that in his anger and distraction Zach hadn't actually closed the front door. I couldn't see them but I could hear them perfectly.

"I'm not going to say this again, Grandmother," Zach was saying.

"You're giving me no choice, Zachary. I was hoping you would come to your senses and be reasonable about this."

"This has nothing to do with you!"

"That's where you're wrong. I won't let some poor trash marry into this family. I realize she's pretty and she likely does things in bed that no respectable woman would do. I've given you time to get it out of your system. It's time to be serious, Zachary. You can't honestly see a future with that woman."

"Get out of my house." Zach's tone was so cold that I actually shivered. Roberta didn't seem bothered.

"I didn't want to do this, but I will if I have to. I know you like this house, though I have no idea why. I've been speaking with a lawyer, and based on some documents I have recently come across, my lawyer believes that I have a very decent chance to have the house given to me, as Walter's widow."

I pushed the door open a crack. It squeaked, but neither of the people inside noticed. They were only just inside the door, Roberta's back to me. Zach's face was hardly recognizable.

"Forging documents is a new low for you, Grandmother."

She sniffed dismissively.

"It won't work anyway," Zach said. "Walter's will was extremely clear. The house is mine and James's."

"But I can stop you from renovating it any further while I tie you up in court."

"That's petty, even for you. And it won't get me to leave Bo."

"Fine. If you don't get rid of her, I'll tell everyone that Alice was pregnant when she killed herself."

I wanted to scream at the devastated look on Zach's face. He stumbled back a few steps, going pale. I was too stunned to move.

Roberta took a step toward him. "I'll tell everyone at Peter's wedding. That should ruin the happy event. I'll give you until June to get rid of the waitress."

Zach collapsed onto the couch. His breaths came in horrible ragged gasps. Roberta stood over him triumphantly.

"I'm just doing what's best for you, dear," she said.

Zach looked up at her with such hatred in his eyes that I started crying.

"Get out of my house," he said quietly.

She opened her mouth to speak and he jumped to his feet so fast she almost fell backward.

"Get the fuck out of my house!" he yelled so loudly that Mop started howling from the kitchen.

Roberta looked for a moment like she was going to argue, but the barely controlled violence in his shaking body seemed to finally sink in for her. She turned and started walking toward me. I had two options: I could stand there and kill her on the front steps, or I could hide and get inside to be with Zach faster. I slunk around the side of the house and watched her walk down the steps. There was no car for her to take back to the hotel. There was a moment of horror when I thought she would turn back but she pulled a cell phone from her pocket. I didn't care how she got home, just as long as she was gone. I ran back to the front door and slammed it behind me.

CHAPTER 45

ZACH WAS COLLAPSED on the couch with his head in his hands. I ran to him, grabbing his wrists and pulling his hands away. His entire body was shaking uncontrollably and tears streamed down his face.

"I'm so sorry," I said, knowing it wasn't enough. I kissed his tears and let my hands run over his shoulders, his back, anything to soothe him. He didn't respond to me. I didn't know if he was shaking from rage or pain.

"Zach? Baby? Will you look at me?" I stroked his face as he stared at nothing and cried without making a sound. He was barely breathing. I didn't know what to do.

Mop walked into the room and cocked his head at us. His large brown eyes were partially shaded by his shaggy coat, but they took in the scene the way only a good dog could. He whined pathetically and pawed at Zach's leg before settling his head on Zach's knee.

Zach looked down at the whining dog that was looking up at him with devotion and adoration. I saw the ghost of a smile on his face as he settled his hand on Mop's shaggy head and ruffled the fur.

"Zach?" I asked.

He looked at me. "Yeah, Bo. I'm OK. Sort of."

Mop knocked me backward as he climbed laboriously onto Zach's lap. The hundred and eighty nine pound dog plastered himself against Zach's chest and began panting happily as Zach struggled to breath. I couldn't help myself; I started laughing.

"Mop, honey, you're not a lap dog," I said through my laughter. I realized I was crying and wiped my tears away.

Zach had his arms around the dog and was shaking his head. "OK, OK, Buddy. I'm OK now. You can get down."

Mop groaned but managed to clamber onto the floor. He resumed resting his head on Zach's knee and begged for more attention.

I looked at Zach, who had stopped crying and shaking. The pain was still in his eyes but he looked human again. I hugged him as closely as I could. He rested his head on my shoulder and held me tightly.

Mop's nose bumped against my butt eventually and I shifted over so I could see Zach's eyes. He sighed and rubbed at Mop's ears.

"Are you OK?" I asked.

"No. I almost hit her, Bo. My own grandmother. I've never been that angry in my life. It scared me."

"You didn't. And you wouldn't."

He nodded and rubbed at his eyes. "How the hell did she find out about Alice?"

"Who knows besides you and me?"

"The doctor, I guess."

"He couldn't have told her. That kind of thing is confidential."

"Roberta goes to the same doctor that Alice did. She either paid for the information, or there is a chance he mentioned it without realizing I hadn't told anyone. It doesn't matter how she knows, just that she does."

I nodded, reaching over to scratch Mop's free ear. I didn't know what to say.

"I can't let her do this," he said, sounding desperate. "I can't let her hurt Charlotte and Carter, my parents, and Rosey. She'll ruin my cousin's wedding. She'll tell all of those people."

"Would she really do it?"

"Absolutely."

I said a nasty word that I reserved for true evil of the female variety. Zach raised an eyebrow but didn't comment. The silence stretched out. I couldn't ask Zach to stay with me if it meant legal struggles for the house and pain to the people he loved. I only met Charlotte and Carter once, but finding out about Alice's pregnancy would devastate them.

"I can't let her do this," Zach said again.

"I'll go," I began.

"Don't you dare." He grabbed my face in his hands. "I am not losing the best thing that has ever happened to me. Don't even suggest it."

I smiled and kissed him. "I was going to say I'll go to Mason's until she leaves for Georgia. You can tell her I left you."

Zach relaxed but shook his head. "She'd know the truth."

"How?"

"She'd pay people to check."

"She'd pay people to spy on us?"

"Evil, remember?" Zach said with forced humor.

I sat back with a sigh. I looked at Zach's profile while I thought. "Well," I said, after a while. "You could beat her at her own game."

"What?" Zach stopped petting Mop who moaned.

"How did you feel after you told me about the baby?" I prompted.

He took a moment to think about it. "It felt good to tell you. To tell someone after keeping it to myself for so long."

"So you can tell Charlotte and Carter."

"It will still hurt them so much."

"I know. But you've carried the weight of knowing by yourself for long enough. It's going to hurt them, but it will help them too."

"Help?" he blinked at me. "How?"

"Because they can share the weight with you. They can be there for you, like they should have been from the start. This secret has been between you for so long. They didn't know about it, but you did."

He sat back against the couch and closed his eyes. "I'm not sure I'm strong enough. I don't think I can go through it again."

I snuggled against him, resting my cheek against his chest. I listened to his heart beating and felt the warmth of him.

"You're strong enough. And if not, you've got me. I'll protect you."

His arm settled around me. "I don't have much of a choice, do I?" he said into my hair.

"Well, I'm not leaving," I said, looking up at him. "And we can't let Roberta ruin everything. So we take away her ammunition."

"She could still announce it at the wedding." He sighed.

"Most of those people don't matter, right?" I asked. "They won't really be hurt by the news? I mean it will be horrible and completely inappropriate, but only Charlotte and Carter would be really hurt?"

Zach nodded. "And my parents and Rosey."

"Your parents?"

He smiled at me. "They loved Alice like a daughter in their reserved way. This would hurt them. And Rosey, it'll crush her. But you're right. No one else would be hurt. It will just be enormously uncomfortable for everyone. I hope once she realizes that I've told the important people she won't go through with ruining the wedding. My cousin doesn't deserve that. Neither does his fiancée."

I kissed him. "So, when are we going to Georgia?"

He kissed my cheeks. "My birthday is four days before the wedding. Alice's birthday. Our birthday. I said I was going to bring her flowers on our birthday this year. We can go down early. I can give Alice and my baby some flowers, and then we can tell everyone the truth."

I held him but he didn't cry again. He breathed steadily, one hand stroking through my hair, the other petting Mop.

"We're gonna be OK," I said. "All of us."

CHAPTER 46

DESPITE THE LOOMING CLOUD of June, March, April, and May were the happiest time in my life. I was in love with a wonderful man who loved me back. Things weren't perfect, but I grew up hard and wouldn't have been happy with perfect anyway. If everything was going right, that meant something was about to break.

Zach bought me a used blue Chevy Colorado and I managed to accept it without too much psychosis. James started working full-time and dating one of the girls he worked with. It meant that Zach and I had the house to ourselves a lot. We took advantage of it.

But Zach was anxious about June. On the second night I woke to find him pacing, I suggested we start renovating the second floor. I knew some walls needed to be knocked down and I figured being destructive was a good thing for him. He dove into the project with renewed energy. James moved into the basement bedroom and we moved our things into his room. Zach knocked the wall down between my room and his to make one large master bedroom. He spent a lot of time on the phone and scratching his head beside plumbers and electricians. The result was a private bathroom off of the master bedroom.

Zach pulled me into the planning process. He showed me plans and diagrams that meant nothing to me despite his explanations. I loved seeing him work. His eyes lit up in a very charming way when he looked at a piece of paper and saw a house.

Because Zach was channeling his fear, rage, and frustration at his grandmother into renovating the house, the master bedroom was done in three weeks. The bathroom took longer and Zach abandoned that project to professionals. He decided to tackle the downstairs.

Rosey was going to come back with us after the wedding and stay a few weeks. Zach wanted to have most of the work done by then. He had the money and time to speed the project along.

The wall separating the living room and kitchen was torn down and replaced by a structural beam. It opened the downstairs up so much it felt like a brand new house. Zach agreed to wait to replace the kitchen counters, floor, and cabinets until after Rosey returned to Georgia. We didn't think it could be finished in time for her visit and I refused to host her without a kitchen. The idea of not having a kitchen, even for a few weeks, disturbed me. The kitchen was the house.

I loved the new setup. I wasn't isolated in the kitchen while I cooked. I could laugh and joke with my brothers as they cluttered up the living room furniture and watched TV. A new slender window beside the front door allowed me to see who was coming up the stairs. What I really loved about the house was that Zach had asked for my input on every detail. It felt like my house.

I was making sandwiches when I heard a knock on the door. I turned to see Maxine holding Danny. I motioned her inside, loving the little window even more. She crossed the large open room.

"Hey, Bo. I have a favor to ask," she said.

"What's up?" I asked, wiping my hands on a dishtowel so I could run my fingers through Danny's soft curls. He grabbed my finger and smiled at me. It shocked me how fast babies grew.

"Can you watch Danny for a little while? I desperately need some adult time." Maxine pulled at her hair. "I just want to go get my haircut. Sit and have a glass of wine, maybe. I just fed him and changed him, so he shouldn't be fussy."

"Of course I'll take him," I said, reaching for the baby. As each month passed I found that Danny was more fun. Now that he was four months old I could dazzle him with shiny objects and make him laugh. The laugh was a brand new thing and I would make a complete idiot of myself to hear it.

"Thank you so much, Bo." Maxine sighed and handed over a diaper bag. "I love him, but I just need a break sometimes."

"You deserve one. Go pamper yourself."

Zach walked in the front door with his arms full of paint, brushes, and rollers. We disagreed about what color to paint the walls so the

furniture had been moved in after the basecoat of white. Seeing as the
room was so open, it would be easy to shove the furniture in and paint
now that I had won the fight over the color. Zach dropped the paint and
kissed Maxine's cheek.

"Hey, Max," he said.

"I'm escaping motherhood for an hour or so," she explained.

Zach had already stolen Danny from me.

"Go on. We've got the football."

Maxine rolled her eyes. "Do not call him that."

"His Daddy does," Zach pointed out.

Maxine threw her hands in the air and left.

I watched Zach with my nephew as I finished making lunch. Zach
was so natural with the baby that it was impossible not to smile. He was
completely shameless about his adoration. I burst out laughing as he
made gooey baby sounds. Danny laughed too.

"We should get you one of those to play with all the time," I said.
The hugeness of what I just suggested made me drop the knife.

Zach was sitting at the kitchen table. He was holding Danny so his
chubby legs were standing on his knee. He looked at me.

"Ah," he said, obviously shaken. "Would you, I mean, someday?"

I looked at the hope and longing in his beautiful eyes. I looked at
the baby in his arms.

"Someday. I'd like to have a baby someday." If he asked me a few
months ago I would have screamed and sworn I would never dare
reproduce. But looking at the man I loved holding a baby didn't scare
me. The knowledge that I wanted to have a baby, Zach's baby, settled in
my chest.

"I don't mean anytime soon. I need to borrow this one for a while.
Get the hang of it," I said to fill the silence.

Zach reached his hand out to me and I took it. He pulled me
toward him and kissed my fingers.

"I love you, Bo," he said.

"I love you too. Now unhand my nephew. It's my turn to make silly
sounds."

I shamelessly used Danny to diffuse the enormity or the conversation
as Zach and I ate our lunch while making fools of ourselves to make a
baby laugh.

CHAPTER 47

THE PLANE LURCHED into motion and Zach made an effort to pry my fingers from the armrest.

"We're not even taking off yet, babe," he pointed out as we were towed backward from the boarding area. I took a deep breath and closed my eyes.

"You sure you don't want those pills?"

"I hate pills. I can handle this." I opened my eyes as the plane started forward. I would be fine as soon as we were actually flying. Taking off and landing were equal in my book to a trip to the dentist.

I needed to distract myself. I looked at Zach, who smiled and gripped my fingers.

"I think I've figured out what I want to do when I grow up," I said.

"Yeah?"

I closed my eyes again as the plane moved toward the runway.

"Bo, tell me what you thought of." His voice was soothing and I tried looking at him, but I could see the ground rolling by behind him and I shut my eyes.

"It's kinda stupid," I said.

"Let me hear it."

"Doggy Daycare."

I still had my eyes closed so I didn't see his reaction, but I knew he cocked his head to the side in confusion.

"What exactly is that?" he asked. "A kennel?"

"No, not exactly. The idea is for people to drop their dog off instead of leaving them home alone while they're at work. That way the dog spends the day playing with other dogs and getting exercise."

"I've never heard of anything like that, but then again, I've never owned a dog."

I almost objected to the statement, thinking of Mop. Whose dog was Mop anyway? I decided not to think about that too much.

"My friend Kol gave me the idea," I said, biting my lip as the plane started going faster.

"Kol?"

"I took Mop out the other day while you were on the phone with that hot Italian guy," I began.

"How do you know Marco is hot?"

I laughed a little and squeaked as the plane left the ground.

"Anyway," Zach said, kissing my temple.

"I was out walking and I ran into Kol. His dog, Blue, is old, so we walk on the same short flat trail. We got to talking about the dogs. Kol's a fisherman, and he used to be gone for weeks at a time. Now he works day boats and Blue gets to go fishing with him. But his mate's dog isn't much interested in the boat. The damn dog has ripped apart his mate's house every time he's left alone. Kol said that Quinn mentioned Doggy Daycare, but there isn't one anywhere locally. So it got me thinking."

"Quinn? The little bartender at the Stowaway?"

"The owner of the Stowaway. She and Kol have been friends forever."

"Wait, is Kol the big blond guy? The one who looks like he could give me a run for my money?"

"That's Kol."

The plane leveled out at last and I opened my eyes. I was surprised to see a jealous look in Zach's eyes.

"How good a friend is Kol?" he asked.

I laughed. "Kol has been madly in love with Quinn's cousin since he was fifteen. He doesn't even notice there are other women in the world. It's not like you to be so possessive."

Zach shifted his weight and looked down at himself harshly. "Sorry. I don't mean to be like that."

"You're not comparing yourself to Kol, are you?"

He looked away from me, confirming it. I laughed. For all his confidence, he really thought he was an unappealing caveman. And in all fairness, Kol was one of the best-looking men I had ever seen, so the comparison wasn't valid.

"Zach, you are so handsome," I said, kissing him.

He grunted.

"So, this Doggy Daycare," he said. "What do you need to get it started?"

I rolled my eyes but allowed him to change the subject. "I need a building to start with. I want it to be a house, actually. With a huge yard. That's gonna be hard to find on the lower Cape. There's not much land available here. Most lots are small."

"Why a house?"

"I want the dogs to feel at home. I want people to feel they are dropping their dogs off to play instead of dropping them off to be stuck in a cage all day. Though I'll need crates and gates and things like that. I imagine I need a license of some kind. I haven't done the research yet."

"You're serious about this?" he asked.

"Yes. There is year round need for it, but I could do a lot more in the summer."

"Why do you say that?"

"Well, tourists who bring their pets get stuck with them. If they want to go out on a charter boat or something, they have to worry about the dog ripping up their rental while they're gone. I could offer a place for them to leave their dogs for a few hours while they did touristy things."

Zach was nodding and I realized his brain was working faster than mine. His favorite thing to do was to start businesses and he was good at it.

"It's a sound plan," he said. "With the right advertising in the summer, it could definitely turn a profit."

"And I would need a staff, so I could hire local people. There are so few jobs; I'd love to be able to make some." I paused a moment, feeling the dread I had been trying to ignore.

"What's wrong?" he asked.

"Well, this all sounds great, but I have a grand total of three hundred twenty-six dollars and thirty-two cents to start it."

Zach shook his head at me and smiled. "I'll back you, babe."

I choked on my instinctive refusal.

"Wow, I thought you were going to bite my head off for offering," he said.

"I'm thinking about it."

"I'd love being a part of it," he said. "And if the money really bothers you, once it makes a profit, you can start paying me back. You could buy me out entirely and have it all to yourself. I just want to make sure you can have this dream. The money isn't doing any good sitting in banks. I'd rather invest it in a sure thing."

"You think this is a sure thing?" I blinked at him.

"*You* are a sure thing," he said, kissing my nose. "You'll work yourself into the ground to make it a success. You won't settle for anything less. And I want to help you, so you don't have to work yourself too tired for sex."

I laughed and rested my head on his shoulder. I looked out the window of the plane. Now that we were flying, I liked the view. I glanced up at Zach's face. I liked the view inside more.

CHAPTER 48

I SAT QUIETLY beside Zach as he told Charlotte and Carter about Alice and the baby. Charlotte burst into tears and Carter held her.

"Why didn't you tell us then?" Carter asked.

"I didn't see the point," Zach said. "It was bad enough as it was."

"We could have been there for you, Zach," Charlotte said, sitting up straight and wiping at the last of her tears. "You shouldn't have had to deal with this alone for so long."

"Why are you telling us now?" Carter asked.

Zach winced and I held his hand tighter. It was more painful for him to admit what Roberta was doing than to talk about the past.

"Want me to tell them?" I asked.

He nodded.

"Roberta doesn't want Zach with me. She found out about Alice and the baby somehow, so she threatened to tell everyone at the wedding if he didn't leave me."

Charlotte's head shop up from Carter's shoulder. "That bitch!"

I was just as startled and caught off guard as the two men in the room. Charlotte jumped to her feet and began to pace, her little body vibrating with fury.

"That horrible, horrible woman," she continued. "And she'd do it too. She'd ruin Peter's wedding, bring out this old nightmare and hurt everyone."

Zach stood up and caught Charlotte in mid-pace. She sagged against him.

"That's why we're here early," I continued. "To tell the people that matter. If everyone knows, then Roberta has nothing to threaten anyone with. Personally, I think he should have told you a long time ago."

"He should have," Charlotte said, looking up at Zach. "It's too much for you to carry alone. You're my son and I won't have you hurting when I can do something about it."

Zach held her and I watched the tension leave him. Carter stood and hugged them both. I closed my eyes. We told James, Rosey, and Zach's parents that morning. There had been anger and tears but mostly outrage at Roberta. Zach's father didn't look at all surprised that his mother would do something so evil and that made me sorry for him.

"Roberta said that I had until the wedding to get rid of Bo," Zach said, bringing me back to the moment.

"What does she have against Bo anyway?" Charlotte asked. She looked at me and smiled.

"I'm trash, apparently," I said.

"Oh, honey, you're not trash. You're wonderful. I couldn't imagine anyone more perfect for my boy than you."

I blinked back tears and stood to hug her. A few months ago her comment would have scared me to death, but not now. I knew where I belonged now.

"What about Roberta?" Charlotte asked when she stepped back. "She could still make a scene at the wedding."

"We're hoping that after we tell her that everyone knows, she'll just let it go," Zach said.

"She won't let it go," I muttered. "The woman hates me."

"For no reason I can see," Charlotte said, patting my shoulder. "But Roberta has always been a miserable, unhappy woman. Don't stress yourself about her. I doubt she'd go through with it if there was nothing to gain."

"She'll try and think of something else to get rid of me." I sighed.

"How much did she offer you?" Carter asked.

I flinched and looked at Zach.

He narrowed his eyes. "You didn't mention that part to me."

"It was only going to make you madder." I shrugged.

"She's that kind of woman," Carter continued. "She doesn't understand that money doesn't buy anything that's really important. No matter what she thinks up or tries, we'll be there at your side, Bo."

I hugged him. "Thank you."

"Now," Charlotte said. "We've had enough tears on this. I baked a pie and there's homemade ice cream to go with it."

As I sat down in their beautiful dining room I marveled at their ability to recover. Only minutes ago they learned about a horrible loss. Instead of wallowing or growing angry, they were serving dessert and talking about everyday things. I found myself laughing with them as the sugar melted on my tongue.

CHAPTER 49

I WOKE UP to the sound of my cell phone alarm clock. Zach groaned and turned over. The plan had been to wake up first and give Zach an early morning birthday present. He beat me to it, though, as usual. Afterward, he rolled over and went back to sleep. My cell phone alarm seemed a bit superfluous.

I had plans for the day and they centered around Zach moving and being coherent in the next half hour. I kissed his shoulder and he purred at me but didn't open his eyes.

"Zach, it's time to get up," I said.

"Already happened, sweetheart. Let me sleep."

I glared at him. I had to get him moving without actually telling him why.

"Rosey is expecting us for breakfast," I said.

"She'll wait."

But the surprise wouldn't. I shoved his shoulder.

"It's my birthday," he grumbled into the pillow. "Isn't it supposed to be my day? I want to sleep."

"It's rude to make her wait," I said.

He opened his eyes. "When have you ever cared about manners?"

"I want breakfast. I'm hungry."

"You'll live," he said, closing his eyes.

I glared at the sleeping giant for a minute. I slid closer. He grabbed me and pulled me on top of him. His arms tightened and held me still. I considered biting him before coming up with a better idea. I shifted my hands around and tickled his ribs. The plan backfired when he convulsively shoved me up and away. I went flying off the bed to land hard on my back on the floor.

He got tangled in the blanket in his hurry to get up. He picked me up off the floor and sat on the bed with me on his lap.

"I am so sorry," he said, kissing my forehead. "Are you OK?"

My butt hurt but I had succeeded in getting him up, so I figured it was a fair trade.

"I'm fine," I said.

"I've told you not to tickle me."

"I didn't realize you were that serious."

"Just ask James. It's not a good idea. I'm really sorry."

"You can make it up to me by bringing me to breakfast. Rosey is making stuffed French toast."

He sighed. "Fine. But you owe me."

"You just tossed me onto the floor!"

"You were asking for it."

I watched him as he got dressed. I would never tire of looking. He had a masculine grace that was mesmerizing at times. He looked at me and I realized I was still naked on the bed, staring at him.

"What?" he asked.

I smiled and jumped off the bed into his arms. "Nothing. Happy Birthday. Let's go eat."

"If you don't get some clothes on, we're definitely not going to leave this hotel room any time soon."

He slapped my butt and I scrambled into clothes.

*   *   *

Zach angled a look at me as we pulled into the driveway. It was almost full of cars.

"So," he said. "This is why you got knocked out of bed this morning? To get me here on time?"

"You didn't make it easy. I didn't want to just tell you they were all here. It would ruin it."

"How did you get them all here at the same time?"

"Why do you think it was me?" I asked, getting out of the car.

"Because none of them would have thought to all get together for my birthday."

I thought that was extremely sad but didn't say so.

"How did you convince my parents to take time away from the hospital?"

I shrugged and opened the front door. "I asked."

Patricia and John, Zach's parents, were seated at the table with James, Carter, and Charlotte. Rosey was in the kitchen humming and finishing breakfast. They rose and hugged Zach, wishing him a happy birthday. I wondered as I sat down how long it had been since they all had a meal together. I wondered if they ever had.

I got up and helped Rosey serve breakfast, despite her protests. There was fresh fruit, stuffed French toast, eggs, bacon, sausage, and the best coffee I ever tasted. The conversation was a little strained at first but Patricia and John warmed up when I asked them about their work. I didn't really understand some of what they said, but I smiled and nodded like I did. I liked John. He was reserved, but there was warmth behind it that showed in the way he looked at his family.

After the meal, I insisted on clearing the table and doing dishes while Rosey enjoyed coffee with the others. I was nervous about the next part. The others hadn't been sure it was a good idea, but I insisted.

"Don't you need to get to work soon?" Zach asked his parents.

"We're taking a long morning," John said.

"We're all going to go and see Alice today," Patricia said with a casualness that I envied. Zach looked around the table and I worried he would object.

"Everyone?" he said, his expression unreadable.

"Yes," Patricia said in a tone that boded no argument.

Zach looked at me. I was afraid he was angry until he smiled. "She was always trying to get us to do things together," he said.

*   *   *

It was a beautiful sunny day and the cemetery was much more welcoming than I remembered. The eight of us made our way slowly to Alice's resting place. I gripped my bouquet of flowers while I watched

Carter and Charlotte kneel down and rest their hands on the headstone. I barely held back my tears as Charlotte told her daughter what happened in the past year and how much she was missed.

Patricia's cold exterior cracked as she moved next to Charlotte and took her hand. Carter and John stood beside each other, quiet but supportive. I realized I had been stupid to ever feel bad for Zach. His birth parents may have been reserved, but they loved. And he had Carter and Charlotte and Rosey. His family was truly beautiful.

A sound beside me caught my attention and I looked to see James crying. I slipped my arm though his and he smiled through his tears at me. I rested my head on his shoulder a moment and glanced at Zach to see how he was doing.

Zach was looking at his two sets of parents and Rosey, who had joined them. He was smiling.

Patricia and John laid their flowers down but didn't speak. Patricia wiped a single tear off her cheek and turned to the group.

"I think we should all come here together from now on. Alice would have liked it," she said.

Everyone agreed and the last of the tears were wiped away and the flowers arranged.

"We have to get going to work," Patricia said.

"I'm going to stay a moment," Zach said. "I'm really glad everyone was here. I'll see you for dinner."

I hesitated while the others left. I wasn't sure if Zach wanted to be alone or not. He didn't let go of my hand so I decided he wanted me with him.

"If I get really corny and clichéd can you resist scoffing at me?" he asked.

I blinked at him. "I won't laugh at you."

He turned to the headstone. "So, Alice," he said, his voice soft. "I promised you that I would come here on our birthday, this time with flowers instead of a bottle. I feel like a total idiot talking to you like this, but if by chance you can hear me, I don't want to miss the opportunity."

He sighed, running his free hand through his hair.

"What?" I asked

"I really do feel stupid talking to her like this," he said.

I shrugged. "Hi, Alice," I said. "I don't think I told you my name last time. It's Bo. I know you loved Zach. I just want you to know that I love him too. I hope you don't hate me for that."

"She wouldn't," he said, pulling me close against him. "You said it yourself; she would want me to be happy. She knew I didn't love her, not like she loved me." He looked over me at the tombstone. "I found that love, Little Bit. I didn't think I deserved to. But Bo was right. If you could, I'm sure you'd pout at me for hiding from happiness for so long." He sighed, resting his chin in my hair. "I'll always love you, Alice. I'm happy now. I'm doing my best to stop blaming myself for the past. I know you'd want me to be happy."

We stood and looked at the garden of flowers. The wind blew quietly and made the leaves of the trees whisper at each other. I may have been a jaded Yankee, but I could have sworn I felt someone touch my cheek.

*   *   *

Zach emerged from the hotel bathroom that night dressed only in his boxers. I looked at him for a moment, trying to figure out what was different. Then I noticed the necklace was missing from around his neck. It was coiled in his hand. He sat on the bed beside me, letting the ring and cross slide around his palm.

"What are you thinking?" I asked.

He sighed and closed his hand around the symbols. "I don't need to carry this with me anymore," he said. "I'll always love Alice. I'll always remember her. But she's gone, and it wasn't my fault."

I took his free hand and looked down at his closed fist.

"What are you going to do with it?" I asked. He stood up and put the necklace into one of the pockets of his bag. "I'll always keep it," he said. "But I won't keep it between us."

He kissed me and I pulled him down to the bed beside me.

"I love you," I said.

"I love you too."

Even a broken heart kept beating, and eventually it could heal and be whole again; especially if there was someone there to hold the pieces together.

CHAPTER 50

ZACH WAS more at home in the dress shop than I was. I would never have walked in the front door given a choice. It screamed money and I didn't have any. But I needed a dress for the wedding. We decided to buy one in Georgia so I wouldn't have to worry about it on the airplane.

"I'll just grab something quick and we can go," I said.

Zach shook his head at me as a pretty redhead in her forties came running at us.

"Zach! There you are. And look at her! She's just as gorgeous as you said." The redhead threw her arms around Zach and kissed his cheek.

"Hey, Courtney. This is Bodel."

The redhead turned to me and hugged the air from my lungs after ignoring my offered hand.

"It's so wonderful to meet you. Zach told me all about you over the phone. I wish he'd sent me a picture. It's hard to pick the perfect dress without knowing what you look like. I wish you had been able to come a week or so earlier. I could have made a dress for you. But I'm sure we can find something and I have time to alter it so it'll look like it was made for you." She was dragging me through the shop toward a back room while she chatted in her beautiful Georgia drawl.

She sat me in a huge pink chair and shook her head at me. "Pink is so not your color."

I could have hugged her again. "No. It's not. I'm not a dress kind of girl, honestly."

"Well, don't you worry, I am. You've got a great skin tone and that lovely hint of something exotic around your eyes."

"That would be my Thai grandmother."

"Well, coupled with those gray eyes the result is truly stunning."

I blushed furiously at the praise and looked at Zach to be saved. Zach had his arms crossed comfortably and was grinning at me.

"It'll be hot out," Courtney continued. "So we'll do something light and airy. And nothing really flashy—colorful, but not bright. I think I have just the thing for you. Wait here. Have some cookies."

She indicated the tray of sweets set out on the table beside me. She was gone before I could speak. The sweets on the table were arranged so beautifully I was afraid to touch them. Zach walked over and picked through the assortment, handing me a few.

"Is she always like that?" I asked.

"Court?" He looked where she had gone. "Yeah. She loves her work."

"How do you know her?"

"She's Charlotte's little sister."

I couldn't imagine having a dress designed and made just for me. I was prepared to go into a store, try on a few dresses and pick the cheapest one that didn't make me look fat. It didn't look like I was going to get off that easy.

I expected Courtney to return with an armful of dresses but she only had one. She held it out to me and I stared at it in fascination.

"I thought of it the moment I saw you. Try it on in there, honey. I guessed your size." She indicated a dressing room and handed me the dress. I was shoved inside and I stared at myself in the mirror. I stripped out of my clothes and pulled the material over my head.

The dress was backless and tied around my neck. It showed a lot of skin but in a classy way. The hem of the dress was too long, ending at a weird length at my knees. The material clung to my breasts and hips but draped attractively over my cookie intake. It was a swirl of smoky blue and pale yellow. The color almost matched my eyes.

I stared at the woman in the mirror. She looked far too beautiful to be me. A knock on the door made me jump.

"Come on out and let me see," Courtney commanded.

I shifted my breasts inside the dress, amazed that the material somehow held them up and in place without clearly displaying my nipples. Still wondering who I was looking at, I left the dressing room.

Courtney clapped her hands and did a little dance. She grabbed my hands and spun me around. I was helpless to stop her and I found myself laughing with her.

"You look absolutely perfect. I can hem this up a bit to land on your legs better. And there's a little extra material here, I can fix that. What do you think, Zach?"

I looked over at him. I never in my life had a man look at me like that before. He didn't need to say anything.

Courtney laughed and closed his mouth for him.

"Am I good or what?" she asked me.

"You are amazing. I never would have picked this out for myself."

"Well, we need some shoes. How do you feel about heels?"

Most of my good humor left me. "I can't walk in them. I have no balance."

"No problem." Courtney grabbed my hand and pulled me barefoot through the store toward the shoes. "It's an outside summer wedding. Sandals with a low thick heel will be perfect for you. These." She picked up a pair of elegant pale yellow sandals.

"I think I can walk in those."

She bustled off to get my size. I turned to find Zach standing behind me.

"That dress," he said, obviously still dazzled by it.

"You like it?" I shifted my hips a little.

He closed his eyes. "Don't do that. I'm this close to dragging you into the dressing room and making love to you till I go blind."

I looked down at myself. This was one damn good dress.

Courtney returned before Zach could drag me off. She slipped the heel onto my foot. They were surprisingly comfortable and low enough that I could actually walk in them without holding my arms out for balance.

"Perfect," Courtney said. She took a few measurements and fussed with the dress for a while. "Leave it with me tonight and I'll do the modifications. It'll be ready tomorrow. Can you two come by and take me out to lunch?"

"We'd love to," Zach said.

"Well, off you go now. I've got work to do," Courtney said, motioning us for the door.

"What about paying?" I whispered to Zach.

"She knows my credit card number by heart."

"It was nice to meet you, Courtney," I called as she hustled off with the dress.

"Likewise, honey. I'll see you tomorrow."

Zach led me out into the Georgia heat, holding my hand.

CHAPTER 51

I FORCED MYSELF not to chew on my painted fingernails as the limo drove us toward the wedding. Only a quarter of the guests could fit in the church and I was relieved we hadn't rated high enough to attend the ceremony. It would have been awkward when I started smoking as soon as I crossed the threshold. It also meant I had more time before I ran into Roberta at the reception.

Zach sat across from me, looking outlandishly handsome in a suit and tie. He was not particularly happy about his attire, seeing as it was mid-June in Georgia. He would rather be in shorts and a T-shirt. He assured me that as the reception progressed, enough alcohol and happiness would be supplied that he could strip down to his T-shirt and no one would care except his grandmother.

Roberta had been strangely absent for the last few days. No one had seen or heard from her, although she was in town. We hoped to corner her before the wedding and tell her that the threat was gone, but no one knew where she was staying.

"Stop doing that." Zach reached across the car and pulled my finger from my mouth. He kissed my hand. "Relax. Everything is going to be fine."

"Relax, right." I went to mess with my hair but had to stop again. Charlotte styled it in a complicated half-up-do with a few braids and tiny bell-shaped blue flowers woven into it. She applied makeup, seeing as I had never owned anything other than mascara and lip gloss. At my request she was subtle because I already felt like a stranger after the manicure, pedicure, hair, and the dress. She had done a wonderful job. I looked like myself, only prettier.

"Bo." Zach moved so he was sitting next to me. I rested my head carefully on his shoulder. "Are you still worried about Roberta?" he asked.

"Not only her."

"Then who?"

"Everyone!" I leaned away from him. "All of these people are going to be looking at me, judging me. I don't know what to say to them."

"You're great at work. Just pretend they're customers," he suggested.

"I don't act like myself at work," I objected. "I put on my happy face and pretend to be interested. I can't pull that off for a whole night. I can barely pull it off for five minutes with my tables. I usually slip and end up making fun of myself to make them laugh."

Zach kissed my nose. "Just be yourself, babe."

"But I'm not," I began. He silenced me with a kiss.

"You are beautiful," he said, adding another light kiss to my lips. "You are smart. You have a great sense of humor. And I love you."

I sighed and gave up. He was convinced I was wonderful. It was too much work disagreeing.

"I love you too."

* * *

The reception was being held outside of the mansion that the bride's parents purchased for the couple. Four large tents were set up on the perfectly manicured lawns. Beautiful gardens separated two of the tents and would provide places to get away from the crowds. Large colored paper lanterns hung from the tents and trees. Detailed cloth butterflies hung with them and were scattered across the tables along with tasteful flower arrangements.

It was the most beautiful setting I had ever seen. And the people took my breath away. The men were all in suits of varying colors. None of them were dressed in the horrible pale blue suit my father owned with the frilly shirt. All the men looked like they had walked out of a magazine. Even the ones that were overweight or had gotten hit by the ugly tree still looked wonderful. I guessed it was the atmosphere.

The women made me want to crawl back into the limo. The dresses were in every possible color and style. I saw corsets, frills, lace, pleating, and every combination. Their hair was all perfect and their makeup magazine quality. There was no way I could walk among these cultured women and fit in.

"Breathe, Bo," Zach reminded me, taking my arm.

"I don't belong here," I said.

"You belong with me," he corrected. "You belong wherever you are. Don't let the polish scare you. They are human, just like you. At least most of them. I'll tell you which to avoid."

I didn't move forward when he did. He sighed and turned to me.

"Chicken," he said.

I narrowed my eyes. He raised his eyebrows in an obvious dare. I grabbed his arm and hauled him toward the tents.

I saw Charlotte and Courtney and dragged Zach with me toward them. I had to let go of Zach while they hugged the life out of me. They both began talking at once about my dress and how wonderful Zach and I looked together. I saw Patricia walking toward us. Her dress was very sexy for a woman who normally projected ice-like control and command. I wasn't surprised by it. I never suggested to Zach that his quiet reserved mother was a lioness in bed. I saw the way John looked at her. No one looked at a freezer like that.

I held out a hand for Patricia. "Nice to see you again, Mrs. Cutter."

She surprised me by ignoring my hand and giving me a quick hug. I wasn't the only one surprised.

"Call me Patricia, please, Bo. You look lovely. Is that one of Courtney's creations?" Patricia asked.

Zach kissed his mother and escaped to go stand with a group of men while we talked about dresses. Part of me wanted to panic without him beside me, but he was only a few steps away. He glanced over periodically and I relaxed. I had friends here.

After a few minutes, Zach pulled me away from his mothers and aunt and into the group of men. I was infinitely more comfortable in their presence as he introduced me. I blanked on names but smiled and shook hands and accepted compliments and kisses on the cheek. As long as I stayed away from the clusters of women, at least those not related to Zach, I would be fine. I spotted Lacey in a large group of frilly pink women. I blew her a kiss and she turned away. The group with her looked at me like I was a cockroach.

"Stay away from that one," one of the men said, noticing the interaction.

"I think Bo taught her a lesson the last time they met," Zach said.

They all demanded to know the story so I gave up and told them. They burst out laughing and shaking their heads. Lacey glanced at me and hustled her group away from us.

"I would have paid good money to see that," one of the men said.

"I'll pay good money to see it tonight. If Lacey comes over my money's on Bo."

"As long as I get the winnings, I'll go pull her hair right now," I said.

They laughed and Zach kissed my hair.

The wedding party arrived and we all moved toward them. The bride was stunning in a flowing white gown that made her look sexy but virginal somehow. The groom was grinning like a fool and was so obviously in love with his new wife not even I could be cynical. I stayed beside Zach as we moved down the line. I kept my eyes open for Roberta. She wasn't in the wedding party but she had been at the ceremony.

I spotted Roberta because she was wearing an ugly gray dress that buttoned from ankle to neck. It would have looked drab at a funeral. At a wedding it was an eyesore. Her face was twisted in distaste and she hadn't even seen me yet.

I tugged on Zach's arm to get his attention. He saw Roberta and I felt his body tense.

"We have to go talk to her, quick," I said.

Before either of us could move, Patricia, John, Rosey, Charlotte, and Carter walked up to Roberta. I gripped Zach's arm hard.

We were too far away to hear what was being said, but Roberta's face flushed red and she looked even more sinister. Patricia actually started jabbing a finger into Roberta's ugly gray dress. John had to pull her away. People were starting to notice the fight that was quietly brewing.

"We need to get in there," I said.

"We need to stop it. What needed to be said has been said by now." But Zach didn't move. "I've never seen my mother so angry."

I looked up at Zach. He looked much like James usually did when Roberta was involved. I tried to pull him forward with me but he didn't move. I gave up and walked into the lion's den alone.

"Roberta," I said with as much icy charm as I could manage. "So nice to see you again."

She looked at me with loathing. I planted myself between her and the enraged parents, my back to her.

"I think we are all sitting at the same table. Why don't we go find our seats?"

The five continued to glare at Roberta a moment.

"We don't want to make a public scene, now do we?" I said quietly.

Charlotte was the first to notice everyone staring. She smiled brightly at me. "Wonderful idea. Let's all go sit down and relax. My feet are killing me in these heels."

Zach had found his balls and was standing beside his father.

"Richard wanted a word with you, Father," he said.

"Let's go find him then," Carter suggested.

Zach and his fathers left in one direction, and his three honorary mothers left with me. Roberta stood in the empty space, red in the face. She looked like the embodiment of evil.

"Nicely done, dear," Rosey said.

"I was about to hit her," Patricia said, sounding stunned. "I just couldn't stop myself. I was so angry."

"She deserves it," Charlotte said. "I wasn't lying about my shoes. Let's go sit."

I moved with the three women toward the tables, but I had a very bad feeling that Roberta would not go so quietly.

CHAPTER 52

I WANTED TO KISS whoever arranged the seating. Roberta was across the tent from the rest of the family. She was seated with a group of elderly women, only one of whom looked happy to be near her. The rest leaned away from her and spoke around her. Roberta sat rigidly and glared at me the entire meal. I was tempted to chew up my food and open my mouth at her, but I resisted.

Everything about the wedding was beautiful: the food, the setting, the live country band. If Roberta would just choke on a dinner roll, the evening might be perfect.

"You OK, babe?" Zach asked me.

"Fine, why?"

"You were staring off into space."

"Actually," James said. "You have that look you get when you are plotting something."

"I'm innocent, I swear," I said, faking a southern drawl.

Everyone laughed and Roberta's glare amped up a few degrees of mean. I couldn't help but flinch and Zach followed the direction of my gaze.

"If she doesn't stop looking at you like that," he said, "we're going to have a serious problem."

"If she hasn't managed to light me on fire yet, it's not likely," I said, hoping to calm him down. He shifted his chair a little and sent a look at his grandmother that made her look away. He put an arm around me and kissed my hair.

Toasts were made as the meal wound down. The best man's speech was truly beautiful and it made me forget about Roberta for a few minutes. The music picked up after dinner and people started dancing.

"I need to dance with you," Zach said into my ear.

I shifted in my chair nervously.

"What?" he asked. "You love to dance."

"But I'm a belly dancer. My dancing is a bit too risqué for a southern wedding." I thought I said it quietly but Charlotte and Patricia overheard.

"You're a belly dancer?" Charlotte asked.

I blushed. "My mom and I took lessons."

"I would love to learn that," Patricia said, shocking everyone at the table. John's eyes lit up at that possibility.

Zach stood up and pulled me to my feet. "You can give lessons later. Come dance with me now."

I let him lead me toward the dance floor, but Lacey and her army of frilly pink women got in our way.

"Evening Lacey, Ruth, Linny, Beth, Susie, Maria." Zach nodded at each woman. "Lacey, you know Bodel, but I don't think I've introduced her to the rest of you."

"Nice to meet you," I lied, determined to be polite.

"We know what you're doing," Lacey said, stepping into my personal space. "I don't know how you've fooled Zach, but you don't fool me."

I could see she was about to go off on an anti-Bo tirade and I'd heard enough of those to last a lifetime. I went to move past her but she but she stepped in front of me again.

"Who do you think you are?" she demanded.

"I'm Zach's lover."

She turned red and would have slapped me if I didn't have decent reflexes. I moved smoothly aside and she lost her balance in her ridiculous heels. She flailed her arms and knocked the wine glass out of one of her companion's hands. The rich red wine splashed down the pale pink of the woman's dress and she shrieked.

I ignored the group of now hysterical women and walked up to the band. They had just finished a song. The singer leaned down toward me. She was a little redhead with a great voice, and I knew exactly what I needed to hear.

"Can I make a request?" I asked.

"Sure thing, sugar," the woman said.

"Do you know 'Only Prettier' by Miranda Lambert?"

"It's not exactly a wedding song." She glanced at the bride and groom a moment.

"Can you say the song is for Lacey from her dear friend Bo?" I asked. The singer looked over at Lacey with obvious loathing.

"No problem. It's a fun song to dance to." She straightened up and spoke with the band a moment. I turned to find Zach behind me.

"What are you planning?" he asked.

I grabbed his arm and pulled him toward the dance floor.

The singer said, "This song goes out to Lacey, from her dear friend Bo." Then she began to sing. We reached the dance floor as the lyrics *I've got a mouth like a sailor and yours is more like a Hallmark card* rang out in her sassy voice.

Zach laughed as he put his hands on my hips. "This may be my new favorite song," he said.

I let myself go, blowing a kiss to Lacey as the singer belted, "Everybody says you gotta know your enemies. Even if they only weigh a hundred pounds and stand five foot three." I danced the way I wanted to but kept it PG because I was at a wedding. Zach did his best to keep up with me, but the way I was moving my hips was obviously distracting him. It made me laugh and he pulled me close and kissed me.

As the song ended, I took note of the dance floor. It was full of people but there was a space around Zach and me. I had a feeling everyone was watching me. Lacey was standing on the side of the dance platform with her arms crossed, trying to kill me with her eyes.

Better women have tried, honey, I thought. I smiled and blew her another kiss. She turned on her heel and stormed off with her pink ladies.

"I owe you for that one," James said, appearing beside us. "I've never seen Lacey that pissed off before."

"My pleasure," I said as he kissed my cheek.

I noticed that three women were approaching me. I held my breath and waited for the assault.

"Where did you learn to dance like that?" the one in front asked.

"I took belly dancing classes with my mom."

"It looks like so much fun." She smiled at me warmly. "I'm Melissa Sanwald."

"Bodel Tavish, nice to meet you."

"How long are you in town?"

I glanced at Zach. "Only a few more days. I have to get home to my dog."

"Well, would you be interested in maybe teaching a few of us to dance like that? If not this time, then maybe when you come down to visit again?"

"I'd love to. I'm not sure I have time this visit. But give me your phone number and I'll give you a call the next time I'm here."

While I exchanged information with a handful of women, I relaxed. Not all of the women here hated me on principle. Zach and I danced to a few songs. He wasn't the greatest dancer, but I managed to dodge his awkwardly placed size fourteen shoes. I took pity on Zach and asked James for a dance.

James was a better dancer than his brother. He waltzed me around and whispered secrets about the people around us. His face sobered and I felt a disturbance in the force. He tried to keep me from spinning us around but I was a better dancer. I turned to see Roberta waiting to pounce on me as the song ended. I knew I couldn't avoid it any longer. I let go of James and turned to face my nemesis.

CHAPTER 53

"HELLO, ROBERTA," I said.

"Grandmother," James said, sounding terrified. "Would you like to dance?"

I glanced at him, surprised he would finally find a spine and try and intervene. But I knew it was no use.

"No. I need a word with Bodel."

I stepped off the edge of the dance floor, stopping just out of her personal space.

"What exactly do you want to say to me?" I asked neutrally.

She narrowed her cold blue eyes. "My offer still stands," she said.

For a moment I had no idea what she was talking about. Then I remembered the money she offered me to leave Zach. I took a step toward her, my hands balled into fists. There was a flicker of alarm in her eyes and it stopped me. I was not going to punch Zach's grandmother in the face at a wedding. I took a few breaths to calm myself.

"Give it up, Roberta," I said. "I'm not going anywhere."

"I will not sit by while my grandson gets manipulated by a whore. You are trash and should have stayed in the gutter where you belong." She raised her voice and it rang out clearly in the silence between songs. Everyone turned to look at us.

"This is your grandson's wedding," I hissed at her. "Are you really going to ruin it?"

"He's not *my* grandson," she said dismissively. "And I warned you. I've given you plenty of time to leave."

"I'm not leaving," I said through my teeth. I realized Zach was rushing toward us. This was only going to get worse.

"Stop this now, Roberta," I said, looking at the stunned people around us. "This is not the place."

"I've had to watch you fornicating on the dance floor all night. You have no place here. Whores like you don't belong in polite society."

"That's enough, Grandmother," Zach said, coming up beside me.

"I can speak my mind," she began.

"Not here," Zach said. "Not like this."

"This woman is trash, Zachary. What were you thinking bringing her here?"

Zach's hands had gone into tight fists. He looked down at Roberta.

"I was thinking that I love her."

"Don't be silly." She dismissed the idea with an imperious wave of her hand. "She has nothing to offer you. She has no money and absolutely no class. She should be working in the garden, not enjoying it."

"You are trying to ruin Peter's wedding. That's really classy," I muttered.

She turned a shade darker red. "I am trying to protect my grandson."

"This has nothing to do with protecting Zach."

"It has everything to do with him. He is an important man here, from an important family. He has a reputation to uphold. I won't have you dragging the family into the gutter."

"That's enough, Grandmother," Zach said through his teeth.

"It surely is. Get rid of her."

"He's not getting rid of me," I snapped. "Do you even realize how miserable he's been for the past ten years? Can't you see he is happy now?"

"He was fine until you came along. He was motivated and ambitious. Then he met you and he's been sitting on that sandbar for months doing nothing."

"I've been renovating the house," Zach said.

"That house should have been mine!" she snapped.

"Why?" I was so angry I was shaking. "Because you tricked Walter into marrying you after your worthless husband gambled away all your money?"

The color left Roberta's face. "You don't know anything about it."

"I knew Walter. He was a good man. And you ripped him apart, used him and left him, taking the only thing he ever really cared about when you left. Walter talked about John almost every day. He was a wonderful kind man and you exploited him and broke his heart. He wanted to leave the house to John but he didn't want to give you a reason to attack your son. So he gave the house to Zach and James. And I'd rather burn it down than have you in it again."

Roberta glared at me for a long time. Then she looked at Zach. "I have to say, you're taste in women hasn't improved much. This one might not kill herself, but that fact alone doesn't mean she's suitable."

I saw red. I jumped between Zach and Roberta as Zach started toward her. I shoved Roberta harshly backward, cutting off her speech. She stumbled back a step and opened her mouth to sputter in outrage.

"Don't you dare say another word," I yelled. "You can call me trash, you can call me a whore. I don't care. But don't you dare talk about Alice like that." I was shaking with rage and it choked me a minute. Roberta was staring at me in shock.

I pushed the rage back enough to yell around it again. "You are the most miserable vindictive woman I have ever met. I may not have money or class, but I'm a goddess standing next to you."

"How dare you," Roberta began.

I stepped into her personal space. "How dare you start this here? This is a wedding. And you are trying to ruin it. Why? Because I was born to a mechanic and a carpenter and I wear jeans? Because I won't lie down and take your abuse? There is nothing you can say or do to get rid of me. I'm here to stay, darling. So you can kiss my nicely-shaped Yankee ass."

I jumped at the applause. I was so involved in my rant I hadn't noticed Roberta and I were standing in a mass of enthralled bystanders. Roberta went white as she realized everyone was clapping for me.

I looked back at her. "I love Zach. I love his family." I looked at the people gathered around us. "And I'm sorry for this scene."

"Let her have it," the groom said, startling me.

I decided to listen to him. It was his wedding after all.

I looked at Roberta. "You truly are pathetic," I said. "I don't think you've been happy a day in your life."

I saw pain flash across the old woman's face. I expected outrage and yelling but my comment had struck home. I was done tormenting her. I had won, and I wasn't the kind of woman to kick someone when they were down.

"You may be afraid of happiness," I said. "I used to be. But I'm not anymore." I turned my back to her to face Zach. He was smiling proudly at me. He looked solid and handsome in his suit. His warm green eyes pulled at my heart. I stepped toward him, taking both of his hands.

"Zach." I took a deep breath, feeling the rightness down to my toes. "I love you. I never dreamed I would find someone as perfect for me as you. Will you marry me?"

Zach's mouth fell open for a second. There was a hush under the tent and I felt all eyes on me. He continued to stare at me in shock.

"Dammit, Zach. Don't leave me hanging," I muttered, looking down at my ridiculous yellow shoes. His hands cupped my chin and lifted my face.

He smiled at me and kissed my nose. "I thought you'd never ask," he said.

"Is that a yes?"

"That's a hell yes."

I jumped into his arms and he swung me around. We laughed and he kissed me like we were the only two people in the world. I rested my head on his shoulder and closed my eyes. His arms were at home around me, holding me close. He would always be there to catch me.

I realized that we were in an ocean of applause. I opened my eyes to Zach's family hovering close. I was pulled away from Zach for hugs and kisses. I got lost in the happiness and love as I was passed around my new family. Zach snatched me away from Carter and held me close.

"Should I have done the proper thing and let you propose?" I asked quietly.

He shook his head at me, tracing my jaw with his fingers. "You're not proper, babe. And I wouldn't have you any other way. I love you, my Yankee harlot."

"I love you too, my southern gentleman."

AN EXCERPT FROM
BECOMING GRACE DIVINE
THE SEQUEL TO *CATCHING BODEL*

THE HARLEY COMMANDED ATTENTION and every eye turned to me. I killed the engine and slung my leg over the bike while I took off my helmet. I ran a hand quickly through my short hair and turned to the family gathered in the yard. My eyes went to the guy at the grill, probably because he was shirtless. He had the kind of body I felt it was a crime to clothe. He was tall and broad and had muscles that made my fingers itch to touch them. He had short brown hair and sunglasses covering his eyes. His jeans hugged his hips and I saw the flash of a tattoo on the back of his right shoulder before he turned to face me.

I scanned the rest of the people as I walked closer. They all watched me walking toward them in my leather. To my immense pleasure the shirtless guy stepped around the grill to meet me.

"Hi," I said, throwing on my best smile and using my 'from nowhere' accent. "Sorry to interrupt your party. I need a mason."

The man grinned at me and it took me completely off guard. He exuded confident alpha male, but the grin had a hint of a playful bad boy. He held out his hand.

"If you're looking for Mason, you've found me," he said as his hand enveloped mine. "If you're looking for someone to lug some bricks around, you're looking for my brother, Axel."

"I might be in the market for both," I said.

ACKNOWLEDGMENTS

None of this would be possible without my family. They have always supported my writing, starting with my poetry as a child, and continuing to become some of the first readers of my manuscript. My family has given me the confidence to pursue my dreams, and I will be forever thankful.

I would also like to acknowledge my writing group, the Tuesday Group that Meets on Fridays. This group of fabulous women started off as strangers with nothing in common but a love of writing, and has become a sensational team. Catching Bodel would not be what it is without them. So thank you, Anita, Barbara #1, Barbara #2, Carol, Iris, Jerry, Joan, Pat, and Yvonne.

Lastly, thank you to Booktrope and the wonderful members of my team for making Catching Bodel into a reality.

MORE GREAT READS FROM BOOKTROPE

A Medical Affair **by Anne McCarthy Strauss** (Fiction) A woman has an affair with her doctor. Flattered, she has no idea his behavior violates medical ethics and state law. The novel is based on solid research of which most patients are unaware.

Haunted **by Eileen Maksym** (Fiction) The Society for Paranormal Researchers, a group of college friends, get involved in a dangerous investigation of a local haunted house.

Keeping Seattle Up **by John Thomas Wood** (Fiction) Wisdom often comes from unexpected places. Looking at love, loss, intimacy and sex with new eyes.

One Day in Lubbock **by Daniel Lance Wright** (Fiction) William Dillinger despises how he spent his life and has one day to find out if rekindling love can change it.

Swimming Upstream **by Ruth Mancini** (Fiction) A life-affirming and often humorous story about a young woman's pursuit of happiness.

Taxicab to Wichita **by Aaron Asselstine** (Fiction) Quinn Jacob is a drug-addicted taxi driver with no options, no money, and no destination. Rocky is a thief with no getaway car, no driver, and no time. In the gathering darkness of a perfect storm, can they trust each other, risk it all, and recreate themselves on the high-wire roads to Wichita?

The Long Walk Home **by Will North** (Fiction) Forty-four year-old Fiona Edwards answers her door to a tall, middle-aged man shouldering a hulking backpack—unshaven, sweat-soaked and arrestingly handsome. What neither of them knows is that their lives are about to change forever.

Discover more books and learn about our
new approach to publishing at **booktrope.com**.

24724943R00152

Made in the USA
Middletown, DE
03 October 2015